TILL DEATH DO US PART

Whitney's eyes took in the length of him. His long, lean body; the sprinkling of black curls at the opening of his silk shirt. He was still so incredibly handsome, so incredibly sexy. So irresistible.

When he was mere inches away from her, a shiver of desire snaked down her spine. With the bittersweet feeling, sanity crept back into Whitney's brain. Sexy or not sexy, she couldn't do this. She couldn't stay here and get caught up in the past. She turned on her heels, determined to leave.

Javar grabbed her arm, and Whitney stopped. The feel of his long, strong fingers wrapped around her slender forearm caused her skin to tingle, and she remembered too easily the way he used to hold her when loving her. Remembered how wonderful last night had been. Knew she wanted to experience that again.

She felt his head nearing hers, felt the heat of his breath on the side of her face. Her knees almost buckled on the spot. His face stopped moving when his mouth reached her ear. With a deep, sexy voice he murmured, "Don't go."

BOOK YOUR PLACE ON OUR WEBSITE AND MAKE THE ARABESQUE ROMANCE CONNECTION!

We've created a customized website just for our very special Arabesque readers, where you can get the inside scoop on everything that's going on with Arabesque romance novels.

When you come online, you'll have the exciting opportunity to:

- View covers of upcoming books

- Read sample chapters

- Learn about our future publishing schedule (listed by publication month *and author*)

- Find out when your favorite authors will be visiting a city near you

- Search for and order backlist books from our online catalog

- Check out author bios and background information

- Send e-mail to your favorite authors

- Meet the Kensington staff online

- Join us in weekly chats with authors, readers and other guests

- Get writing guidelines

- AND MUCH MORE!

**Visit our website at
http://www.arabesquebooks.com**

EVERLASTING LOVE

Kayla Perrin

Pinnacle Books
Kensington Publishing Corp.

http://www.arabesquebooks.com

Dedication

To Dexter Graham, for all your help regarding the world of architecture. Thanks so much!

To Pearl, Judy, Henry and Pat at TGH, for letting me use their computer while I was on deadline!

And to Brenda and Kesley, a very dear sister and brother— this one's for you.

PINNACLE BOOKS are published by

Kensington Publishing Corp.
850 Third Avenue
New York, NY 10022

Pinnacle, the P logo and Arabesque, the Arabesque logo are Reg. U.S. Pat. & TM Off.

First Printing: July, 1998
10 9 8 7 6 5 4 3 2 1

Printed in the United States of America

Prologue

Rain, heavy and menacing, fell in large droplets on the windshield of her late model, royal blue Chevrolet Cavalier. Her hands clenched on the steering wheel as she maneuvered the car, Whitney Jordan worried her bottom lip. Filling her lungs to their full capacity—to the point where it hurt—did nothing to calm her frantic nerves. If she had known it was going to rain when she had left her mother's, she would have delayed this trip.

It was always worse when it rained—the images, the memories. During those times, she didn't even have to close her eyes in order for the terrifying memories to surge forth. And they were there now, in the forefront of her mind, as strong and as real as the night it had happened.

She could still see the bright lights coming toward her, feel the blood freeze in her veins as icy fear enveloped her body. She could still hear the horrifying crunch of metal and the ominous crack of the windshield.

But the sound she could never forget was little J.J.'s scream. The shrill, terrified sound. And she could never forget the sight of his twisted, bloodied, motionless body on the ground.

The horrifying sight of J.J.'s body zapped into her mind with such velocity that Whitney's jittery hands caused the car to swerve into the oncoming lane.

Gasping, she righted the car, then inhaled a deep, steadying breath. She held back her tears, tears that always accompanied the memories. Everything for her had changed after the accident, and her life would never be the same. She had come out of the crash with her life, but she had lost everything else that mattered.

And now, she was returning to the place where it had all happened. The place where one tragic event had shattered her entire existence. Perhaps that was why the pain and the memories seemed so much stronger now.

Whitney sucked in a sharp breath and let it out slowly, willing herself to calm down. She would get through this. She had to. Once she had accomplished her task, she could leave Chicago and get on with her life.

Without Javar. A wave of nostalgia washed over her as she thought of Javar and of how she would now be closing the door on their life together forever. It wasn't something she wanted to do, but her husband had given her no choice. Some marriages just couldn't survive the challenges thrown at them. Theirs was one of those marriages.

And after an almost two-year separation, it was time to officially end their marriage and get on with their lives.

Glancing in the rearview mirror, Whitney noticed a set of headlights in the distance behind her. Her eyes darted to the road, then back to the rearview mirror. The lights were getting closer as the car gained on her, clearly speeding despite the road conditions. As the car neared her bumper, its driver flicked on the high beams, nearly blinding her. Whitney squinted, trying to lessen the effect of the offending bright lights.

"Okay, okay," she muttered. The car was right on her tail now, doing sixty miles an hour. Mumbling an unladylike oath, Whitney hit her blinker, signaling her intention to enter the right lane. But as she started changing lanes, she noticed that the car behind her was swerving to the right as well.

"Impatient," she grumbled, directing her car back into the left lane to let the restless driver pass her.

But before she could completely cross over the line, she felt and heard the impact of metal against metal as the car behind her crashed into her car. That was all it took to send Whitney's car sliding on the rain-slicked roads straight into the path of oncoming traffic.

Her heart thundering in her chest, Whitney's mind screamed, *It's happening again!* Panicked, and desperate to avoid a head-on collision, she turned the steering wheel to the right. But it was too sharp a turn, because the car began to spin violently, heading toward the shoulder of the road and the large oak tree that loomed ahead of her.

Shielding her face when she realized there was nothing else she could do, Whitney Jordan screamed as the passenger's side of her car collided with the tree trunk.

The next moment, darkness overcame her.

Chapter One

Somewhere in the back of her mind, Whitney thought she heard hushed voices and soft sobbing. The sounds were hazy, but were growing clearer each second. She had no idea where she was, only the definite feeling that she shouldn't be here. And despite her mind's haze, she felt sore. The entire left side of her body screamed with pain, and her head felt as though someone had tightened it in a vice.

She had to wake up. Her mind wanted to, even if her limbs felt like lead. Whimpering softly, Whitney shifted in the bed and forced her eyes open as much as she could. A blinding jolt of pain in her head caused her to wince, and she let her eyes flutter shut.

"Whitney? Whitney, honey?"

She felt someone gently squeeze her hand.

"She opened her eyes!" a woman shouted excitedly. "Cherise, go call the nurse!"

It was her mother, Whitney realized, feeling a sense of comfort. Fighting the pain, she opened her eyes once again. Lord, it hurt. And all she could see was a blur of shapes. Why was she here, lying on this foreign bed? What had happened?

A startling mental image hit her—the body of a little boy—and Whitney's heart instantly went berserk. Cold, numbing fear slithered through her veins, and as panic seized her, she fought to suck in small gulps of air.

It felt as though someone was strangling her, forcing the very life out of her.

She tried to speak, to ask the questions she so desperately needed answered. But she couldn't. She could only gasp and cry as she struggled to fill her lungs.

She heard the voices around her grow frantic, and she sensed that people were trying to help her, but she wasn't sure what they were doing. Her eyes, although open, couldn't focus on anything.

And then, everything started fading. The shapes, the voices. The frantic movements around her grew faint. Even the memories eluded her now.

Sleep was beckoning her, and Whitney closed her eyes, welcoming the painless oblivion.

Javar Jordan squeezed his forehead with a thumb and forefinger as he looked down at the sketches before him. Close, but not quite right. He wanted to secure the bid for a new shopping plaza in Phoenix, and these sketches that one of his senior associates had produced were good, but lacked the creative edge necessary to land the job.

And he wanted to land the job. Thus far, after eleven years in business, his architectural firm was one of the most successful in the Midwest. But he had yet to accomplish his big dream: to be among the ten best architectural firms in the entire United States. It was a dream that, with time, he knew he could make a reality. Already, several large clients across the country contacted him directly, offering him substantial jobs. In the Midwest, he was always on the short list for government contracts, and when it came to private projects, he was always one of the first architects to be approached.

So, while his financial security didn't depend on this bid, he wanted it. Michael Li of the Li Development Corporation was one of the most affluent commercial property developers in the country, and if he could land this bid, his dream would be one step closer to becoming a reality. For service and value, his firm, Jordan & Associates, was second to none, and once Michael Li learned what Javar's company was capable of doing for him, he would no doubt offer the firm more lucrative jobs in the future.

If he hadn't been busy working on the Milwaukee hotel project, Javar would have done the sketches for the Phoenix bid himself. Clearly, he thought wryly, he was going to have to.

Javar rubbed his tired eyes, but found that useless in relieving the grit-like feeling that assaulted them. What he needed was some sleep, but he'd have to settle for a short break. Pushing back his black, Italian-leather swivel chair, Javar stood and strolled to the left side of his floor to ceiling windows, and glanced out toward the west. His office was on the thirtieth floor and offered him a magnificent view of downtown Chicago. On Lake Michigan, he could see several boats sailing on the glistening water. Below, he could see West Madison, the street where his firm was located. Crowds of people swarmed the waterfront and Grant Park, enjoying the Taste of Chicago festival. Attracting millions of people each year, the summer event could only be described as a big, street food party. Because of the festival, and the fact that it was Friday, traffic was already jammed in the downtown core. And it wasn't even noon yet. Not that Javar had to worry about rush hour. If he was lucky, he would get out of the office by midnight when the streets would be quieter. The sketches for the Li bid had to be revised right away.

The shrill ring of the telephone on his large, mahogany desk interrupted Javar's troubled thoughts. Expelling an aggravated breath, he turned and reached for the receiver. "Yes?" he barked.

"Mr. Jordan, I know you asked not to be interrupted, but—"

"That's right, Melody," he told his administrative assistant. The strain of another stressful day was evident in his voice. "Tell whoever it is to go away."

In her soft-spoken, delicate voice, Melody explained, "Uh . . . they said it was important. It's someone from your insurance company."

"My insurance company?" Irritation caused Javar's brow to furrow. If this was about his BMW, he didn't have time for it. "Did he say what this is about?"

"It's a she," Melody corrected. "And no, she didn't say. Only that she needed to talk to you immediately."

Running a hand over his wavy coif, Javar groaned and said, "Put her through."

Three seconds later, a deep female voice asked, "Mr. Jordan?"

"Yes, this is he." Javar's tone was curt. "What's this about?"

"Mr. Jordan, this is Gwynne Creswell. I'm calling about Wednesday's accident. I need to know what garage you had the car towed to, so we can send an adjuster out to examine the damage. I'll also need a copy of the police report, so if you could tell me what district did the investigation . . ."

Javar rolled his eyes. He was going to have to change insurance companies—soon. This was the second time in the last year they had screwed up his claim.

"Ms. Creswell," he began, his voice calmer than his perturbed feelings, "I haven't had any accident. My car was stolen. As for the district that did the investigation, I've already given all that information to Robert Blacklock, my regular broker."

"Mr. Jordan, I realize that you weren't involved in the

accident. I'm talking about your wife," Ms. Creswell explained, her tone indicating that she was sure Javar knew what she was talking about but was just feigning ignorance.

For goodness' sake, Javar thought, groaning inwardly. This woman had no idea what she was talking about. And why was *she* calling him? Was reliable Robert on yet another vacation?

"Ms. Creswell, I have to tell you, I'm not very impressed with Rathburn Insurance at the moment. This is the second time you've screwed up my claims in the past eight months. Not only are my wife and I separated, but she's nowhere near Chicago. She's down South, in Louisiana."

Javar heard Gwynne sigh. "Okay," she stated in a placating tone, "is your wife not Whitney Jordan?"

A silent alarm bell went off in Javar's head, and he lowered himself into his chair. "Yes," he replied, his tone guarded.

"Well," Gwynne continued, "according to the call I got from Avery Rentals, your wife was in a serious accident on Wednesday night, and her rental car was badly damaged."

My wife? Javar's stomach tightened in horror. Impatient, he asked, "What exactly has happened?"

"Surely the police must have contacted you, Mr. Jordan. All I know is that the rental car is supposedly a write-off, and since your wife had your insurance policy transferred to the rental car—"

"My wife has been in an accident?" Icy fear slithered up Javar's spine, causing the short hairs on his nape to stand on end.

"According to Avery Rentals, yes."

"Oh my God. Is she all right?"

Clearly flustered, Gwynne said, "I . . . I don't know. What's going on here, Mr. Jordan?"

Javar didn't have time to answer her. He didn't have time to hang up the receiver. He only had time to grab his gray Armani blazer and rush out of his office.

* * *

Whitney had the strange sensation that someone was watching her and her eyes flew open. Something was wrong, she knew, and immediately, her stomach coiled with dread. Focusing her eyes while she glanced around anxiously, she saw both her mother and her cousin sitting to the right of her bed, worried expressions etched on their faces. This wasn't her mother's place, neither was it her cousin Cherise's. Curious, her eyes took in the orange curtain that was on the left side of her bed, before noting the intravenous stand and bag that were connected to her arm.

She was in a hospital, Whitney realized. Why? What had happened? Her gaze narrowed on her mother's coffee-colored face, taking in the sight of her red, swollen eyes. Whatever had happened must have been something awful, but she couldn't remember what that something was.

"Oh, Whitney!" her mother said as she looked at her, relief evident in her deep voice. "Oh, thank God!"

Whitney didn't like the confused feeling that plagued her. Her mind was a groggy haze, and her body was thrumming with pain. Drawing in a ragged breath, she struggled to sit up.

Electric jolts of pain shot through her head and back, causing her to groan.

Her mother's gentle hand was instantly on her shoulder, softly easing her back down. "Eh eh eh," Carmen Elliston's mild voice warned. "You just lie back and relax, Whitney. Cherise, go call the doctor."

Whitney saw Cherise's warm smile and bright brown eyes that were swollen from crying before she scampered toward the door. Her mother and her cousin were here, the two people who mattered most to her. But despite the presence of her family, the wary feeling that overwhelmed her just wouldn't go away.

J.J.! her mind screamed, and her pulse quickened. Whitney's throat constricted as haunting images—blood, broken glass, a small lifeless body—flooded her mind. Terrified, she reached out and gripped her mother's hand with all her strength. Her voice was hoarse as she asked, "Where's J.J.?"

Carmen's eyes widened with surprise as she stared at her daughter, but she quickly softened her expression. Bringing her hand to Whitney's face, she stroked her cheek in a gentle soothing motion. "Just lie back and go to sleep, honey. You need your rest."

"Mom, where's J.J.?" Whitney repeated, more frantic this time.

A soft sigh fell from Carmen's lips. "Oh, honey." Worry flashed in her dark, hazel eyes. "J.J., he's . . . don't you remember, honey? It's been two years. . . ." Brushing at a tear that escaped her eye, Carmen bit down on her bottom lip.

Two years, Whitney thought, fighting hard to remember what was eluding her. And then she did. She remembered it with such force that her body shook. J.J. was gone.

But not recently; two years earlier. So why did it feel so fresh, like it had only just happened?

"W-what happened?" Whitney inquired, swallowing against the grief lodged in her throat.

Whitney's mother returned her eyes to her daughter's. "Oh, honey. I don't want you to worry about that. You're gonna be okay now, that's all that matters."

Whitney tried to shake her head, but couldn't. The discomfort was too intense. Instead, she said, "Tell me."

Carmen unleashed a weary sigh. "Honey, you . . . You were in an accident, but don't you worry. Everything's gonna be all right now."

An accident? Whitney was shocked, and her mind fought hard to fill in the blanks. Suddenly she remembered the high beams, and driving in the rain.

"It was wet," Whitney said aloud, hoping that the rest of the puzzle would come together.

"Don't even think about that now," Carmen said, patting Whitney's hand. "You need your rest."

The shuffle of footsteps drew Whitney's attention to the left, and she watched as Cherise and a young, attractive woman entered through the curtains.

The young woman, dressed in a white lab coat, strode purposefully to the right side of the bed, and Carmen stood to let the woman get closer to Whitney. Beaming down at Whitney, the woman said, "Welcome back."

Whitney managed a small smile.

"I'm Dr. Farkas," the woman told Whitney, then proceeded to check her pulse. Her olive complexion and striking features indicated a Middle Eastern background. But she was so small and seemed so young, Whitney found it hard to believe this woman was old enough to be a practicing physician.

"Your pulse is normal." The doctor slipped her hand into Whitney's saying, "Can you squeeze my fingers?"

Whitney did.

"Great, Whitney." Dr. Farkas then shone a light in both Whitney's eyes. "Your pupils are fine, indicating no damage to your brain. How does your head feel?"

"It hurts."

"That's understandable." Dr. Farkas smiled and crossed her arms over her chest. "You are a very lucky young woman, Mrs. Jordan."

"I was in an accident?"

Dr. Farkas nodded, her short, dark brown hair, gently swaying. "Yes. Do you remember what happened?"

Squeezing her eyes shut, Whitney tried again to remember. Only fragments would come to her—the bright lights, the rain on the windshield. Nothing else. She shook her head, then cringed in pain. "No."

"We're going to keep you another night or two for observation, but the good news is, your injuries are only surface. I hear the tree wasn't so lucky." Again, Dr. Farkas smiled down at Whitney.

Whitney found it hard to get excited about Dr. Farkas's good news. She didn't feel lucky. Not when it hurt to open her eyes or to shift her body even slightly.

Dr. Farkas asked, "Do you need something for the pain?"

Weakly, Whitney nodded. The doctor gave her two small pills and water to wash them down. Whitney prayed they would help ease her discomfort.

"That should help you rest, as well as lessen the pain," Dr. Farkas explained. "I'll be back to see you later today. In the meantime, if you need anything, you can ring for the nurse." Turning to Whitney's mother, Dr. Farkas placed a hand on her shoulder and said, "Mrs. Elliston, don't worry. She's going to be just fine."

"Thank you, doctor," Carmen replied. Then, closing her eyes for a brief moment, she added, "And thank you, too, God."

Smiling, Cherise moved to the side of the bed the doctor had vacated and took Whitney's hand in hers. "Hey cuz, you okay?"

Whitney forced a smile. "I will be."

"You certainly know how to scare a person. Sleeping for two days straight." She smiled weakly. "The next time you want some attention, just let me take you out on the town."

A chuckle that sounded more like a groan escaped Whitney's throat. It was just like Cherise to try to cheer her up with her playful sarcasm. "I'll remember that."

"Good." Cherise light brown face grew serious, and she ran her free hand through her long, thin braids. "You get well, Whitney. We can't lose you. Not now."

Whitney gave Cherise's hand an encouraging squeeze, surprised that she had the strength. "I'll . . . be fine. You . . ." She paused to swallow. "You don't . . . have to stay here. You need to work."

"Work can wait," Cherise told her. "You're what's important now."

Whitney tried to turn onto her side, and grunted in agony. Giving in to the pain, she collapsed onto her back. The surge of energy she had recently experienced was now passing. Despite the fact that she wanted to stay awake and spend time with her mother and her cousin, the only two people in Chicago who cared about her welfare, her eyelids were getting heavy, and she longed to close them.

She suddenly realized that Cherise had said, "two days straight". Widening her eyes, she looked at Cherise and asked, "How long have I . . . been here?"

Sadness marred Cherise's features as tears filled her eyes. Quickly, she brushed them away. "Two days."

"Two?"

"You were unconscious for the first day, then started to wake up, but you never really did. At least not for long. Dr. Farkas said you had a slight concussion."

"Oh, God," Whitney uttered, feeling alert once again. "The car. Where is it?"

"Girl, I tell you that you've been unconscious for two days and you're worried about some dumb car?" Cherise flashed Whitney a sardonic grin. Whitney held her gaze, and Cherise continued. "The car's a write-off. But don't go crazy worrying about that. Your mother has already contacted the rental company."

Relieved, Whitney released a breath she didn't know she was holding. "Thank God . . . I had insurance."

Cherise's eyes bulging, she said, "Thank God you're okay. Now why don't you close your eyes and get some rest? Your mom and I will both be here when you wake up."

Whitney glanced at her mother and saw her smiling. Her heart warmed. She knew at that moment that she would be okay. She had her family with her.

Drawing in a comforting breath, she closed her eyes, accepting the temporary peace sleep offered.

"Where is she?" Javar demanded at the information desk on the first floor of Cook County Hospital. After calling the local police stations in Chicago to inquire about accidents while sitting in traffic, Javar discovered that his wife had been taken here. The description of the accident scene was hard to comprehend, and as he stared down at the young black receptionist, beads of sweat popped up on his brow. He had to see Whitney. He had to know that she was okay.

"And who would 'she' be?" the receptionist asked, a small smile lifting her full lips.

"Oh. Oh, of course." Javar drew in a deep, calming breath, then continued. "My wife. Her name is Whitney Jordan."

"Thank you." The receptionist checked her computer. Several seconds later, she smiled up at Javar. "She's in room four-nineteen, sir. You can take the elevators at the end of the hall."

Whirling around on his heel, Javar called "Thank you" over his shoulder.

When he stepped off the elevator on the fourth floor, Javar was instantly aware that the hallway was crowded with people. Patients on gurneys in the corridor were groaning and crying from their injuries, and several men and women of varying ages surrounded their sick loved ones or sat on benches or lined the walls. The horrible memory of the last time he had been to this hospital entered his mind, and he stopped, swallowing, fighting the unpleasant emotions the memory stirred. Praying for strength, Javar

forged ahead and found room four-nineteen. He hurried
inside.

Orange curtains closed off both bed areas. Boldly, he
pulled open the first flimsy curtain, but the person he saw
there was not Whitney. A young woman with a cast on her
arm lay sleeping, and a man and young boy, probably
father and son, sat piously beside her bed. The boy was
older than J.J. had been, probably ten, but still the sight
of him brought back vivid images of J.J. lying on a hospital
bed, his small body bruised and damaged. Javar's throat
constricted, remembering how it had been too late for his
son. Only a few hours after arriving at the hospital, J.J. had
died. Javar apologized for the intrusion, then made his
way to the other partition.

Carmen Elliston's saddened expression was the first
thing he saw as he pulled back the curtain and stepped
inside. One look on the middle-aged woman's troubled
face and Javar assessed the severity of the situation. It was
bad. Alarm gripped him, and as he tried to suck in a breath,
he found his lungs wouldn't hold more than a mere gasp
of air.

He didn't want to glance down, didn't want to look at
Whitney. He didn't want to know that she was injured
to the extent that she might die. But even as the thought
hit him, Javar knew he had to turn his gaze toward her.
He had to see his wife, no matter how badly she was
injured. Because if she was nearing the end of her life,
then he would spend every minute of it by her side.

Anxiety causing his heart to beat rapidly, Javar's eyes
moved to the bed. The sight he saw there made his
stomach twist into a tight knot, and he almost cried out
in pain. Whitney was lying on the small hospital bed, her
head bandaged, her eyes closed. Her normally vibrant
honey-brown skin was pale and bruised around her eyes.
And her round face was drawn, thin—not full the way
it had been the last time he had seen her almost two
years ago.

But he could see the soft rise and fall of her chest, the faint, yet steady, breath of life.

Relief washing over him, Javar expelled a hurried breath and stepped further into the curtained area.

Whitney was alive.

Thank God.

Chapter Two

"What are you doing here?" Carmen asked, her hazel eyes shooting daggers in Javar's direction.

"What do you think?" Javar asked, not bothering to try and hide his annoyance. He wasn't about to let Carmen bully him into leaving. Whitney needed him. But as he looked at Carmen and the bitterness in her eyes, he felt regret tug at his heart. Once, she had loved him like her own son. Not anymore.

Outrage sparking in Carmen's eyes, she rose from the black vinyl chair at Whitney's side and approached Javar, determination in her steps. "You have a lot of nerve coming here, Javar. I suggest you leave before Whitney wakes up. You know as well as I do that she doesn't want to have anything to do with you."

Javar stared down at his estranged wife's mother, meeting her cold eyes with an equally hard gaze. "I'm still her husband."

Carmen snorted, then threw Javar a distasteful glance. "Like you know the meaning of the word."

Javar didn't reply because the last thing he wanted to

do was argue with his mother-in-law over the events of the last two years. Now was not the time nor the place. He only wanted to visit with Whitney. He needed to determine for himself how well she was doing. Brushing past Carmen, he made his way to Whitney's side.

His breath left him as Javar sank into the chair beside Whitney's bed. She looked so fragile, so vulnerable ... His gaze steadfast on Whitney, he said to Carmen, "Tell me what happened."

Tension-filled silence permeated the air. Evidently, Carmen felt she owed him no explanations. After several seconds of waiting for his mother-in-law to answer him, Javar turned and faced her, his eyes imploring her to give him the answer he craved.

She frowned. Then sighed as resignation passed over her features. "There was an accident," she stated monotonously. "Whitney was heading to see you, and ..." Carmen's deep voice cracked, and she wrenched her gaze away from Javar's. It took her several seconds to regain her composure, and when she did, she again faced him with anger in her eyes. "Once again, Javar, you're the cause of my daughter's pain."

"How am I responsible for this?" Javar unleashed an irritated breath. "I didn't even know she was back in town. And if anyone should be upset here, it should be me. Whitney's been here for two days and you didn't even call to let me know?"

Carmen was silent, her face contorted with ire. She could quietly fume all she wanted, but she couldn't say anything in response to Javar's statement because she knew he was right. He was still legally Whitney's husband, and he had a right to know what happened to her. Shaking his head, Javar pondered the thought that he might have been too late. And if Whitney had died before he'd gotten a chance see her, he would never have forgiven his mother-in-law.

Closing his eyes for a long moment, he tried to assuage his stormy emotions. Whitney hadn't died, and what was important now was seeing her get well. Moments later, his voice calm, he said, "Will you just finish the story please?"

Carmen cleared her throat and continued. "The roads, they . . . it was raining. The police don't know exactly what happened, but somehow Whitney lost control, and she collided with a tree. It was awful, the accident scene."

"I . . . I remember seeing something on the news a couple nights ago. . . . Oh, my God." The wreckage he had seen on the news had been horrifying. How could Whitney have come out of that accident alive?

"The police and doctors say it's a miracle she's still breathing."

She could have died. It was as though the realization only now truly hit him, and his stomach lurched painfully. Why? His mind screamed. Why did this happen? Why Whitney? She had suffered so much already. Pushing those thoughts aside, Javar reached forward and delicately stroked the soft, pale, honey-brown skin of her face. In spite of the severe bruising under her left eye, and her swollen, bruised lips, she was still incredibly beautiful. As always.

He swallowed. Until this moment, he had deluded himself by saying that he could go on with his life alone, without his wife. In the almost two years that Whitney had been gone, he had resigned himself to a life without her; his anger had made that resignation easier. But seeing her now, and realizing that he had almost lost her a second time, he knew that he would never truly be fulfilled if he didn't have her in his life again. How could he go on without her, when he knew deep in his heart that he had never stopped loving her? It was time to put aside all the hurt and bitterness and move on.

He brought Whitney's frail hand to his lips and kissed it, then held it against his face.

"Touching, Javar," Carmen muttered sardonically. "But just a little too late."

"What's he doing here?"

Javar didn't have to look up to recognize whose face went with that high-pitched question. It was Cherise Burnett, Whitney's feisty, hot-headed cousin.

Feeling her presence upon him, Javar gazed up at Cherise. Her brown eyes were cold and harsh as they stared down at him, telling him in no uncertain terms that she most definitely did not approve of him being here. Too worried about Whitney to deal with Cherise's wrath, Javar returned his gaze to Whitney's bandaged face. He continued to hold her soft hand against his cheek.

"You actually have the audacity to show up here?" Cherise whispered in a lethal tone. "If you know what's good for you, Javar, you'll get out of here."

Javar ignored her; arguing with Cherise would get him nowhere.

"This is ridiculous," Cherise continued, exasperated. "Aunt Carmen, I'm gonna get the nurse to call security." Pinning Javar with an icy glare, Cherise said, "And Javar, you better be gone when I get back."

That comment was Javar's undoing. "And what do you think the nurse or doctor, or security for that matter, is going to say, Cherise? I'm her husband, in case you've forgotten."

"You're the one who conveniently forgot that, now didn't you?" Cherise retorted, her face distorted with anger. If looks could kill . . .

A soft moan came from Whitney's lips and Javar returned his attention to his wife. Seemingly restless, Whitney stirred.

"Keep your voice down," Javar said softly, casting a side-long glance at Cherise. "You're disturbing Whitney, and she obviously needs her rest."

Javar heard Cherise huff, and he could imagine that frown she wore so well pasted on her lips. She got quieter, but the icy quality was still evident when she said, "Well that's another reason you should get lost. For once, think of Whitney, not yourself."

Not bothering to dignify Cherise's comment with an answer, Javar rose from the chair at Whitney's side. This visit wasn't going the way he had expected. He'd hoped for some quiet time to sit with Whitney, but he should have known that her family would be with her, and considering the way things had ended between him and Whitney, he should have known that her family wouldn't be happy to see him. Sighing, Javar brushed past Cherise and Carmen, then strode to the door and opened it.

When he stepped into the hallway, the emotions he'd been holding inside overcame him. Relieved, he expelled a soft moan and leaned forward, bracing his hands against his knees. *Whitney's alive!* His mind screamed. *Whitney's alive!*

And according to Carmen, she had been en route to see him when the accident happened. After all this time and his own stubborn pride preventing him from going to see her, she had finally been the one to make the effort to see him.

And now she was lying in a hospital bed because of it.

It was all so hard to believe. How could the vibrant, lively woman he'd met five years ago now be lying in a hospital bed, fighting for her life? One serious car accident was bad enough to have suffered, but another one?

Maybe it was seeing Whitney in such a dismal state that had Javar remembering a happier time. Whatever the reason, he couldn't help remembering the first time she had entered his life. She'd been a twenty-two-year-old cocktail waitress then, and he was nine years her senior. Still, he'd been fiercely attracted to her. He could remember their meeting like it was yesterday . . .

Javar followed his brother through the crowd at The Rave, one of Chicago's most popular nightspots. The men were outfitted in dress pants and silk shirts, and the women were all decked out in their sexiest outfits. As Javar made his way through the crowd, he realized that it had been a long time since he'd relaxed. All work and no play, his brother would say about him. At his brother's requests, Javar had finally agreed to an evening of fun.

Khamil, his younger brother by a year, definitely appreciated a beautiful woman, and right now, his eyes were roaming the crowd. Turning, Khamil smiled widely at Javar. "Mmm mmm," he hummed. "The ladies are looking super-fine tonight."

"Down boy," Javar said, then chuckled. "Let's wait until we've had at least one drink before you go on the prowl."

"Why wait?" Khamil retorted. "You know what they say: Wait too long and life passes you by."

Rolling his eyes playfully, Javar patted his brother on the shoulder. "Just remember we're here together. Don't you dare find some honey and take off on me, like you did the last time."

The music was loud, and the walls and floors in the two-level club were vibrating with each beat. The large dance floor, which was to their left, was packed with people energetically moving their bodies to the funky tune. Javar smiled. It had definitely been too long.

"Why don't we go upstairs?" Javar suggested, and he was relieved when Khamil led the way to the winding stairs that would take them to the second level.

It was a wonder they even made it upstairs before the end of the night. Along the way, Khamil met, hugged, and conversed with so many beautiful young women, Javar lost count. It was one thing to be well-liked, which his brother certainly was, but it was quite another to know almost all the single women in a given club.

His brother certainly got around.

As Khamil whispered in the ear of a beautiful, dark-skinned woman, Javar leaned forward and whispered in his ear. "Believe me, Khamil, 'getting around' is overrated."

Khamil threw Javar a dubious glance. "Get real, J. Maybe

if you're the Pope, but not when you're young, dark, and handsome, like I am.''

Folding his arms over his chest, Javar chortled. His younger brother certainly wasn't lacking in the self-esteem department. In fact, it was obvious he had enough to spare.

When Khamil finally drew himself away from the beautiful woman, he turned to Javar and said, "Javar, this is April. April, this is my brother, Javar.''

April looked up at Javar from lowered eyelids, grinning at him seductively. Javar flashed her a quick smile. "Hi, April.'' Then, turning back to his brother, he said, "Can we go upstairs now? You promised me a drink, and I'm getting pretty thirsty.''

Khamil shrugged apologetically at April, and when they were out of her earshot he turned toward Javar, pinning him with a puzzled expression. "Are you crazy?''

"No," Javar replied coolly. "Why do you ask?''

Khamil's mouth fell open in complete surprise. "April— she's a TKO, man! And she likes you! What's up with you?''

Javar smirked and stated simply, "She's not my type.'' One look at April, and he could tell that she was the type of woman who was out for a good time, not a long time. She was also the type who thought all men should worship the ground she walked on, merely because she was beautiful. She probably wasn't rejected too often. Well, let him be one of the few to reject her. Javar was too old to play dating games. He was thirty-one, and he'd already made one big mistake in his life: Stephanie Lewis. Stephanie was gorgeous, and after she'd pursued him relentlessly, he'd finally given in to her seductive charms. He had found out the hard way that she wasn't interested in settling down, merely in having a good time and spending his money. Now, three years later, he had custody of their two-year-old son J.J..

Khamil slapped Javar on the shoulder. He may have been Javar's younger brother, but Khamil was taller than him by about half an inch. "There's a table over there, man. Let's go sit down and I'll buy you that drink I've been promising you.''

"Sounds like a plan," Javar said. Within seconds, he and his brother were seated at a small table near the railing, affording them a view of the dance floor below.

"Holy . . ." Javar heard Khamil murmur, and Javar lifted his eyes from the view of the people below. Khamil's mouth was hanging open and his eyes were lit up with interest as he looked over Javar's shoulder. A woman, Javar figured, smiling wryly. Turning slowly, he saw the object of Khamil's desire. *Holy was right,* Javar thought, sitting taller in his seat. His own lips parted as he observed the waitress approaching their table. To say she was beautiful was an understatement. She was exquisite, the most attractive woman he had ever seen in his life. A form-fitting red top and black miniskirt allowed Javar a fairly unrestricted view of her body, and he liked what he saw. She was probably five foot six, with a small frame, but curves in all the right places and legs that seemed to go on forever. Her skin was a rich, honey-brown complexion. Her face   and her eyes were bright and wide, and as she smiled at him, he could see two small dimples peeking at him from her cheeks.

"Good evening, gentlemen," she said, her soft, silky voice gently washing over Javar. "What can I get you to drink?"

Javar couldn't speak. He was completely mesmerized. The gorgeous woman standing before him had affected him the way no other woman ever had. She was exquisitely beautiful, exotic—her round face and almond-shaped eyes indicated an Asian influence—yet there was an innocent quality about her, a genuineness.

Khamil snapped his fingers before Javar's face. "J., she asked you a question."

Embarrassed, Javar lowered his gaze and swallowed— hard. What was wrong with him?

"You'll have to excuse my brother," Khamil said, flashing the waitress a wide smile. "He doesn't get out much."

Javar's lips twisted into a crooked grin, directed at his brother. Turning to the waitress, he said, "Don't listen to him." Her radiant smile nearly blinded him.

She chuckled softly. "Can I get you something to drink?"

Javar's throat was suddenly very dry. "Sure," he managed to say. "I'll take a draft beer. Whatever you have on tap."

She took Khamil's order next, but Javar barely heard a word they said. His eyes were fixated on her full, sensuous lips, and his thoughts were completely focused on how he could get to know her better.

When she walked away, he watched the gentle sway of her hips. As soon as she was out of his sight, he released a breath that sounded suspiciously like a whistle.

Khamil smiled at him. "So that's the kind of woman it takes to wake you up, huh? Too bad she was checking me out, not you, big brother."

"Is that right?" Javar bit his bottom lip and raised an eyebrow in a challenging manner. "Well, I hate to disappoint you, bro, but you're definitely not her type."

Khamil laughed. "Hey, the ladies have a hard time passing up a fine brother like me."

"She's not like all your women, Khamil," Javar stated, knowing deep down that he was right. The waitress was different. Although beautiful, he could tell she wasn't the flaky type of woman Khamil seemed to like.

It wasn't a moment too soon when she returned to their table, carrying a small tray with their drinks. Javar stood to his full six foot one inch frame and reached into the back pocket of his black dress pants. He extended a twenty to her, but as she reached for it, he pulled it away. "Before I give this to you, tell me your name."

Curious eyes met his determined ones. "Excuse me?"

Javar sighed, wondering what had gotten into him. Sure, he was attracted to her, but he wasn't used to losing his cool with women. And he certainly wasn't into cheesy pickup lines or games. And to make matters worse, she looked about twenty—definitely too young for him.

He handed her the twenty. "I'm sorry if I offended you. Keep the change."

"Thanks." The waitress's lips curled into a full, genuine smile, exposing her perfect white teeth. She stuffed the twenty in her apron and spun on her heel. When she had walked away a few steps, she turned back and faced Javar. "And since you're interested, my name's Whitney." . . .

"Excuse me, sir. Are you all right?"

The sound of a female voice pulled Javar back to the present and the unpleasant reality. He looked up at the pretty nurse who stood before him. He was still hunched forward with his hands on his knees, and instantly, he stood. No wonder the woman was concerned about him; he must have looked like he was going to be sick.

Javar smiled down at the slim nurse, appreciating her concern. "I'm fine. Thanks."

She looked at him as though she didn't believe him, but after a moment the nurse scampered off.

"Wow," Javar mumbled, thinking of how caught up with the past he had just been. A soft smile touched his lips as he remembered his brother's shock that Whitney had been interested in him. By the end of that first night, Javar and Whitney had exchanged numbers, and two weeks later, they were dating steadily. Despite his mother's protests that she was a gold digging child who wanted to sleep her way into their family's money, Javar married Whitney eleven months after they had met.

He sighed. In recent years, whenever he thought about Whitney, he also remembered J.J., the accident, and how everything had taken a turn for the worse in their relationship.

Now was no time for a trip down memory lane, he told

himself. He needed to speak with Whitney's doctor. Running a hand over his short hair, Javar made his way to the information desk.

A middle-aged nurse smiled warmly at him. "May I help you, sir?"

Javar nodded. "Yes. My name is Javar Jordan. My wife is Whitney Jordan. Who is her doctor?"

"Let me just check for you," the nurse said, directing her gaze to a chart. A few second later, she looked up at Javar and said, "Dr. Farkas is her supervising physician."

"Is Dr. Farkas available?"

The fair-skinned nurse pursed her lips and shrugged. "I haven't seen her in a little while. She's still working, I know that. I can page her for you."

"Please do." Stepping aside and leaning against the counter, Javar squeezed the bridge of his nose. Whitney. He had to believe that she was going to be okay. He had to do whatever it took to make sure that she would be okay. And that meant getting her out of Cook County Hospital and to a place where the doctors weren't so overloaded with patients that they might ignore his wife's needs.

He couldn't lose her . . . not now.

"Mr. Jordan?"

Javar turned to face the petite young woman before him. She extended a small hand. "I'm Dr. Farkas."

Javar's eyes widened, unable to shield his shock. Surely this woman standing in front of him wasn't old enough to be a doctor, especially not Whitney's doctor. All the more reason to get her moved to another hospital immediately.

Apparently reading Javar's concern, Dr. Farkas announced, "I assure you I'm quite qualified."

Embarrassed that she had read his thoughts, Javar cleared his throat, then took Dr. Farkas's small hand in his large one, shaking it firmly. "Sorry. You just look . . ."

"Young?" Dr. Farkas supplied, then smiled. "I know."

Rubbing the back of his neck with his right hand, Javar

nodded absently. "Please, tell me about my wife's condition."

Dr. Farkas folded her arms over her chest. "Mr. Jordan, your wife is a very lucky woman. Since she was admitted two days ago, she's been in and out of consciousness, but she's recently woken up, and I'm happy to tell you that she appears quite lucid. Despite the severity of the accident, her wounds are superficial. She did suffer a mild concussion, but has recovered from that."

Javar met Dr. Farkas's steady gaze with questioning eyes. "What do you mean, 'superficial'? I've seen her, and sure, she's breathing, but she looks like she's in a lot of pain."

"She was in a serious car accident and she's bound to experience a lot of discomfort. Unfortunately, the pain is something she can't escape. But fortunately, she didn't have any internal injuries—"

"What about her head?"

A weary look flashed in Dr. Farkas's eyes. "I understand your concerns, Mr. Jordan, but I assure you the wounds to her head are all superficial. The lacerations will heal nicely."

"How do you know that there's no serious internal damage?"

"Because we've run all the tests possible to detect that, Mr. Jordan," Dr. Farkas replied, her tone authoritative.

"An MRI?"

The doctor's eyes darkened a shade. "Yes, Mr. Jordan. I assure you there's no reason to worry about your wife's recovery."

Frustrated, Javar exhaled. He glanced around the hospital hallway, seeing the numerous patients on gurneys and their concerned family members. Dr. Farkas seemed certain that Whitney was going to be okay, but he couldn't be convinced of that. Not if she remained at this facility. He had already lost one person he loved at this hospital. He wasn't about to lose another.

"Well, Dr. Farkas, I do worry," Javar said, turning to

meet her gaze once again. "Cook County clearly has too many patients to care for. I would feel much better if my wife were moved to another facility."

"I have to object, Mr. Jordan. She's had a head injury, and it's inadvisable to move her in her condition."

"I thought she was fine?" He watched as Dr. Farkas's olive complected skin turned a shade of crimson red. He sensed she was angry, that she felt her competence was being questioned. Javar realized he was being demanding without offering any explanations. "Dr. Farkas, I have no doubts that you are a qualified physician. The problem isn't you." He paused. "Two years ago, I lost . . . my son died here. And whether I'm justified or not, I feel that moving my wife to another hospital will . . . It will make me feel more comfortable."

Dr. Farkas nodded. "I understand where you're coming from, but I assure you—"

"Please, Dr. Farkas," Javar said.

Looking up at him with concerned eyes, the doctor nodded tightly. "Very well."

"Thank you. I'll make the arrangements now." Turning, Javar strode toward the pay telephones, reaching into his pocket for some change.

Ten minutes later, he had all the arrangements made to have Whitney moved to Rush North Shore Medical Hospital in the Chicago suburb of Skokie. Skokie was much closer to his home in Kenilworth, anyway, and he trusted that hospital's medical care much more than he did Cook County's. Rush would not look like a war zone, which was the way Cook County did. Whitney deserved the best medical attention available. J.J. hadn't been so fortunate.

He returned to Whitney's room with an open mind, but the moment he arrived Cherise threw him a hateful look. Carmen's hazel eyes were swollen and red, and as she looked at him, what he could see behind the anger was sadness . . . and fear.

He was afraid too. That's why he was having Whitney moved to another hospital.

He cleared his throat before speaking. "I just want you to know that Whitney will have the best care available. I'm having her transferred to Rush North Shore Medical Hospital, where I'm sure she will get the attention she needs."

Carmen's mouth fell open in horror, and she gasped. "She's too weak to be moved to another hospital."

"That's right," Cherise added. "God only know why you're here Javar, but if it's guilt, get over it. She doesn't need you."

"The arrangements have already been made, and an ambulance is on its way. What you can do for Whitney now is get her things ready."

Rising, Cherise said, "You can't do this."

"I happen to be her husband, and she's still on my insurance policy. So, yes, Cherise, I can."

A muffled groan escaped Whitney's throat, and instantly Javar made his way to her side. "Sweetie?" He watched as her face contorted, but her eyes remained shut. "Sweetie, it's Javar. I'm right here."

Whitney's eyelids fluttered open, and her chestnut-colored eyes met Javar's. Confusion flashed in their depths, and her eyes widened. But the next moment, they narrowed, then closed. When she opened them again, her eyes were heavy-lidded, and it seemed like it was a major effort to keep them open, but she did.

Grinning, Javar ran a finger along the silky smoothness of Whitney's cheek. Thank God she was waking up.

"Don't you worry, sweetie," he said, his voice filled with emotion. "I'm here now, and I'm going to take care of you."

Chapter Three

"Javar?" Whitney's voice was faint.

Relieved laughter bubbled from his throat as Javar beamed at Whitney, pressing her soft hand against the stubble on his cheek. "Yeah, sweetie. It's me."

Whitney groaned. "W-what . . . why . . . ?"

Javar pressed Whitney's delicate fingers to his lips, remembering the way things used to be between them. For a brief moment in time, they had been deliriously happy. Her fingers, now cold and frail, had once lovingly caressed his face, his body. Regret washed over him, and he swallowed the emotions that were lodging in his throat. "All that matters is that I'm here now, Whitney. And I'm going to be here until you get well."

Carmen appeared at the other side of Whitney's bed. "I can make him leave, honey. Just say the word."

Whitney's eyes moved to her mother, then returned to meet Javar's gaze. Suddenly, her eyes grew wide, and her chest heaved as she started to cry.

Javar's stomach churned as he watched Whitney, his heart aching for the pain she was in. He brushed her forehead with his fingers, hoping to soothe her. "What is it, Whitney? What's wrong?"

"J.J." she sobbed, clenching his hand. "Where's J.J.?" Confusion clouded her face. Then, as though everything became clear, she gasped, then started crying harder. "I— I'm sorry," she cried. "I'm sorry."

Javar leaned forward and nuzzled his nose against Whitney's cheek. "Shh," he cooed. "Whitney, sweetie, it's okay."

"I—it's my fault," she said, her words choked between sobs. "J.J.—he's—Oh God!"

Carmen threw her hand to her mouth, but wasn't able to hold back her tears. Javar looked up at her, perplexed, worried. "What's going on?"

Sniffling, Carmen wiped at her tears. "When she awoke before, she was confused. She seemed to think that she was in the accident that . . . that killed J.J. But then she remembered. Oh, dear Lord, what's happening to her?"

Javar watched Whitney cry, his own heart breaking. Dr. Farkas obviously didn't know what she was talking about. Whitney's injuries were more than surface. Was she suffering some type of memory loss? Javar bit down hard on his bottom lip, overwhelmed with emotion. Then, turning to Cherise, he said, "Go get the doctor!"

Fighting her own tears, Cherise ran from the room.

"It's okay, it's okay," Javar repeated to Whitney, but his soft words didn't stop her tears. Moments later, Dr. Farkas appeared, followed by Cherise.

"Doctor, something's wrong," Javar explained. "She's almost hysterical."

As Dr. Farkas moved to Whitney's side, Javar stepped aside. "What's wrong with her?"

"She needs a sedative," Dr. Farkas replied. "I'll be right back." Minutes later, she returned with a syringe and inserted it into the tubing hooked up to Whitney's intravenous bag. "This should calm her down."

"She doesn't seem lucid at all, Doctor. She thinks she was in an accident that happened two years ago."

"She's going through a lot of physical and emotional stress. Most likely, her actions now were a response to a dream. I have to tell you, Mr. Jordan, I strongly object to transferring her in this state."

Javar leveled a steady gaze on the doctor. "No offense, but I'm now more convinced than ever that my wife needs to be moved."

Dr. Farkas pulled her lips into a thin, taut line. "As you wish. You'll need to settle your wife's bill at the reception desk."

"I'll be out there in a minute." Javar averted his eyes to Whitney, whose breathing was now calmer, and her tortured expression had relaxed. He walked over to the bed, leaned forward and planted a soft kiss on her forehead.

Whitney was clearly tortured. The accident had injured her physically, but guilt was making her suffer far worse than any physical pain. Gritting his teeth, Javar realized that he had done nothing to help Whitney overcome her guilt when she had needed him most. Instead, he had turned his back on her.

Seeing her like this, in so much agony, pained him. A large lump constricted his throat, making it hard to swallow. He had almost lost her before they'd had a chance to make things right.

Javar moved from the bed and went to the small closet in the corner of the room, where he found Whitney's clothes. "Is this everything?" he asked, turning to face Carmen and Cherise.

Her lips curled downward in a frown, Cherise nodded.

"Good. Please get Whitney's other things ready. I'm going to settle the bill before the ambulance arrives."

* * *

The trip to Rush North Shore Medical Hospital was uneventful, and Whitney was now comfortably resting in a private room. The sedative Whitney received at the other hospital had helped her to relax, and other than the occasional nervous twitch, she didn't seem to be in any pain.

Carmen and Cherise had decided not to make the trip to the new hospital, no doubt because they didn't want to see any more of Javar than was necessary. But they had told Javar they would visit Whitney the next day.

Dr. Adu-Bohene, a longtime friend of Javar's parents, and an excellent physician, was supervising Whitney's care. Javar hated to leave her before he knew the extent of her injuries, but having been told that the doctors wouldn't know anything conclusive until they ran some tests, he decided to head to his office to take care of some business. Now that Whitney needed him, he was going to be there for her. And that meant limiting his time at the office.

It was after four in the afternoon when Javar entered his office building. Murphy's Law dictated that on the one day he just wanted to get to his office to take care of business, the elevator would stop on almost every floor before he reached his destination. When he finally reached the thirtieth floor Javar rushed off the elevator and headed to the office of Duncan Malloy, one of his two senior associates. He spent half an hour going over the specs for the renovations of a waterfront estate in Highland Park, a wealthy suburb of Chicago. The estate was an older home, and some of the remodeling the client wanted just wasn't feasible, at least not without tearing apart part of the foundation, and that kind of work wasn't within the client's budget. However, Javar was certain that Duncan could make alternative suggestions that the client would find satisfactory. As for the bid for the Li project, Javar explained to Duncan that he would be personally handling the project from this point on. He should have realized that Duncan wasn't the right architect for the kind of project Mr. Li wanted; he had a more conservative style, and Mr. Li liked innovative, larger-than-life designs. Javar had just been too busy to take on the project himself. In return, he gave Duncan two of his current sizable projects.

Next, he went to see Harvey Grescoe, his other senior associate. Harvey was clearly surprised when Javar named him acting principal for an unspecified period, but Javar avoided the curious man's questions. While he was good friends with Harvey, he didn't want to get into the complicated story of what was going on in his life right now. He trusted Harvey implicitly, and knew that when he returned, the office would still be running smoothly. When Harvey flashed him a concerned look, Javar smiled faintly and promised to check in with him on a daily basis.

It felt weird, reassigning his duties in order to take a leave of absence. It wouldn't be a true leave; he would still be working on the sketches for the Li bid as well as other business, and he would call the office on a regular basis. Still, it felt strange. Javar had built Jordan & Associates from the ground up. In the beginning, he'd spent long hours at the office, and then long hours at home, determined to prove to his parents that he wouldn't fail. But once he had become established, he still hadn't cut back on his work hours. Even when he had married Whitney, he'd continued to burn the candle at both ends. That was something Whitney had constantly complained about, claiming that he wasn't investing as much time in his marriage as he was in his career. She'd suggested on several occasions that the firm was too large for one man to control, that he should accept either of the senior associates' requests for partnership. Javar hadn't wanted to do that, and as a result, he'd put in the hours necessary to run his business successfully and single-handedly, not thinking of the consequences for his marriage.

And then, after J.J. died, and Whitney had left him, his work had become his life.

Burying the thoughts of J.J. and Whitney in the back of his mind, Javar marched across the plush gray carpet, approaching the double mahogany doors to his office. He'd taken care of most of the urgent matters, but still needed to tie up some loose ends before heading back to the hospital.

Melody had the phone secured between her shoulder and ear when Javar stopped at her desk and looked down at her. When she noticed him, Melody's lips curled into a wide grin, and she promptly ended her call.

"Any messages?" Javar asked.

Melody nodded as she searched the message pad on her desk. "I've got some brief ones here. But check your voice mail." Smiling brightly, she handed Javar the pink message slips.

"Thanks." Javar turned to leave, then halted. "Melody, I'm going to be out of the office for a little while. I'm not sure how long yet. Whatever can't wait until I get back, please give to Harvey Grescoe to handle."

Melody's dark brown brow furrowed with concern, and her eyes narrowed. "Are you sure, Mr. Jordan? What if someone insists on speaking with you, not Mr. Grescoe? Should I contact you at home?"

"That won't be necessary. I will check in with you once a day, as well as Harvey. If there are any emergencies, either you or he can relay them to me then."

Melody stood and rounded the corner of her wide oak desk. She placed a soft hand on Javar's. "Is everything okay? The way you stormed out of here earlier, I was a bit worried."

"Well, don't be," Javar said succinctly, and immediately regretted his abrupt tone. At her startled look, he forced a smile. "I'll be fine."

Javar knew that Melody was interested in him, and physically, he found her an attractive black woman, but after his disastrous relationship with Stephanie Lewis, he'd vowed never to get involved with someone who worked for him again. He'd never returned Melody's obvious affection, yet she still persisted. Never overtly, but subtly, with gestures and heated glances. She had liked him even when he'd been married, and then when Whitney had moved away, Melody had started wearing provocative outfits to work, no doubt trying to get his attention. Although professional, her skirts were definitely tighter and shorter, and her necklines were lower, revealing her ample bosom. Her new style of clothes hadn't been a distraction for him, but it had certainly been a distraction for several other men in the office. Javar was immune to that kind of thing; he had fallen for one too many pretty faces, and he'd learned his lesson.

Besides, after falling in love with Whitney, he knew there would never be another woman who would steal his heart.

Looking at Melody now, her full lips pursed in a concerned pout, he thought for the millionth time that he should have hired an older, frumpy woman to be his administrative assistant. Now more than ever, he didn't need the hassles of unwanted sexual attention. But Melody had been the best candidate after Stephanie, and at the time he had hired her, she'd been married, so Javar hadn't anticipated any complications in their work relationship. But she'd gotten divorced shortly after she had started the job, and ever since the ink was dry on her divorce papers, she'd had her sights set on him.

It was ironic, Javar thought, that there were several women vying for his heart, yet he wanted the one who'd had the strength to walk away from him.

"I appreciate your concern, Melody." Javar turned his attention to the message slips in his hand and began to flip through them. With a small grin, he left her standing at the corner of her desk and strolled into his office.

There were three messages from his mother, all of which said, "Urgent". He would have to return her calls, but only after he had taken care of office business.

He spent the next hour checking his voice mail and returning calls. Satisfied that everything was under control for the next couple of days, Javar stood and inhaled a large gulp of air. Moving to the window, he looked out at the spectacular view of Lake Michigan, which was glittering enticingly under the sun's strong rays. It was another hot late June day in Chicago.

But he had no time to worry about beautiful views, or any frivolous thing like that. Flicking his wrist forward, Javar looked down at his gold Rolex. Five forty-three. He was anxious to get back to the hospital and see Whitney, but he knew his mother would never forgive him if he didn't return her calls. When Angela Jordan said something was urgent, she expected to be contacted promptly. By now, she should have been home from Mercy Hospital, where she worked as a surgeon.

Javar picked up the telephone receiver and punched in the digits to his parents' home. After two rings, Gretta Kurtz, the lovely older German woman who was his parents' housekeeper, answered the phone. "Jordan residence," she said pleasantly.

Even after all the years she had been in the United States, Gretta's voice still held a distinct German accent. "Hello, Gretta. It's Javar. Is my mother home?"

"Oh hello, Javar. Yes, your mother's here. One moment, please."

Several moments later, Angela came to the phone. "Javar?"

"Hello, Mother."

"My goodness, where have you been?" Angela Jordan chastised. "I've been trying to reach you for hours."

It was just like his mother to skip the "Hi hon, how are you?" And give him the third degree.

"It's been a long day," Javar replied, his tone making it clear that he didn't want to answer any questions about his whereabouts. "What's so important that you called me several times at work?"

Angela made a sound somewhere between a huff and a snort, the way she always did when she didn't like the response she got. His mother loved to control—her husband, her children, and anyone else who would let her. She had his father wrapped around her finger, and for years while Javar was growing up, he, too, had done everything possible to please her. Not anymore. Javar was too old for her power games.

"I was just calling to remind you of the dinner party tonight, dear," his mother replied, her tone sugary. When Javar was silent, she added, "The one with Judge Harmon and his family."

And Judge Harmon's daughter, Althea, a successful criminal attorney in Chicago. The perfect woman for him, according to his mother. Javar rolled his eyes heavenward. "I'm sorry, Mother. I can't make it."

Angela gasped. "Why on earth not? We're all expecting you."

"Mother, I never promised that I would be there, only that I'd try. And I can't make it. I've got work to do." The last thing he wanted to do was explain that Whitney was back in town and in the hospital. The mere mention of Whitney's name would make his mother livid.

"In other words, you forgot?" Angela asked, clearly not pleased. "Is that it?"

"Actually," Javar began, "I did forget. I've been very busy working on the Milwaukee hotel project I told you about, and—"

His mother's cold words cut him off. "This is about Whitney, isn't it?"

All the blood drained from Javar's face. "W-Whitney?" he stammered, thrown aback by his mother's question. How did she know?

"Yes, Whitney," Angela replied, saying Whitney's name as though it were some horrible disease. "I heard she was back in town."

There was no point denying the truth now. "Yes," Javar responded, his tone deceptively calm. "She is. And she needs me now."

"Because of the accident?"

Javar's brow furrowed. "How did you know about that?"

"Word gets around in medical circles," she replied succinctly. The next moment, her tone softened. "What can you do for her now, Javar? She's in the hospital, they're taking care of her. She doesn't need you."

An agitated sigh escaped Javar's clenched teeth. His mother had never approved of his relationship with Whitney, and she would never understand his need to stand by her now. But that was her problem, not his.

"Mother, please relay my deepest regrets to Judge Harmon and his family. I will not be able to make it this evening. Good-bye."

As he replaced the receiver, he could hear his mother's loud protests. He didn't care. He didn't have time for dinner parties and mindless conversation. And he definitely didn't want to be paired with Althea all evening, thinking of things to say to her, and listening to her ramble on about all her important cases.

All he wanted to do was head back to the hospital and be with Whitney. Grabbing his blazer, Javar headed out of the office.

Whitney awoke with a start. Fear gripped her. Darting her eyes around the spacious room, her stomach coiled in apprehension as she realized that she didn't recognize her surroundings.

Where was she?

She was still in a hospital, that much she could ascertain, but not the same one as before. This one was nicer.

A polished oak table was to the right of her bed, on which sat a crystal pitcher filled with ice and water, and two crystal glasses. In the far corner of the room near the large bay window were two plush sofas and a small oak coffee table. Across from the bed, built into the wall, was what looked to be a twenty-one inch television. A vinyl recliner rested on the left side of her bed.

No, this definitely wasn't Cook County Hospital.

Gathering strength, Whitney reached for the nurse buzzer resting on the oak table. She pressed down on the small, blue button. Less than a minute later, a middle-aged woman dressed in a light pink nurse's outfit entered her room.

"How are you feeling?" The woman asked, an amiable smile gracing her lips.

First Whitney looked at the name tag pinned to the woman's shirt. It read, "Hazel McDonnell, R.N.". Then, she lifted her gaze to Hazel's, staring at the pleasant looking woman through narrowed eyes. "Where am I?"

"You're at Rush North Shore Medical Hospital." The nurse proceeded to take her blood pressure, then checked her pulse.

Whitney knew this was going to sound like a dumb question, but still she asked, "Why am I here?"

"Your husband had you transferred from Cook County Hospital earlier."

Javar. . . . Concentrating, she remembered him being at the hospital, but little else.

"Open, please." Whitney complied, and the nurse stuck a thermometer under her tongue. After about a minute, she removed it. "Are you in any pain?"

Whitney nodded, slightly. "My head."

The nurse clucked her tongue, then gave Whitney's hand a reassuring squeeze. "It's gonna be all right, dear. I'll get you some painkillers, and now that you're awake, the doctor would like to see you."

As the nurse left the room, Whitney laid her head back, willing the pain to go away. She wondered where her family was.

And more specifically, where was Javar?

* * *

"How is she, Dr. Adu-Bohene?" Javar asked the dark-skinned African man as he stood outside Whitney's private room.

"Surprisingly, well. The swelling on her head is already going down, and the bruises are starting to heal. All our tests indicate no serious head trauma, or other type of internal injury."

Relieved, Javar exhaled a gush of warm air. "Thank God."

"She'll need to take it easy for a while, of course. I can't say how long it will be before she makes a full recovery."

"I understand." Anxious to see her, Javar averted his eyes to her closed door. "But at least she's out of danger?"

Dr. Adu-Bohene's shoulders rose and fell in a noncommittal shrug. "It looks that way, but we can never be too cautious with a head trauma, as far as I'm concerned. I suggest she stay here at least another couple of days for observation."

Javar nodded, his expression grim. Dr. Adu-Bohene patted his back in an effort to comfort him. "Don't worry, Javar. I'll make sure she's fine . . . at least physically. As for emotionally, I know this must be hard on her, especially after the earlier tragedy."

"Have you spoken to her?"

Dr. Adu-Bohene nodded.

"How did she seem? As I told you before, I'm concerned she may have a memory loss."

"When I spoke to her, her mind seemed very clear. She didn't mention the previous accident, only her desire to speak with you. Why don't you go in and see her? I'm sure she'll be happy to see you."

His heart warmed at the doctor's words. If Whitney was asking for him, that had to be a good sign. And he couldn't wait to talk to her. Flashing Dr. Adu-Bohene an appreciative smile, Javar said, "Thanks." Then he turned the doorknob and slowly entered the room, careful not to disturb Whitney.

She lay sleeping as he gazed at her. Peaceful, serene, without worry . . . that's how she looked. *Thank goodness*, Javar thought. She deserved some peace. He was anxious to talk with her, but he wouldn't disturb her now. Her rest was much more important than what he wanted.

Quietly, he made his way across the gray marble floor until he reached the black recliner beside Whitney's bed. Easing himself onto it, he took Whitney's hand in his, stroking her soft flesh. As he laced his fingers with hers, he closed his eyes, thinking. So much had gone wrong in their marriage. When they had said their vows in the backyard of his waterfront home that sunny day in May four years ago, he had never in his wildest dreams considered that they might separate, much less after only two years of marriage. But things had gone terribly wrong, and they *had* separated. Was there a chance they could make it right again?

Moaning, Whitney stirred. Javar opened his eyes, throwing his gaze to her face. When he'd seen her last, the day she had moved out, she hadn't been as thin as she was right now. He wondered if she was eating.

Whitney's eyes flew open, and when she saw Javar, she looked startled. After a few minutes, a small grin lifted her lips. A weak smile, yet her cute dimples were clearly evident.

Javar smiled back. "Hi."

"Hi."

A strained silence fell between them, and Javar realized how awkward this situation was. The last time he had seen her, she'd been crying; he'd been angry. Most definitely, they hadn't parted on good terms. Now, here he was at her bedside, playing the doting husband. More than anything, he wanted to right things between them.

"I'm sorry," he murmured, looking down at their joined hands, then into Whitney's dark eyes.

Whitney flashed him a questioning look. "Sorry?"

Javar nodded. "Yes, I'm sorry. For everything." He
paused as a wide range of emotions washed over him. "For
the pain you're feeling now . . . for all the pain I caused
you to feel before. I know you were coming to see me
when you had the accident."

"My mother told you?"

Chuckling mirthlessly, Javar said, "Did she ever."

Whitney closed her eyes pensively, then reopened them.
"I'm sorry if she offended you."

"She didn't. She's just worried about you, and I can't
blame her."

Whitney nodded.

Javar brought his free hand to his wife's face, and softly
ran his fingers along her cheek. It felt so good to touch
her. He wondered how he could have been such a fool to
let her walk out of his life. "You came back."

"Mmm hmm."

"I'm glad."

Whitney was uncomfortable, and she shifted in the bed
until she found a position she liked. She now lay on her
side, facing Javar. "You are?"

Javar nodded, a smile brightening his nutmeg-colored
eyes. "Yes, Whitney. Does that surprise you?"

Whitney's eyes roamed the hard, masculine edges of his
oval face, the wide, full lips, the thin mustache, the black
stubble that lined the sides of his golden-brown face. He
was still so handsome, so sexy. But when it came down to
it, looks didn't count for anything. Dedication did.

"Kind of," Whitney replied. It did surprise her that he
said he was happy to have her back. After the way things
had been between them when she left, she hadn't known
what to expect when she saw him again. She certainly
hadn't expected him to be at her bedside, holding her
hand.

"Well, don't be surprised. Things are going to be different between us." His smile faded into a soft frown. "I know
I was stubborn before. I was just in pain, and I didn't know

how to deal with my anger. But that's all behind me now. I promise you."

A nervous sensation spread through Whitney's blood as she realized the implication of what Javar was saying. He was talking like they had a future to look forward to . . . together.

Maybe it was the thought of almost losing her that had him thinking of a reconciliation. Or maybe he was just feeling guilty for the way things had ended between them. Whatever the reason for his sudden, bizarre display of emotion, it didn't change the fact that there wasn't a future for them. Their marriage ended nearly two years ago.

After the way he had pushed her out of his life then, she knew that he had never truly loved her. And if he *had* loved her, his love hadn't been strong enough to survive the horrible challenge they'd had to face.

"I'm glad you had the strength to come back, Whitney," Javar was saying when she focused on his words again. "I was wrong to ever let you walk out of my life. But you're back now. And that's all that matters."

How simple, Whitney thought, a wave of coldness sweeping over her. So, Javar was just ready to pick up the pieces? She didn't think so. She was playing by her rules now, not his.

And she had to end this charade before it went too far. The excited gleam in Javar's eyes said he thought she had come back to Chicago for a reconciliation. But after the dreadful pain she had suffered, Whitney knew that she could never turn back the clock to the happier times they had once shared. She didn't want to.

Softly moaning as a jolt of pain hit her, Whitney eased herself higher on the bed. "Javar."

"Yes, sweetie. What is it? Somewhere hurting? You need some water?"

Closing her eyes, Whitney took a deep breath. This wasn't the way she had wanted to tell Javar, but it was clear to her that it was necessary to set him straight now. "About why I was coming to see you . . ."

"It's okay, sweetie. You don't have to talk now. We've got our whole lives ahead of us." He softly stroked her cheek.

"No." Whitney's word was loud, final.

Javar flashed her a concerned look.

Whitney leveled a steady gaze in his direction. "There . . ." She paused, gathering strength. "There is no future for us, Javar."

Javar looked at her through narrowed eyes, clearly bewildered. "No . . . don't think like that Whitney. You survived the accident. You're going to be fine."

"That's not what I mean," Whitney retorted, her tone abrupt. She watched as confusion washed over Javar's face again. It wasn't easy, she realized, asking for a divorce even though their marriage was clearly over. Swallowing, Whitney lowered her eyelids, finding it suddenly hard to meet his questioning eyes.

In a voice barely above a whisper she said, "Javar, I want a divorce."

Chapter Four

Javar stared down at Whitney in stunned silence, his lips parted. Surely, getting a solid right hook to the gut couldn't wind him more than Whitney's last statement just had. Her expression solemn, Whitney had turned her head slightly to the left, avoiding his probing gaze.

Was this why she had come back to Chicago? To get a divorce and get on with her life?

"Whitney, you don't mean that. . . ."

"Yes," she said, then paused. "I do."

Javar shook his head as he looked down at his wife, as though that could make Whitney's words go away. "I know that we've had some rough times, but . . . I think we can. . . ."

"No," she replied, softly this time. "It's too late, Javar. Are you honestly going to tell me that you want to get back together?" Her eyes narrowed, speculatively. "I don't need your pity, Javar, and I know that's where this attitude must be coming from."

"No—"

"Well, it doesn't matter," Whitney continued, cutting

Javar off. "It's been almost two years since we separated. That's why I was going to see you. It's time . . . we set each other free."

"Whitney . . ."

"Please, Javar. Don't fight me."

A shiver passed over him. It couldn't be true. She couldn't really want this. Anger, hurt, and sadness flooded through him, and Javar bit his inner cheek to fight the unpleasant emotions.

A divorce? No, he couldn't accept that. "You know, now isn't the time to talk about this. You're in pain. . . ."

"But my thoughts aren't impaired. I know what I want, Javar. And that's to get on with my life."

Without him. Why the sudden hurry? he wondered, but didn't ask. She'd been content with a legal separation for almost two years; while they hadn't divorced, they had both gone on with their lives . . . apart. Frowning, he supposed he always knew this day would come, but nothing had prepared him for the emptiness he would feel when he actually heard her say the words.

He couldn't help asking, "Is there someone else?"

Whitney sighed, then winced as though in pain. Instinctively wanting to ease her discomfort, Javar brushed his fingers across her forehead. Whitney moved away from his touch, and Javar recoiled his fingers as quickly as if he'd been stung by a deadly snake's poison.

She stared at him for a long moment, as though she couldn't believe he'd asked that question. "No," she finally said. "I don't want a divorce because of some other man."

"Then why?"

"How can you ask me that?" She hesitated, then continued. "I thought you'd be elated that I'm finally asking for a divorce. I hear you're dating some lawyer. Maybe she can draw up the divorce papers."

Stunned, Javar's eyes bulged. She must be talking about Althea Harmon. "Where did you hear that?"

"It doesn't matter."

No, he agreed silently, it didn't matter. There was only one person who would have relayed such a story to Whitney: Cherise. He didn't know how she did it, but Whitney's cousin had a knack for discovering all kinds of sordid gossip. "It's not true," Javar told her, praying she believed him. "I . . . I haven't dated anyone since we separated."

Whitney shrugged her petite shoulders. "That's really not the point. I . . . our marriage failed." Her eyes challenged Javar to disagree. "What point is there in continuing to be legally married, when we aren't really married in the true sense of the word?"

Javar clenched his teeth, not liking what he was hearing at all. He wanted to have a real marriage. The vows he had taken he'd meant, and right now, he was willing to do whatever necessary to earn Whitney's trust, and her love. And if she had meant the vows she'd taken before God four years ago, then she at least owed it to him to make the same effort. Calmly, Javar said, "I don't want a divorce."

Whitney unleashed a ragged sigh. "Please, Javar, I don't want you to contest this. It's over—irrevocably. For goodness' sake, you've never even tried to contact me in the two years we've been separated."

"That's because you wanted to be left alone."

Whitney threw him a dubious glance. "If you'd really wanted our relationship to work, you would have tried harder than that. You knew exactly where I was."

He had known; she'd been living with an aunt in Louisiana. But he'd been too angry to contact her in the beginning, and then, after awhile, he'd just pushed all thoughts of her to the back of his mind. He had suffered unbearably after the death of his son, and quite frankly, he had shut down his emotions for months.

"As I said, I was in pain then. I didn't know how to deal with it."

Whitney stared at Javar in disbelief. "And I suppose I wasn't in pain?"

"I never said that. But you hadn't just lost your son—"

"He *was* my son, Javar. I may not have given birth to him, but I loved him as my own. And I had to live with the worst part of it all—I still do. If I had made sure that he was still buckled in. . . ." Unable to go on, Whitney's voice broke.

An intense pang of guilt hit him. God, he was an insensitive fool! Javar took her hand in his and gave it a comforting squeeze. "I'm sorry. Whitney, I didn't mean that the way it sounded. Please, forgive me."

"You see, Javar, this is exactly what I'm talking about. You were never able to recognize *my* pain, let alone forgive me for the accident. Based on what you just said, I don't think you ever will."

"That's not true," Javar replied. "I have forgiven you."

Whitney was shaking her head and grimacing. "You haven't, Javar. If you look deep inside yourself, you'll realize that."

Tears filled Whitney's eyes and Javar felt his insides constrict, but he didn't know what to say or do to make her feel better. It was still painful for him to think about the accident that had caused his son's death.

"Whitney, I . . ."

"Don't," Whitney said, tears now spilling onto her cheeks. "Don't say anything you don't mean, Javar. I just want you to leave."

The loud sounds of a funky tune on WGCI 107.5 FM filled Javar's car as he sped along John F. Kennedy Expressway. Gripping the steering wheel, Javar pressed down hard on the gas pedal, accelerating at an extremely fast rate. Seventy, eighty, ninety . . . The wind felt wonderful against his face as he whipped his red, convertible Dodge Viper through traffic at dangerous speeds. One hundred, one-ten. . . . He hit the brake as he came upon some fool in the left lane who refused to let him pass. He slowed to about seventy before he snuck into the immediate right lane in front of another car, then sped up and cut in front of the slower car in the passing lane.

He was driving like an idiot, but he was mad. Nothing was going right in his life and he needed to do something to alleviate his stress. He was in no frame of mind to work on the Li bid, so he could kiss that good-bye. And Whitney's words still rang loud and clear in his mind: "I want a divorce."

Javar floored the gas pedal, taking his Viper to an even higher speed. He'd been driving since he was fifteen, and knew how to handle a car well. And right now, flying through traffic seemed like the only thing he could control in his life.

A soft, love ballad filled the airwaves and Javar searched the passenger seat for a cassette he could play instead. He picked up an old S.O.S. Band tape, then tossed it aside. He didn't want to hear its unrealistic take on love. Continuing to search, he found a tape of George Clinton. Old-school was his style, and he threw the cassette into the tape deck.

The sounds of "Flashlight" blasted through the speakers, and he tapped his thumb against the steering wheel to the beat. He was so focused on the road before him, he didn't notice the police cruiser until it was right on his tail.

"Damn!" Javar lowered the volume of the music, then began to gradually slow down. He heard the loud blast of the police air horn, and cursing under his breath, he downshifted gears, making his way onto the left shoulder.

He slowed to a complete stop, put his car in park, then opened the car door and stepped out onto the shoulder. He felt the enormous force of other cars zooming by at the legal speed limit, and realized just how much of a madman he had been.

"Get back in the car!" the police officer bellowed as he approached Javar, and Javar immediately did as he was told.

A few seconds later, the officer, a young black man who must have been at least six foot five, reached the driver's side of his car. With the hard top off, Javar felt small compared to the man's height, and suddenly, he didn't feel too in control.

"Do you realize you were doing one hundred and eleven miles an hour?" the officer asked, his look saying Javar had to have known but just didn't expect to be caught.

Javar was used to being stopped by police officers, especially because of the expensive cars he drove. But he was always happy when stopped by a brother; if nothing else, presumptions that he must be involved in something illegal in order to afford such an expensive car didn't exist.

Javar looked up at the police officer and smiled. Being polite was the first step in being able to talk his way out of this ticket. "Officer . . ." he looked at the name tag, "Williams. I do apologize for my idiotic behavior, but if you'd give me a chance to explain . . ."

"License, registration, and insurance please."

His hope fizzling, Javar complied, searching the glove compartment for the requested items. He handed them to the officer. "I'm not normally this crazy, but I just found out some bad news. My wife's been in a bad accident—"

"Mr. Jordan, I don't have time for excuses. And there is no excuse for the speed you were driving."

"No, you're right," Javar conceded. This cop wasn't going to be a pushover. How could he expect him to be when he had been driving like a madman? Time to try plan B.

"If you'll just wait a minute, I'll be right back," the cop said, and started walking back toward the cruiser.

"As you can see, my name is Javar Jordan," Javar called to him. "Nephew of the late Marcel Jordan, who died only a year ago in the line of duty, while serving and protecting the citizens of Chicago."

Officer Williams stopped in his tracks. He turned around

and walked back to Javar's car, eyeing him skeptically. "Your uncle was Marcel Jordan?"

Javar nodded. He felt lousy using his deceased uncle to get out of a citation, but at the speed he was going, he wouldn't just get a ticket for speeding, he'd get a notice to appear in court.

"Marcel Jordan trained me when I first started on the job. I rode with him for six months."

"Really?" Javar's eyebrows rose with interest.

A small smile lifted Officer Williams's lips as he nodded. "Yeah. He was a great man. It was too bad, him getting shot like that."

"Yes, it was." A wave of nostalgia washed over Javar as he remembered his uncle. Always laughing, always willing to lend a helping hand. He didn't deserve to die the way he did, gunned down at a routine traffic stop.

"I know," Javar said softly.

"Here." Officer Williams returned Javar's information. He smiled. "I'm not about to give any nephew of Lieutenant Jordan's a ticket. But I have to ask you to please slow down."

"Thanks." Javar nodded solemnly. "I really appreciate this. And yes, I will slow down."

Officer Williams tapped the side of the car. "Have a good evening, sir."

"I will. And thanks again."

As Javar started his car and eased back into traffic, he thought about the donation to the Chicago Police Department he would make in his uncle's name. It was something he had planned to do before, but never got around to it.

He would do it soon.

By the time Javar stepped into his waterfront mansion in Kenilworth, a suburb of Chicago along the coast of Lake Michigan, it was well after nine P.M. He had continued to drive after being stopped by Officer Williams, only at a much slower speed, and instead of the expressway, he'd driven along North and South Lake Shore drives, enjoying the view of the water beside him. Surprisingly, he found the calm, scenic drive even more soothing than his mad rush on the expressway. After having worked out his anger he'd had some time to reflect.

While he was angry with Whitney's request for a divorce, he had to admit that he was also angry with himself. He had hardly been the loving, forgiving husband he should have been. Rather, he'd been cold, spiteful, too blinded by pain to offer forgiveness. She didn't believe he could ever truly forgive her. Was she right, Javar wondered. If he was honest with himself, he'd have to admit that he wasn't really sure.

Javar hopped up the steps on the *Gone With the Wind* staircase in his home two at a time. Turning left when he reached the top, he walked down the large, brightly lit hallway to J.J.'s room. He hadn't changed a thing—not even the bedspread—since J.J. had last been in there alive and well. Inhaling a steadying breath, Javar opened the door, but as the hinges creaked softly, he couldn't bring himself to step inside the room.

Finally, he entered. He took one cautious step, then another, until he was beside the bed. J.J.'s favorite stuffed animal, a large brown teddy bear, lay atop the Mickey Mouse bedspread. Martin was the name J.J. had given his favorite bear. A smile touched Javar's lips as he remembered how Martin went everywhere with J.J. Ironically, he hadn't had it with him the day of the accident.

Javar wasn't sure when it had happened, but sometime during the last year, the intense emotional pain he'd originally felt when he'd lost his only son had lessened. It still hurt to think about his death, but instead of the horrifying images of the accident and his dying son entering his mind when he thought of J.J., Javar remembered the happy times they had shared. Before, he couldn't even enter this bedroom without breaking down. Now, to his own surprise, he at times found it necessary to visit J.J.'s room, to feel closer to his son, to remember the love and happiness J.J. had brought to his life. People had always told him that time would ease the pain, but he hadn't believed them. Two years later, Javar had to admit that those people were right. He would never forget his son, but now, instead of only sadness, J.J.'s room gave him a sense of peace.

But would he ever overcome his guilt? That sudden, unexpected thought disturbed him, and Javar made his way down to his den, where he poured himself a scotch—straight. Sooner or later, the nagging guilt he felt over losing his son always crept into his mind, threatening to drive him insane. He didn't want to think about his guilt, about the fact that he believed losing his son was his ultimate punishment. The drink would help. But as Javar reached for the glass, he couldn't make himself pick it up.

He turned, dragging a palm over his face. Alcohol wasn't going to make him feel better. When he had turned to it after J.J.'s death, it had only postponed the pain. It was time to find a way to overcome his pain and guilt. Perhaps a little more time.

Feeling a small sense of victory at overcoming the temptation, Javar went back upstairs to his bedroom where he grabbed his keys. Returning downstairs, he made his way to the garage and to his car. The only thing that mattered now was Whitney. He had to make her believe that they had a second chance.

That goal consuming his thoughts, Javar drove from his driveway out onto the tree-lined, dimly lit street. Turning left, he headed toward Skokie, and Rush North Shore Medical Hospital.

Whitney hated hospitals. The bright white walls, the smiling nurses and doctors, the antiseptic smell of medicine and cleansers. No matter how much they tried to make a hospital aesthetically appealing with things like colorful paintings, nothing could mask the aura of sickness and death, not even the maternity ward.

She wanted to go home.

Glancing at the clock on the wall opposite her bed, Whitney saw that it was eleven eighteen. Now that visiting hours were over for the evening, she felt very alone. Her mother and her cousin had spent a couple of hours with her earlier, and by the time they left, she'd felt much better than she had when she'd asked Javar to leave earlier. He had left in a huff, and Whitney could tell that he was fuming. But what did he really expect? That she'd jump at his suggestion of a reconciliation? Had he conveniently forgotten how horribly their short marriage had ended?

Whitney groaned and threw her head back onto the pillow, frustrated. Immediately, a sharp pain exploded in her head. She tried to relax, hoping that would help the agony subside. As much as she hated sitting still, it was necessary that she take it easy.

Ten minutes later, the pain in her head was even worse. Although she didn't like to take medications, Whitney finally gave in and rang for the nurse, who brought her two powerful painkillers.

As Whitney closed her eyes and she felt sleep pulling her into its peaceful darkness, she wondered if Javar was ever going to come back.

Although Whitney had told him to leave, Javar found that he just couldn't stay away. He heard what she had said. He just couldn't bring himself to believe it.

Careful not to make any noise, Javar made his way into Whitney's private room. As her husband, he was allowed to spend the night. And that was exactly what he was going to do.

One look at Whitney sleeping peacefully, and Javar's heart warmed. She lay on her side, her lips slightly parted, the soft sound of her breathing filling the room.

In the closet, Javar found an extra blanket. He took it out and flung it over a shoulder. As he made his way to the small sofa near the window where he intended to sleep, Javar unbuttoned his white silk shirt. He slipped it off and tossed it onto the coffee table, then undid his belt. After dropping his pants to the floor, he bent, scooped them up, and placed them next to his shirt. Now he wore only a pair of white briefs, a white undershirt, and black nylon socks.

Whitney had fallen asleep with the bedside lamp on. Moving across the cold marble floor, Javar went to the small table where the lamp rested and turned it off.

He was about to go back over to the sofa when he heard Whitney's soft moan. His eyes flew to her. Her frail form was bathed in the soft glow of the moonlight.

She looked so beautiful.

Mesmerized, Javar merely stood there, observing Whitney. He'd forgotten how she looked when she slept. Her legs were drawn up in front of her, and she was curled in a fetal position. So childlike and so innocent . . .

The need to touch her was so great it was like a tangible force, drawing him to her. Unable to stop himself, Javar reached out and touched Whitney's face, trailing a finger along the length of her jaw. But the touch wasn't enough; he needed more. Leaning forward, he planted a soft, lingering kiss on her cheek.

The kiss warmed him all over, made him feel more alive than he had felt since she left him. It had been too long since he'd been loved, he realized. Way too long. He and Whitney had their problems, but they would work them out like married couples should. If it was the last thing he did, he would get her back.

Whitney Jordan, the murdering little witch, was back in town. Like a pesky cockroach, she had refused to die. But that didn't mean she wouldn't. Only that it would take longer than planned.

Caution was the utmost priority. However Whitney died, it had to look like an accident. There could be no questioning, no speculating as to the actual cause of death.

So, there was no time to waste. There were things to consider, like the best way to do the deed. Forget another car accident; she was probably so scared now, she wouldn't get behind the wheel of another car. But what? A drowning? An accidental overdose?

Something that would look like a suicide, that would be perfect. After all, Whitney had at least pretended to feel guilt over J.J.'s death, so who would doubt that she had gone crazy and had decided to end her life after years of living with the guilt?

Hmm. This definitely was going to be fun. Planning the perfect murder was going to be the sweetest revenge.

Chapter Five

Javar was dreaming. About food. Eggs, crispy bacon . . .
He stirred. No, he wasn't dreaming. *Carlos must be making
breakfast,* he thought, as he realized the scrumptious smell
of eggs and bacon drifting into his nose was very real. As
if in response to the tantalizing smell, his stomach growled
long and loud. Stretching, Javar yawned and opened his
eyes.

Immediately, he bolted upright. He wasn't in his bed.
He wasn't at home.

Whitney.

Throwing a glance over his shoulder, Javar saw Whitney
sitting up in the hospital bed. A tray of food was in front
of her, and she nibbled on a strip of bacon.

When she saw him looking at her, Whitney's lips curled
into a timid smile. "Morning."

That smile . . . Javar's blood grew warmer. His wife's
smile had always been her best feature. Warm and sexy at
the same time, that smile had wooed him on many an
occasion.

"Morning," Javar muttered, then swung his feet to the

floor. He was about to throw off the flannel blanket draped over his bare legs, but stopped himself. It had been a long time since he had woken up in the same room with Whitney. A tingling sensation washed over him, one of sexual awareness, but also worry. Would Whitney be uncomfortable with her half-dressed husband in the room?

"Still working like an obsessed man, I see," Whitney said, her chestnut eyes meeting his own. "It's after eleven o'clock, and you're just waking up."

Although he didn't doubt her claim, Javar threw a glance in the direction of the wall clock. He couldn't believe how long he'd slept. Obviously, he had needed the rest.

Today, Whitney looked much better and her bruises had faded significantly. Javar's heart expanded in his chest, overjoyed. For the first time, he felt absolutely positive that Whitney was going to be all right.

"How did you sleep?" he asked.

Whitney washed down the bacon with some orange juice. When she finished swallowing she answered, "Fine. The nurse gave me some painkillers last night, and I was out like a light."

"You look better. How are you feeling?"

"A lot better," Whitney replied, emphasizing each word. "Yesterday, I didn't know how I was going to get through this. Today, I feel like a whole new person." A bright smile lit her eyes for a quick moment before she returned her attention to her food.

"At least you've got an appetite."

Munching on another strip of bacon, Whitney nodded. "The doctor says that's a good sign. I was getting tired of the drip." She glanced at the intravenous bag beside her bed which was connected to her arm.

A slight grin touched Javar's lips. "I'd say so. If you're getting your appetite back, then I'd say you're well on your way to recovery."

Whitney couldn't help chortling. Javar was referring to the fact that she loved to eat. Besides great sex, food was her next favorite passion. If she wasn't able to eat, that was a sure sign that she was gravely ill.

Javar yawned, and Whitney watched as he stood and gave his tall frame a long, hard stretch. The blanket that had covered his legs fell to the floor, revealing the sexy white briefs he sported. Large muscles grew taut in his corded arms and powerful, long legs as he stood on his toes and extended his body. When he finally relaxed his physique, the appealing shape of his sexy muscles was still evident. Javar's body had always been incredibly gorgeous. His brawny chest was evident beneath his thin white undershirt. His arms bulged in all the right places. But Whitney's weakness had always been Javar's firm, cute butt, which looked ever enticing in his skimpy underwear, even though she only had a side view of it.

As if he read her mind, Javar turned and faced the bay window, allowing Whitney a full view of his behind. Her eyes instantly fell to his lower body, taking in the sight of his sexy butt, and then his golden brown thighs and calves before venturing back up to the part she loved the most. Almost two years had passed since she'd had this kind of view of his behind, and she found herself wishing that the briefs would disappear.

Get a grip! her mind screamed. What was wrong with her, lusting after her husband like some lovesick teenager? Swallowing a sigh, Whitney realized that that was the perfect description for her. Since the breakup of her marriage, she hadn't been physically intimate with any other man.

Now, to her surprise, she realized just how much she had missed. The fact that she was lying in a hospital bed recovering from bodily injuries didn't prevent her body from growing taut with sexual awareness. White-hot desire pooled in her belly, then spread throughout her body.

"Looks like it's going to be another scorcher," Javar said, turning to face her.

Heat engulfed Whitney's cheeks. She looked down at her food, hoping that she had averted her eyes quickly enough; she didn't want Javar to realize that she had been ogling him. If he did, he might just get the impression that she was interested in saving their marriage. Which she wasn't, despite her sexual attraction to him that clearly hadn't died.

"Yes, it looks like it," Whitney replied, pondering the double meaning of their words. She was eyeing the scrambled eggs intently, as if they held the answers to life's questions.

Javar suppressed the grin that wanted to escape. It had only been a quick flash, but he'd seen the desire that had flickered in the depths of his wife's eyes. She was still sexually attracted to him.

They had a chance.

Not that sex alone could repair their marriage, but it could probably work wonders. In the past when they'd argued, they'd always ended up in bed, passionately resolving their differences. Maybe that was what they needed now.

If only it could be that easy. Not only had too much time passed for sex to be an answer, but Whitney was recovering from a major accident. The last thing he should be thinking about was making sweet love to her.

He couldn't stop himself.

But he had to. Moving to the coffee table, he retrieved his slacks and stepped into them. He was tempted to strip and go take a shower, but he didn't want to startle Whitney into a relapse. He had to concentrate on getting her well before he thought of ways to seduce her.

A soft rapping sound at the door drew Javar's attention from his carnal thoughts, and he threw a questioning glance at Whitney. Her eyes meeting his own, Whitney shrugged, letting him know that she had no idea who was at the door. As he continued to button his shirt, Javar sauntered to the door, opening it. What he saw disappointed him.

It was Derrick Lawson, an old friend of Whitney's. A

sudden, unpleasant attack of jealousy caused his stomach to lurch. What was Derrick doing here?

"Javar," Derrick said, acknowledging him with a tight nod.

"Derrick." Javar forced a smile. "What are you doing here?"

"I'm here to see Whitney," he replied.

"Well, she's occupied right now," Javar told the tall, fair-skinned man.

Derrick's determined eyes met Javar's. "This is official business," he said, then brushed past Javar.

Derrick strolled into the brightly lit room, and Javar gritted his teeth as he closed the door.

"Derrick!" Whitney exclaimed, a wide grin forming on her lips. A grin Javar didn't like one bit.

"Hey, girl." Derrick strode to the bed and threw his arms around Whitney. She hugged him tightly.

Javar would have mentioned that Whitney had just survived an accident and was suffering physically, if it weren't for the fact that she was giggling like a schoolgirl as Derrick held her. Instead, he folded his arms over his chest and bit his tongue.

Pulling back from Derrick's embrace, Whitney said, "What are you doing here?"

"What do you think?" Derrick flashed a smile that was all charm. "You know whenever you get yourself into any trouble, I'll be here to help you out."

Whitney giggled happily. "Yes, of course. How could I forget?"

It was completely irrational, but Javar wanted to grab Derrick by the collar and drag the man away from his wife. However, he couldn't do that. He would upset Whitney, and Derrick would probably charge him with assaulting a police officer. But he could make sure that Derrick got down to "business," whatever that may be. Clearing his throat, Javar approached the opposite side of the bed from where Derrick had made himself comfortable. "You did say this was official?"

Derrick threw Javar a quick glance, nodding. "Actually, what I need to ask Whitney, I have to do in private."

Javar's body went rigid, and he shot Derrick an I-don't-think-so look. "Whatever you have to say to my wife you can say in front of me."

Derrick's light brown eyes met Javar's head-on. His lips lifted in a wry smile. "No, Javar. I can't. It's about the accident, and I hear you weren't even at the scene. So if you don't mind, I'd like to interview Whitney alone."

Sure you would, Javar thought. His stomach lurched again. He had no right to be jealous, but God help him, he was. What he needed to do was calm down. He couldn't start acting like a possessive fool whenever another man was around Whitney. "Fine," Javar replied, his tone flippant. "I'll just sit over there."

"Javar." Whitney's voice was stern, and he stopped mid-pivot to face her. A weary look stretched across her face. "Please . . . just give us a few minutes."

Not wanting to leave Whitney alone with Derrick, a man he knew had always had a thing for his wife, Javar merely stared at Whitney with uncompromising eyes. She met his gaze with a firm, but pleading one.

Finally, Javar sighed. "All right. I'll be outside the door."

"Thank you," Whitney said.

Javar spun around and walked out.

When the door clicked shut, Whitney turned and faced Derrick, beaming at him. "I'm so happy to see you, Derrick. It's been so long."

"I know." Derrick took her hand in his large one and squeezed it. "I have definitely missed that beautiful smile."

"And I've definitely missed your friendship." Derrick had been one of her good friends since grade school. "How's the force?"

"It's good. I'm a detective now."

Whitney smiled. "For real?"

"Yeah, for real."

Whitney was impressed, but she had always known that Derrick would move up the ranks of the police force quickly. "How do you like it?"

"I love it. I'm doing a bit of undercover work here and there, going after drug dealers and other lowlifes. I'm having a lot of fun."

"I'm happy for you." From the time Derrick was a child, he had wanted to be a police officer. His family hadn't supported his decision, especially with the high rate of crime in some areas of Chicago and the danger that police officers naturally face. But Whitney had understood his urge to help his community; she too had been drive to into the field of social work for the same reason. Unfortunately because of his job, Derrick found it hard to maintain a long-term relationship; women were usually afraid of losing him in the line of fire.

"Things are going well," he said.

"And how's your family?"

"Good. Mom's great. She's enjoying being a grandmother. And Karen is working for the Chicago Board of Trade."

"Mmm hmm." Whitney threw him a suspicious glance, trying to figure out what he was *not* telling her. Her curiosity got the better of her and she asked, "Any special woman in your life?"

Pursing his lips, Derrick shook his head. "Naw. Too busy."

"That's it? Too busy?"

Derrick chuckled and looked at her through narrowed eyes. "I thought I'm the one who's supposed to ask the questions."

Whitney giggled. Derrick was a master at avoiding her more personal questions. Oh well. One day he would find the perfect woman. "Okay, Derrick. What do you want to know?"

"It's about the accident."

"You're assigned to my case?"

Derrick nodded, then reached into the pocket on his black blazer. He withdrew a small police notebook. "Yep. Like I said, whenever you're in trouble, you know I'm going to be there."

Hugging her elbows, Whitney inhaled deeply. Until this moment, she had avoided thinking about the accident. Derrick's presence on behalf of the Chicago Police Department now made that impossible. And remembering the accident the other night meant remembering the accident two years ago; an accident that she had survived, but her stepson had not.

Whitney inhaled again, hoping the deep breath would calm her. It didn't. From what the doctors had said, it was a miracle that she was alive. A miracle, yet she didn't feel very lucky. She'd finally hoped to put all her painful memories behind her, including the guilt she felt over the first accident. But the second accident had just made the haunting memories fresh.

Derrick's deep, smooth voice brought Whitney's thoughts back to the present. "Do you remember what happened?"

Rain. Oh God, she remembered the rain. A tremor hit her, causing her to shudder. She hugged her elbows tighter.

"It was raining."

Derrick jotted something down in his notebook. "Do you remember what caused you to lose control of the car? Did you swerve to avoid an animal, maybe?"

Whitney shook her head. Felt her nerves go haywire. It had been raining, and . . . "I was driving in the left lane, along North Lake Shore Drive. There was someone behind me. Another car. Some impatient driver who gave me the high beams, so I indicated to go into the right lane. Only, by the time I was going into the right lane, so was he."

"You say he," Derrick pointed out, interrupting her. "Did you get a look at the driver?"

Whitney clenched her fist, trying to stop the shaking. "I . . . no. It was dark. I-I just assumed that it was a man. Most women don't drive like that."

"Did you get a look at the car?"

Scrunching her forehead, Whitney thought hard. The action brought discomfort with it. But she had to remember. After several moments, she groaned. Nothing. She couldn't remember seeing a particular kind of car, only bright high beams. "No," she replied, frustrated.

Derrick jotted down some more notes. "So what happened to cause you to lose control?"

Running a hand over her limp hair, Whitney tried again to remember. It had all happened so fast. "I remember that when I was going into the right lane, so was the other driver. As I said, he—or she—was impatient. Probably late for something. I swerved back into the left lane, and that's the last thing I remember. Except trying desperately to gain control of the car, but I couldn't."

"It is possible the car hit you?"

Exasperated, Whitney expelled a pent-up moan. "I—I don't know. I can't remember."

"It's okay. Forensics will check the car for any evidence that the other vehicle may have hit you."

Whitney buried her face in her hands and moaned softly. Moments later, she lifted her head, focusing on Derrick's kind face and the warmth it offered.

He seemed to sense that she needed comfort, and he ran a large hand down her arm, lifting her hand into his. "I know this is hard for you. But I have to ask these questions. I just want to get to the bottom of this."

"I know."

Derrick winked at her. "You're strong, Whitney. You're going to get through this."

Despite her frustration, Whitney was able to smile. "Thanks. That means a lot." The smile faded, and she bit down on her lower lip, shaking her head. "It was a stupid accident. Probably preventable, but it's too late to turn back the clock."

"Yeah." Derrick looked away for a moment, then returned his concerned gaze to Whitney's face. "How are you doing . . . emotionally?"

"I'm doing better." Sometimes, she wondered if that was really true. She would take two steps forward, then four steps back. She could never escape the horror of the memories, but she prayed she would be able to live with them.

"Coming back to Chicago is a really big step. I know how much courage that must have taken." Derrick raised a suggestive eyebrow, and his lips twisted in a frisky grin. "If it means anything, I'm glad you're back."

"You're too much." Whitney chortled—however weakly—then playfully punched Derrick's arm. Was he merely being friendly, or something else? She couldn't be sure. All she knew was that he was a friend she could trust, count on. "I guess it won't hurt to tell you," she said softly. "I'm only back because I'm asking Javar for a divorce."

"It's about time."

Whitney flashed Derrick an amiable, don't-go-there look. Derrick had never liked Javar. No doubt, because he'd once had a crush on her. A silly grade-school crush, but ever since then, Derrick had been protective of her, telling her in no uncertain terms what he thought of the men she went out with. Thinking back, Whitney realized that Derrick had never approved of any of the men she'd dated.

Whitney hesitated, shrugging. "You're right. It is time." She remembered Javar's plea for a reconciliation, and felt regret wash over her. So many dreams, so many promises . . . all of them broken.

Derrick's eyes softened as he held Whitney's gaze. "I know this can't be easy. You loved him once."

Her heart pounded at the word *loved*. It sounded so final. . . . But it was accurate, wasn't it? She cared about Javar, would always have a special place for him in her heart. But that was all. Their romantic passion for each other had died two years ago. Now, she loved him like she loved a friend or family member. She kept those thoughts to herself though, because nobody would understand that after all that had happened between them, she still cared deeply for Javar. Sure, she wanted a divorce, but not because she was bitter, angry, or even hateful. Their problems were too monumental to work out, and there was no point in delaying the inevitable.

Hopefully, one day, she would find the man with whom she would spend the rest of her days, blissfully happy.

One day, if she could be so lucky twice in a lifetime.

Javar had a plan.

Maybe it was seeing Whitney's reaction to Derrick that had him realizing he had to act soon if he wasn't going to lose her. Hell, who was he kidding. He still felt uneasy—jealous—not knowing what was going on behind the closed doors of his wife's hospital room.

He tapped his fingers against the polished oak table next to the chair he was sitting in, while he waited for Dr. Adu-Bohene. He prayed the doctor would go along with his plan. He thought it was feasible, fair, reasonable. And it might be the only chance he had to win Whitney's love back.

Sensing a presence, Javar looked up. Dr. Adu-Bohene stared down at him.

"You wanted to see me?" the doctor asked.

Javar stood and smiled. "Yes, Dr. Adu-Bohene, I did."

* * *

Fifteen minutes later, Javar strolled into Whitney's room, a lively bounce in his step. Dr. Adu-Bohene, the good man that he was, had agreed to go along with his plan. All that was left to do was to break the news to Whitney. If he made it appear like the good doctor's idea, what could she say? Besides, the Whitney he knew had always hated hospitals, and he was sure she would do anything to get released, even if it meant accepting Dr. Adu-Bohene's conditions.

Dr. Adu-Bohene had assured Javar that the most recent tests had confirmed the findings of the first ones. Whitney was going to be fine. She hadn't completely recovered yet from the surface wounds, but Dr. Adu-Bohene had no doubt that she would, soon.

Javar was pleased to find Whitney standing at the window, looking outside. When she heard him enter the room, she turned. Her wide eyes quickly narrowed with suspicion as Javar approached her, a foolish grin on his lips. "What?" she asked.

"Where's Derrick?"

"He had to go back to work."

"Good." He hoped that Officer Derrick Lawson was finished questioning his wife.

Whitney's forehead wrinkled as caution flashed over her features. "That's why you're so . . . happy?"

Javar shook his head. "Actually, I have some good news for you."

Still suspicious, Whitney asked, "You do?"

Javar nodded. "You want to go home, don't you?"

Whitney looked at him with anticipation, a half smile on her lips. "I can go home?"

God, Javar felt wonderful seeing Whitney standing, excited even. He took a step closer, wanting to take her in his arms and brush his lips against the velvety soft ones he remembered. He needed to taste her honeyed sweetness, feel her body respond to his the way it once did. . . .

In time, Javar. In time.

He swallowed, then spoke. "Yes, Whitney. That's the good news. I've spoken with your doctor, and he says you can go home . . . today."

Whitney squealed, delighted. Turning on her heel, she scampered to the closet, no doubt intending to gather her belongings. She was so much stronger than yesterday. Life had been cruel to her, yet it hadn't weakened her spirit, her zest.

He watched her for a moment before adding, "On one condition."

The excitement fizzled out of Whitney's eyes as she turned and faced him.

Her tone was wary as she asked, "And what condition is that?"

Chapter Six

"No."

Javar merely smiled, an arrogant, confident smile. Whitney wanted to slap it off his face.

"I mean it, Javar," she added, her hands clenched at her sides. "If that's the condition, then I'm staying right here."

"Oh, come on. The way you hate hospitals. . . . You can't be serious."

How dare he do this to her! That cocky smile was the tell-tale sign that he had put Dr. Adu-Bohene up to this. Whitney was certain that the doctor had not suggested Javar take her home to *his* place where she could recuperate. With the help of a hired nurse, of course, to make his proposition seem legitimate. The weasel! Javar knew how much she hated hospitals.

Grunting in frustration, Whitney turned from the closet and marched to the bed. Pain shot through her left hip as she hastily climbed onto the soft mattress. Unable to cover her distress, she cried out softly. Javar was immediately at her side.

Glaring at him, Whitney said, "Don't touch me."

Dark brown eyes held hers. "Whitney," Javar began in a placating tone, "don't you think you're being just a little ridiculous? You know as well as I do that you're going to get well a lot quicker at home, where you can go out to the backyard and relax, soak up some sun. . . ."

"No," she reiterated.

Javar's lips twisted. "I've already hired a nurse. Everything is arranged."

Everything is arranged—like that meant she was obligated to agree! Whitney's eyes were uncompromising. "Well *un*arrange it. I won't agree to that condition."

"Whitney—"

"No."

Javar eased himself onto the bed beside Whitney, his eyes precarious as he regarded her. A frown stretched across her beautiful lips, a sexy pout if he ever saw one. But they weren't playing a lover's game of cat and mouse here. Whitney really wanted nothing to do with him.

Javar wanted to run his thumb along her tempting lips, to kiss the bruises on her face and make all her pain go away. But he knew that was the last thing Whitney wanted. Instead he dug his nails into his fists as he clenched them, hoping that would dull the ache in his groin.

"Whitney, do you really hate me so much that you can't stand to be around me, even to the detriment of your own health?"

She was still pouting, refusing to look at him. Finally, she cast a sidelong glance in his direction. Javar couldn't help thinking how much he loved her eyes. They were the most magnificent eyes he had ever seen, a deep chestnut-brown with a thin layer of royal blue around the outer edge of her irises. Unusual, yet striking. That little touch of royal blue added a peerless spark.

"I . . . I don't hate you," Whitney finally said, her voice low. "It's just that . . . I know what you're trying to do, and I don't like it."

Javar raised a questioning eyebrow. "And what is it that I'm trying to do?"

Whitney's beautiful eyes rolled toward the ceiling, and not in a playful manner. She was deadly serious. A chill snaked down his spine.

"Javar, I want a divorce. Getting me into your house is not going to make me change my mind."

He knew it, saw it in her eyes before she said the words, yet when she repeated her intentions, Javar's insides tightened painfully. Was he making a mistake by forcing her to go home with him? Would his plan backfire? No, he decided, not if he took things slowly. He lowered his eyelids and said, "Well, if you're so certain of that, then what's the problem?"

"I just don't like your deception."

"Whitney, I know you may not believe this, but all I really want is for you to get better." That was the truth. Her health came first. "No, I don't want a divorce, but I can't force you to stay married to me against your wishes. Think about it. This arrangement will be perfect. You can get well in a much more appealing environment, not some depressing hospital. You'll have a nurse at your side twenty-four hours a day for as long as necessary. And if anything, *anything*, seems wrong with your health, we can always have you readmitted to the hospital." Javar shrugged. "I don't know about you, but that certainly seems like a great plan to me."

"I'm sure it does."

"Do you have a better idea?"

Whitney drew in a deep breath and lowered her eyes. Javar made it sound so wonderful, so simple. And boy did she ever hate hospitals! She found them more hazardous to her health in this stage of recovery than helpful.

She looked at Javar. A small grin tugged at the corners of his lips, and his nutmeg-colored eyes regarded her warmly. She didn't want to lead him on. Obviously, he still cared about her. But how would he feel if she went along with his plan, then still pursued the divorce when she got well? Would he hate her? God, she couldn't handle that. There was enough animosity between them.

She was crazy for even considering his proposal. "Javar, if I . . . go home with you, it won't . . . change anything."

Whitney suspected his emotions weren't as calm as his voice when he replied, "I understand."

"All right, Javar." She hoped she wouldn't regret her decision. "I'll go along with your plan. But don't think for a moment that I believe this was the doctor's idea. I know you're behind it."

Javar opened his mouth to say something, but Whitney put her hand to his lips, stopping him. A familiar rush of longing spread from her fingers down her arm. How she wished she could erase the events of the past and love Javar the way she had vowed to do.

But she couldn't.

She recoiled her fingers, looked down, then continued. "Javar, please be sure about this. If you're entertaining thoughts of a reconciliation, please don't. I meant what I said. When this is all over, when I'm completely healed, I'm still going ahead with my plans for a divorce."

Half an hour later, Whitney was dressed in jeans and a T-shirt and sitting in a wheelchair waiting to be formally released from the hospital while Javar was settling the bill. Earlier she'd spoken with her mother and had told her about the doctor's condition for her release. Her mother hadn't liked the idea and was very worried about Javar pressuring her into a reconciliation while Whitney was vulnerable. But Whitney had assured her mother that she would be well and out of Javar's house soon.

During a final examination by Dr. Adu-Bohene, he replaced the bandage on her forehead with a fresh one, and confirmed that she was recovering nicely. The large gash beneath the bandage was healing, and the bruises were changing color. A little makeup and she would look as good as new.

She'd nearly had heart failure when the doctor told her and Javar that if she felt up to it, lovemaking would not be a problem. Of course, with caution, he'd added, then smiled knowingly. Whitney hadn't dared to look at Javar's face, since her own embarrassment—and probably longing—would have been evident.

A middle-aged black nurse accompanied Javar as he strolled toward Whitney from the reception desk. The nurse took hold of Whitney's wheelchair, moving her across the sparkling gray floor toward the elevators. Javar followed, silently.

When they reached the first floor, the nurse rolled Whitney's wheelchair to the front door, then said warmly, "Here we go."

Javar helped her out of the chair, then turned to the nurse. "Thanks so much for your help."

The nurse's eyes lit up with unmasked longing. Whitney felt a strange pull in her stomach, remembering the same look of desire on so many other women's faces who had found her husband attractive.

"It was my pleasure." A sheepish grin lifted the woman's lips.

As the nurse sauntered away, Whitney felt an unpleasant surge of jealousy sweep over her. Javar seemed unaware of the nurse's flirtatiousness, as he had with the other women. The countless other women. There were so many, so willing. . . . After J.J.'s death, Whitney had wondered if Javar was seeing someone. He had refused to make love with her, eventually moving out of their bedroom, and he'd spent more and more time at the office, no doubt with Melody, his lovely secretary, hanging all over him.

Whitney pushed that unpleasant thought to the back of her mind. Her husband was an attractive man, and it would be stupid to get upset whenever a woman gave him a sidelong glance, or a bold one for that matter. Besides, he was still legally her husband, but he had stopped being a real one to her a long time ago. So jealousy was the last thing she should be experiencing.

"You ready?" Javar asked, his words interrupting her troubled thoughts.

He was so handsome when he looked at her like that. She exhaled harshly. She would get through this. "I'm ready," she replied. "Lead the way."

Javar wrapped an arm around her waist, leading her out the main doors of the hospital, then across the street to the hospital parking lot. He carried her small suitcase with his free hand. She had to admit she felt comforted by his touch. She felt strangely warm as she leaned into him for support. Why did he still have to look so good? And why, after all the pain he had caused her, did she still find him attractive? Wryly, she wondered if the bump on her head had anything to do with her body's convenient memory loss; clearly, her body didn't seem to remember Javar's betrayal of his vows.

A few minutes later, Javar stopped beside a gorgeous sports car, a red Dodge Viper. This must have been one of his new "toys". She hadn't seen it before.

"New car?" she asked, realizing that it was dumb question after the words left her lips.

Javar opened the passenger door for her as he replied, "Yeah. Just got it a few months ago."

In time for the beginning of the spring. How nice.

Javar slipped Whitney's small suitcase into the cramped backseat. This car obviously served only one purpose: to get attention.

"Do you like it?" Javar asked.

Whitney's eyes roamed the gleaming, cherry red surface of the car. What wasn't to like? It was gorgeous. "It's beautiful."

"I'd take the top off, but we're not far from home, so there's no point."

Whitney nodded absently. She slipped onto the soft,

gray leather seat, running her hand along the edge as she did. Javar's money had allowed her to drive a sporty BMW while they were together. Unfortunately, that was the car that had been totaled in the accident with J.J. But Javar had also driven a top-of-the-line BMW, and from what Whitney remembered, that was his favorite car.

"What happened to your BMW?" she asked.

"It was stolen."

"Stolen?" Whitney repeated, shocked.

Javar nodded. "Yeah. A few days ago. Right out of my driveway."

The moment Whitney walked into the three-story mansion, a gripping wave of nostalgia washed over her.

She stopped. Stared.

It had been so long.

The black marble floor glittered beneath the sun's bright rays, which flowed through the high ceiling's skylight. The *Gone With the Wind* staircase with a second level balcony looked grand and majestic as it took center stage in the colossal octagon-shaped foyer. Four of the foyer's eight walls boasted high archways leading to hallways and other rooms on the main level. Hanging above the center of the floor was an elegant silver and crystal chandelier. On the walls to the immediate right and left of the double front doors hung two large paintings depicting Africans in the traditional dress of their native Ghana. Javar had traced his family's roots back to that country. The beautiful paintings had graced the walls when Whitney had left almost two years ago. In fact, looking around, everything appeared the same. Even the small mahogany table to her right had the same white, lace doily on it she remembered. And the large crystal vase atop the doily was filled with fresh orchids. Her favorite flower.

Just like the day she had left.

The exterior of the house looked the same, as well. Pink

and white rosebushes lined the long, U-shaped walkway from the sidewalk to the front door of Javar's ultramodern, cream-colored estate. The California-styled roof was an orange-brown. The house had several dozen windows— many bay styled, squared, and circular. Having bought more than two acres of land with a moderate-sized house, Javar had demolished the older one and constructed his dream home. Later, he had shown Whitney the blueprints for the house, explaining that he had designed one with lots of windows because he felt sunlight added life to a home. He'd also told her that his dream house hadn't become his dream home until she had moved in and shared it with him.

"Mrs. Jordan. Welcome back."

Whitney lifted her eyes from the orchids she didn't realize she was staring at until she heard the warm, familiar voice of Carlos Medeiros, Javar's longtime butler. He smiled, excitement dancing in his eyes as he regarded her for the first time in almost two years.

Whitney returned the smile. "Thank you, Carlos."

She hesitated only a moment before moving to him. Wrapping her arms around him, she kissed him on the cheek. Carlos was the one to end the hug, stepping back. Whitney remembered that he wasn't prone to physical affection, at least not with his employer's family. He probably worried that he would offend Javar if he got too close.

Carlos looked down at the small suitcase. "This is all your luggage?"

Whitney saw the surprise in Carlos's eyes and wondered what Javar had told him. "Yes. For now at least." She had more clothes at her mother's, which she would pick up later.

"I'll bring the suitcase upstairs, Carlos," Javar told the man. He turned to Whitney. "Are you hungry?"

Whitney flashed him a knowing look. Was she hungry? When was she not?

Javar chuckled. "Silly question. Carlos, why don't you

make some French toast for Whitney. I'm sure she'd like that."

"Absolutely sir," Carlos said, then turned and headed toward the arch at the back of the stairs that led to the kitchen.

Whitney looked at the stairs a few feet away from her. Sunlight spilled onto the winding staircase partly from the skylight and partly from the large, circular window at the top of the stairs. Thick, cream-colored carpeting covered each step. The wood was a polished mahogany, Javar's favorite, that gleamed enticingly under the sun's rays. Throughout the house, Javar had implemented a style of whites and creams contrasting with black, and the result was quite striking.

"Would you like to lie down?"

Whitney glanced at Javar, at his handsome oval face. Memories were still flooding her, like the time he carried her over the threshold of the patio doors after their garden wedding under the clear, blue sky. Or the first time Javar had carried her up those *Gone With the Wind* stairs to their bedroom, where they had made sweet, passionate love for hours. There also was the time she had made a path of scented rose petals from their bedroom to the pool room, where she had seduced him in the Jacuzzi. The memories were of years ago when they were first married, yet they seemed so fresh, so current.

"Actually," Whitney said, contemplating what she should do as she spoke, "I think I'd like to walk around."

"All right. Your room is the first one on the left, at the top of the stairs. The nurse will be here shortly."

Whitney nodded, then turned to her right, walking down the long corridor. She glanced in a sitting room with floor to ceiling windows facing the backyard. She poked her head in Javar's library, graced with rich wood paneling. Books of all types, including fiction and nonfiction, filled the numerous shelves. Further down the hallway was Javar's home office, and stepping inside she saw his large drafting table near the vast windows. Pictures of houses and commercial properties he had designed and renovated framed the walls, including a poster sized picture of his own waterfront home. An image of the time she had worn a skimpy red number down to Javar's office, seducing him from his work entered Whitney's thoughts. The memory was bittersweet. Her husband had been an obsessed workaholic, even through their newlywed stage. She often had to physically distract him from his work in order to get some love and affection. She didn't mind at first, knowing she could tempt her husband, but later it wasn't as easy to divurt his attention. And she had become frustrated.

Whitney stepped out of Javar's office, and continued strolling down the great hallway. She kept walking until she rounded a short corner and reached the double glass doors that led to the indoor pool and Jacuzzi. Opening the door on the right, Whitney stepped inside.

The smell of chlorine hit Whitney as she entered the room. The aqua-blue water in the large, kidney shaped pool glistened beneath yet another skylight. At the opposite end of the pool from where she was standing, thick wooden doors led to a sauna. The Jacuzzi, which was quite large, was beside the pool on the left. Whitney swallowed as a clear image of a very naked Javar in the Jacuzzi, his wet body pressing against hers, invaded her mind.

Whitney shook off the memory, then walked toward the Jacuzzi and the patio doors beside it. She looked out into the backyard, where another inground pool, a hexagon-shaped one, lay beyond a large concrete deck at the foot of the steps. Unlocking the patio doors, Whitney stepped out onto the peach-colored patterned concrete and looked over the deck's wrought-iron railing. This was where they'd had pool parties with friends, with chicken and steaks grilling, and loud music pulsating out of the patio speakers.

Whitney walked down the deck steps, past the pool area until she reached the vibrant green grass. The backyard was enormous. A variety of flowers were interspersed throughout the colossal backyard in a brilliant display of colors. On the left was a tennis court as well as a basketball court. To the far left, red rosebushes lined a cobblestone path that led from the back of the house to the beach. Whitney walked along the grass until she reached the opening to the path, the sweet scent of azaleas, petunias, lilacs, and roses filling her nose. She followed the path's curving trail down to the shore of Lake Michigan.

The waters of Lake Michigan splashed against the shore, hitting *Lady Love*, the twin hull catamaran Javar had given to her as a wedding gift. The memories were everywhere.... She couldn't escape them. And she couldn't help smiling as she remembered her excitement when Javar had led her down the softly lit, winding rose path the night of their wedding, to the beach, and to her surprise....

"Come on, Javar. Tell me what my surprise is."

Her husband of several hours flashed her a sexy smile. "It wouldn't be a surprise then, now would it?"

Whitney curled her lips downward in a playful pout. "I know, but ... I hate surprises."

"Patience, my dear," Javar said, wrapping his arms around her from behind and kissing her cheek. Desire shot straight through her entire body at Javar's touch. The whole day had been an incredible aphrodisiac—the intimate ceremony, the stolen glances exchanged with her husband, the intoxicating smell of fresh flowers, the orchestra, the exchange of personal vows. Now, the last of the guests from the wedding celebration had finally left, and Whitney hadn't yet made love to her husband. They'd agreed to wait until their wedding night, and Whitney found herself unable to wait any longer.

"Come on." Releasing his hold on her waist, Javar took Whitney's hand and jogging, led her down the path. She couldn't help giggling. When they finally reached the moonlit beach, Whitney's mouth fell open.

"Ta da!" Javar turned and faced Whitney, the love in his eyes making her want to cry. "There you are, sweetie. There's your present."

It was beautiful! Whitney threw her hand to her mouth as she approached the gleaming white boat. The words *Lady Love* were painted on the side in bold, red letters. Whitney didn't know much about boats, but she certainly knew that people didn't tend to name catamarans. "You got me a boat?"

"Yes," Javar said proudly.

Whitney's eyes grew misty as she looked at him. "You named it?"

"What? People can't name catamarans?"

She held the tears at bay, laughing instead. "Not usually. Aren't names reserved for bigger boats?"

"Well, I like to be different," Javar stated with a quick shrug of his shoulders. Then, as he regarded Whitney, his smile faded and his eyes narrowed. "You do like it, don't you?"

Whitney gaped at her new husband. The man she planned to be deliriously happy with for the rest of her life. She threw herself into his arms. "Like it? I love it! Oh, Javar, thank you!"

"Really?"

"Of course, really! This is the best gift I've ever received!"

Javar gazed into her eyes. God, he looked so gorgeous when he smiled at her like that, his eyes crinkling. "Good," he said. "How 'bout a moonlit sail?"

"How about this?" Sliding her hands up Javar's large back, over his corded muscles and wide shoulders, Whitney laced her fingers around his neck. A deep, carnal groan rumbled in her husband's chest. She felt it against her own and her longing intensified. Pulling his head down,

Whitney whispered, "You've kept me waiting long enough."

Whitney sighed against Javar's lips as they met hers, smooth and sweet. She kissed him slowly, somehow controlling all the pent-up passion that needed to be released.

Unzipping her simple, knee-length white silk dress, Javar slipped his fingers beneath the material and trailed them up her back. She moaned. This felt good, so good. A tremor of longing rocked her body, and heat engulfed her inner thighs. She stood on her toes and arched against him, feeling the evidence of his desire. Javar groaned and deepened the kiss, delving his tongue deep into her mouth.

Gripping her back, Javar pulled her close. Ever so slowly, he trailed one hand around up her back to her shoulder, nudging the dress off. Then softly, he stroked the fullness of one breast. Whitney's nipple immediately hardened, and when Javar tweaked it with his thumb and forefinger, she thought she would die of the pleasure.

"Oh, Javar!" she moaned against his lips.

Tearing his lips away from hers, Javar brought his hot tongue down onto her throbbing nipple, drawing it into his mouth and suckling. Nothing had ever felt this good. Sensations she'd never before experienced—searing, dizzying sensations—overwhelmed her. The pleasure was so intense that it shocked her, tore the sound from her voice.

Finally, the moan that wanted to be unleashed found the voice to accompany it. The sound was loud and rapturous as it escaped her lips, and sounded foreign to her ears. She felt slightly embarrassed, but she couldn't stop the sounds. The feelings of pleasure were so exquisite. . . .

"Let's move to the boat," Javar murmured.

When Whitney nodded, Javar scooped her up in his arms, carrying her to the catamaran's tramp. . . .

"You're remembering, aren't you?"

Startled, she whirled around and saw Javar standing a

couple of feet away from her, a peculiar expression on his face. Her own face was flushed and she was definitely hot with longing. Her heart beat an erratic tempo.

Lord, what was wrong with her? How had she gotten so caught up in the past? The memory had seemed so real. . . .

Javar took a step toward her, and despite her urge to move away Whitney found she was rooted to the spot. Desire sparked in the depths of Javar's beautiful brown eyes. Holding her gaze, he pulled his bottom lip between his teeth.

Whitney sucked in a sharp breath.

He reached out and ran his thumb across her bottom lip. Why couldn't she respond, why couldn't she stop him? Because the simple touch of his finger on her mouth felt so good.

"You are, aren't you, Whitney?"

Whitney's throat was suddenly so dry and tight it ached. She couldn't say a thing. She wanted to walk away. She wanted to feel Javar's sensuous lips on hers.

"Whatever else went wrong, sex was always wonderful for us, wasn't it Whitney? We used to love passionately."

She couldn't deny that.

"We can have that again, Whitney. It can be so good."

Whitney's lips trembled under the seductive touch of Javar's thumb. Her breath was so shallow, she wasn't sure she was breathing. Her lips parted, remembering, inviting . . .

Whitney's pulse quickened as Javar leaned forward, lowering his lips until they were a fraction of an inch away from hers. His lips lingered there, taunting her. Javar's musky, masculine smell flirted with her nose, mesmerizing her. Nervous, she flicked her tongue out, running it across her bottom lip.

And then his lips were on hers, capturing her mouth in a soft, sweet, mind-numbing kiss.

But he ended it almost as soon as it began, leaving Whitney surprised and frustrated.

Javar backed away from her, his eyes holding her captive. "I'll leave you to your thoughts. I just wanted to let you know the nurse has been delayed but will be here as soon as she can."

Then, ever so calmly, as though he hadn't been affected by the meeting of their lips, Javar turned and walked away, strolling casually up the winding path.

Whitney watched him leave in stunned disbelief.

When he was out of sight, Whitney sank into the sand. She wanted to grab a rock and hurl it at him for toying with her the way he had. What she really wanted to do was get away from this place. She couldn't believe how flustered she felt. One quick kiss, and her entire body was thrumming with wanton sexual desire.

Anger soon replaced her frustrated longing. Javar wasn't going to do this to her. He wasn't going to get her worked up to the point where *she* went after *him*.

No way.

Her days of loving Javar Jordan were long over.

Heaving herself off the sand, Whitney rose and started jogging up the path back to the house. She went in through the back patio doors and scampered through the pool room and back down the corridor she had originally followed. She didn't bother to take her shoes off when she ran up the stairs and straight to her room.

Whitney slammed the bedroom door behind her and locked it. Her head pounded from overexerting herself. She paused to catch her breath. Then she marched to the phone beside the bed. Picking up the receiver, she held it between her shoulder and ear while punching in the digits to Cherise's home.

The phone rang five times, and just as Whitney was about to hang up, Cherise answered.

"Cherise," Whitney said, breathing a sigh of relief. "I need you to come pick me up . . . No, I'm at Javar's . . . I know, I know. It's a long story . . . Cherise, I really want to get out of here, so if you don't mind, I can tell you the details later . . . Okay, cuz. Thanks a lot . . . See ya soon."

As Whitney hung up the phone, she dropped herself onto the edge of the king-sized canopy bed, needing to rest a moment. She lingered there for a few minutes, then made her way to the closet where she grabbed the suitcase and opened it. Her clothes were hanging neatly in the closet.

Without regard for the garments, Whitney grabbed them off their hangers and dropped them into a pile in her suitcase. How could she have agreed to Javar's ridiculous proposition? Coming here was a mistake, and she wouldn't stay here a minute longer.

She had to get out of here before Javar made a further fool of her.

Chapter Seven

When she heard the doorbell, Whitney grabbed her suitcase and made her way to the bedroom door. She prayed Javar was busy doing something else, and that Carlos would answer the door. Carlos would be surprised that she was leaving, but she could scurry out before he was able to stop her, or alert Javar. She wanted no hassles.

As she stepped into the hallway, she felt the powerful urge to look to her left. Toward J.J.'s room. She inhaled a deep breath, remembering everything. Little J.J. as he played with her, as he asked her thousands of questions about everything. She had loved that child as if he was her own, yet nobody could understand that.

Swallowing a sigh, Whitney averted her gaze and hurried toward the stairs. The sooner she got out of here the better. The sooner she got away from the pain . . .

She hurried down the stairs. As she reached the bottom, she saw Carlos and Cherise. The smile on Cherise's face gave her the strength to go on.

Carlos's eyes narrowed as he saw the suitcase in Whitney's hand. She did the only thing she could: lie. "I'm going to get the rest of my stuff. This suitcase is empty. I figure I'll need it."

Carlos nodded. "I see."

"I shouldn't be too long. There's no need to tell Javar that I'm even gone." She turned to Cherise. "Let's go."

Cherise took the suitcase from her, then the two hurried to the door. She was stepping over the threshold when she heard Javar's voice.

"Carlos, is that the nurse?"

Whitney closed the door and started down the concrete steps. Cherise's Toyota was several feet away, but if they hurried. . . .

"Whitney!"

Whitney halted at the sound of Javar's voice, but didn't turn around.

"Whitney, where are you going?"

"Uh . . . I'm going to get the rest of my stuff."

Cherise looked at her. "Why don't you tell him the truth?"

"Look at me, Whitney," Javar commanded.

She didn't have to look around to know that he was only a few feet behind her. Slowly, she turned. "Javar, I . . ."

"Give that to me." He indicated the suitcase in Cherise's hand.

Cherise looked at Whitney, as though for approval, and Whitney shrugged. "Go ahead," Whitney instructed her cousin.

Eyeing Whitney skeptically, Javar took the suitcase from Cherise. After a moment his eyes narrowed. "If you're only going to get the rest of your stuff, then why is this suitcase full?"

Whitney felt like a child who had been caught with her hand in the cookie jar. And she shouldn't feel that way. She was an adult who could make her own decisions.

"Well?" Javar prompted.

Cherise walked the several feet to the car, giving Whitney and Javar some privacy. Whitney watched as Cherise rounded the back of the car and went to the driver's side before speaking. "I'm leaving."

"That isn't part of the plan."

"I've changed my mind."

"We had an agreement."

"I'm a big girl, Javar. I'm allowed to change my mind."

"Not in this situation, you're not."

Whitney turned, looked at the old maple trees that lined the borders of his property. Their vibrant green leaves rustled softly as the light breeze flirted with them. The scent of the various roses, some of which she had planted and pruned while she'd lived here filled her nostrils. Once, she had been happy here. Now, she only wanted to leave.

Javar's voice interrupted her thoughts. "You weren't even going to tell me you were leaving? Why? Why are you so anxious to get away from me?"

Whitney opened her mouth to speak, but stopped herself. She couldn't tell Javar that just being around him, being in his home, was unnerving. She didn't want to give him any reason to hope, to read anything into her flustered feelings. "I . . . just . . . this makes no sense. We're getting a divorce."

"You may be willing to risk your health to get away from me, but I won't let you." He paused, holding her gaze, making sure she knew he was serious. "For my own peace of mind, I want to make sure you're one hundred percent better—no matter how things end between us."

The fact that he sounded so sincere made Whitney feel somewhat guilty. But why should she feel guilty? She was doing the right thing.

The sound of tires on concrete caused them both to look toward the driveway. A Ford Probe was making its way up the curved path. Moments later, the car pulled up behind Cherise's Toyota and parked. An attractive, fair-skinned woman whose hair was a rich amber color, hopped out of the car and hurried toward them. The pale blue outfit she wore made it clear she was the nurse.

"Are you Mr. Jordan?" she asked when she reached them.

"Yes," Javar replied. "You must be—"

"Elizabeth Monroe," she supplied. "Your nurse."

"Nice to meet you," Javar said shaking her hand.

"I'm sorry I'm late," she continued. "When I got the call from the agency . . ."

"It's okay," Javar said.

Elizabeth Monroe seemed to only now realize that Whitney was standing there. Turning to her, the woman smiled. "Oh, hello."

The wrinkles around her eyes when she smiled were the only indication that she was in her mid-to-late forties. Whitney returned the woman's smile. "Hello."

"This is my wife," Javar explained, moving to Whitney and resting a hand on her shoulder. "She recently came home from the hospital. In fact," he turned to Whitney, looking down at her, "we should all go upstairs so Ms. Monroe can examine you."

"Please call me Elizabeth."

Whitney glanced at the blue car where Cherise sat, waiting. Then she turned back to Javar. "In a moment."

Quickly, she walked to the driver's side of Cherise's car. Cherise saw her and immediately opened the door, stretching her legs out onto the concrete. She seemed confused and perhaps a little annoyed as she asked, "What's going on?"

"I—I'm staying. Sorry."

Cherise's lips twisted. "Okay."

"That's the nurse," Whitney explained. "Javar hired her for me."

"Give the man a medal." She sighed. "They're waiting for you. I'm gonna go."

"No," Whitney said. When Cherise flashed her a perplexed look, she added, "Why don't you stay—visit with me."

She shrugged. "Sure."

Whitney waited until Cherise exited the car before starting back toward the house. If Javar wouldn't let her leave, she'd surround herself with her family. With people who really cared about her.

In the short time Elizabeth had been here, she had set up Whitney's room with the necessities of the modern medical world. Blood pressure equipment stood to the left of the bed as well as a nurse's stand, on which lay a box of latex gloves, a stethoscope and other gadgets Whitney wasn't familiar with. There was even a special pager to summon Elizabeth, if necessary.

"Your blood pressure is high," Ms. Monroe said. She plucked the thermometer from Whitney's mouth and examined the reading. "Your temperature is normal."

"Tell her she needs to rest. She won't listen to me."

Whitney gazed at Javar, frowning. She'd tried to convince him he wasn't needed during this examination, but he had insisted on being here.

Elizabeth spoke to Whitney much the way an adult would speak to a child. "Whitney, you need to rest. Your blood pressure is high, so it's critical you also avoid stressful situations. You may feel better, but you haven't completely healed from the accident. Please, take it easy. That's the only way to ensure your complete recovery."

The nurse ended her visit by giving Whitney two small capsules. "Take these."

"What are they?"

"One's a Tylenol for pain. The other's lorazepam for stress."

Whitney did as instructed. It would do no good to argue. The nurse left immediately afterward, leaving Whitney alone with Javar. She didn't look at him.

"Whitney—"

"The nurse said I have to avoid 'stressful' situations."

"And I'm causing you stress?"

"Yes." She knew her response hurt him, she could feel it, but she wouldn't take it back. Wouldn't offer him any comfort. "I'd like to see Cherise now."

Javar didn't argue. Looking out a window, she only heard the soft sound of his feet on the carpet as he left the room.

Whitney pushed the niggling of guilt aside, or tried to, at least. Maybe she was acting like a spoiled child, but it wasn't easy for her being here. Why should it be for Javar?

Minutes later, Cherise, who had been waiting in the family room down the hall, entered the room. Her gaze was wide-eyed, like a child in a candy store who couldn't decide which of the treasures to sample first. "Wow," Cherise said, running her hand over the delicate carvings in the oak post on the canopy bed. "This room is gorgeous!"

"This isn't the first time you're seeing this house."

"It's just been so long." Cherise's eyes darted around the room, taking in everything with excitement. Whitney followed her gaze to the cream-colored lace canopy, the antique oak dresser, the Queen Anne chaise, and the extravagant entertainment center. "My God, this room is almost as big as my whole apartment."

"This is a big house," Whitney said simply.

Cherise was still exploring. She strolled to the far end of the room near the bay windows and entered the ensuite bathroom. "Holy . . ." she called from inside. Moments later, she reappeared. "That tub is so big, you can swim in it!"

Shrugging, Whitney changed the subject. "Where are Tamika and Jaleel?"

"With their father," Cherise replied sourly. "For a change."

Whitney knew that Paul, Cherise's ex-husband, was a sore spot with Cherise. They'd been married only four years when Cherise had discovered that her husband was sleeping with other women. Before, she had suspected as much, but hadn't had any proof. When she'd found him in bed with a neighbor, she'd taken her two small children and left him. It hadn't been easy, especially since Paul wasn't regular with his child support payments nor his visitation, but Cherise had survived.

"At least he's spending some time with them. That's positive, right?"

"How positive can it be when he sees them once in a blue moon? He's more of a stranger to Tamika and Jaleel than anything else. And Jaleel is so vulnerable. He needs his father. But Paul is too busy getting his freak on with anything that moves, the K-9."

Silence fell between them. Whitney was suddenly tired and wanted to lie down. But she didn't want to send her cousin home. At least not yet.

When Whitney looked up, Cherise was standing before the entertainment center, fingering the selection of compact discs. "Now Javar," Cherise suddenly said, "he was a good father. Loving, devoted, and wealthy. Man, if the accident never happened, you'd still have all this." She gestured to the room.

Whitney propped her foot on the bed, hugging her knee to her chest. "To tell the truth, things weren't that great in our relationship. In fact, I think that sooner or later we would have broken up, regardless of the accident."

Cherise threw her a look of disbelief. "Are you crazy? Why would you ever leave him? Men like Javar do not come along every day."

"Men like Javar love their work more than their families."

Slipping her hands into the back pockets of her form-fitting jeans, Cherise walked toward her. "He's a hardworking man. Look at all he gave you."

Cherise made it sound like it was only the material things that mattered. Sure, while Whitney had lived here she hadn't wanted for anything that money could buy. She had wanted her husband's love and affection, and that was something she hadn't been able to pay for in dollars—or she would have.

Whitney looked up at Cherise. "All this," she waved a hand around the room, "is overrated."

Cherise rolled her eyes. "Of course. It's always those who have money who say it's overrated."

"I didn't always have money. Or a big house. Or a fancy car. You know that. I grew up on the South side of Chicago, just like you. And I'd choose the South side over this posh neighborhood any day, if I could have the love I wanted."

Cherise shrugged. "I'd choose the money. 'Cause when men decide to wander—as most do—at least you'd have the money to make you feel better. When you're with some fool who can't even hold a job, when he screws around all you have is heartache . . . and hungry mouths to feed. I'd take the money any day."

That is classic Cherise, Whitney thought as she stared at her cousin, chuckling softly. But she had two young children who'd suffered because their father didn't have the decency to support them. But Whitney had lived the fairy tale. She was a student struggling to pay the bills when she'd met Javar, when he'd stolen her heart and swept her up into a dreamworld. A dreamworld that had ended with a bitter nightmare.

"Well, cuz," Whitney finally said. "I'd gladly trade places with you. I would. Because without the rest of the package, money just doesn't mean anything to me."

Whitney felt the strangest sensation, like something was surrounding her, trying to keep her down. Something evil . . .

Her eyes flew open. She found herself in darkness. The blinds were closed, and only a sliver of light filled the room. She didn't even remember falling asleep.

There . . . a sound. Shuffling. The bedroom door opened, then closed with a soft click.

She threw her gaze to the door, but saw nothing. She

shivered. Someone had been in her room. She held still, paralyzed beneath the bedsheets.

Moments later, she sighed deeply. She was overreacting. It was probably just Elizabeth, or Javar who had been in her room, checking on her.

Still, as Whitney closed her eyes and tried to fall back to sleep, she couldn't shake the cold, eerie feeling that someone was watching her.

Chapter Eight

Whitney stirred, opening her eyes, then bolted upright. It was morning now; bright sunlight spilled into the room from behind the blinds. But that wasn't what had awakened her. Something else had.

Voices. She heard voices. Loud, angry voices. Throwing the blanket off her body, Whitney eased herself out of the king-sized canopy bed. The robe she'd worn last night was strewn across the Queen Anne chaise, and she picked it up, slipping into it.

Tying the belt on her white silk robe, she opened the door and stepped into the hallway. The voices were coming from downstairs in the foyer, and they were growing louder. When she reached the mouth of the winding mahogany stairs, she looked down and saw Javar. He was talking with a woman.

Whitney made her way down the thickly carpeted steps. She made no sound as she descended. When she neared the bottom of the stairs, she saw clearly who Javar was talking to—Stephanie Lewis. The street-fine beauty was dressed in a black cat suit and high, thick heeled boots.

Dressed to seduce, as always. Whitney paused on the steps, fighting a sudden bout of nervousness. Then, gathering courage, she continued, stepping at last onto the cool marble floor.

"Hello, Stephanie," she said softly.

Stephanie's dark brown eyes flew to Whitney, bulging as she took in the sight of her. Returning her ice-cold gaze to Javar, Stephanie said, "You sonofabitch! So it *is* true. How *dare* you let my son's murderer stay here!"

Whitney cringed. Stephanie's harsh words shouldn't have startled her, but they did. Time had done nothing to heal the woman's pain. She was still angry and bitter, and no doubt still believed that Whitney belonged in jail. Whitney could understand her pain—how could she not—but she had suffered, too, probably more than Stephanie ever would. It was she who relived the accident almost every night, she who questioned her own negligence for not buckling J.J. into his seat. It was she who would take the horrifying images of the accident to the grave with her, as well as her profound guilt.

But for now, she needed to fully heal, then get on with her life. Coming downstairs had been a mistake. "Excuse me," she murmured, pivoting on her heel to leave.

"Bitch, don't you walk away from me!"

Stephanie's crude name-calling caused Whitney's back to stiffen with angry indignation. That was uncalled for. Whipping her head around, she faced Stephanie with a sneer. "No matter what you say to me, Stephanie, your son is never coming back."

"You little . . . I'll kill you! I swear I'll kill you!" And with her deadly threat, an enraged Stephanie lunged at Whitney. Javar grabbed the angry woman before she could reach her intended victim. Screaming at the top of her lungs, Stephanie flailed her arms and legs, demanding that Javar let her go.

"That's enough, Stephanie," Javar said sternly. "You're making a fool of yourself."

"You should be dead!" Stephanie ranted, staring at Whitney, then succumbed to angry tears.

Whitney watched as Javar dragged Stephanie to the door, a wave of numbing pain sweeping over her. Carlos had arrived and he opened the door.

"Don't come back here again," Javar told her, then deposited her on the front step. Quickly, he closed the door, but Stephanie's crying and ranting was so loud, she could still be heard.

Javar moved to Whitney, a troubled expression etched on his face. "Are you okay?"

She trembled. She was cold, frightened, and she felt so . . . alone. Stephanie's anger had opened old wounds, causing her to remember all the hatred she had experienced after little J.J.'s death.

"I'm so sorry." Javar wrapped Whitney in the safety of his arms, squeezing her tightly. He was an anchor, a lifeline in a troubled sea. Unable to contain her emotions any longer, Whitney let the tears that longed to fall gush from her eyes and spill onto her cheeks.

"Don't cry," Javar said into her hair, his voice soft and gentle. "Please, don't cry."

Whitney couldn't stop the flow of tears. She let Javar hold her until she had cried all the tears she could possibly cry.

The nightmare was starting again. She'd suffered enough of Stephanie's wrath almost two years ago; she didn't want to relive that now. Nobody, not even Javar had understood the anguish she had suffered, the unbearable guilt she carried in her heart every day. But Lord help her, if she could turn back the clock, she would. She'd bring little J.J. back to life, even if it meant exchanging her life for his.

She should have let Javar come to Louisiana and get the divorce there. She should have stayed away from Chicago. People hated her here. Hated her for something she hadn't been able to control, or prevent. After the accident she'd received numerous death threats. They had come in the form of letters and telephone calls. The letters had never been sent to her home, but to her job, the All For One community youth center in Chicago's Near West. The phone calls had been at home and at work. It had gotten so bad that she'd been afraid to even leave the house.

When, four months after the accident, Javar was still being cold toward her and the death threats hadn't stopped, the decision to leave Illinois and go live with her Aunt Beverly and Uncle Theo in Louisiana had been made easily.

Javar pulled Whitney close. "Stephanie . . . she's an angry, unhappy woman. Don't let what she says bother you."

That Stephanie was angry and unhappy was an understatement. Whitney pulled back and looked up into Javar's dark eyes. "Stephanie is a lot more evil than you give her credit for."

Javar shrugged. "She's suffering. Pain can make people do crazy things."

"Like threaten to kill someone else?"

Javar ran his hands down Whitney's arms, taking her hands in his. "She didn't mean that."

Whitney shrugged out of Javar's embrace, a wave of anger washing over her. "Why are you so sure, Javar? You heard what she said." Whitney huffed. "She's probably behind all those death threats nearly two years ago."

Javar's eyes bulged as shock sparked in their depths. "Death threats? What are you talking about? I don't remember any death threats."

The sudden memories caused a chill to pass over her, and Whitney wrapped her arms around her body. "I . . . after the first accident, I received numerous death threats . . . after J.J. . . . ."

"What?" Disbelief sounded in his voice.

"It's one of the reasons I left."

Troubled lines etched Javar's golden brown forehead.

"Let me get this straight. You were receiving death threats while you were living here and you didn't tell me?"

Whitney didn't like the anger in his eyes. Unable to face him, she turned her back to him. Javar immediately grasped her arm and spun her around. He looked down at her with eyes that said he couldn't believe what she'd done. "Answer me, Whitney. Why wouldn't you tell me something like that?"

"Because."

"Because? That's your answer?"

Tears poured from Whitney's chestnut eyes and spilled onto her bruised cheeks. Javar's gut clenched. He wanted to comfort her, but how could he when he felt so ... angry? Yes, he was angry. He was her husband, and she hadn't trusted him.

"Whitney, you owe me an explanation."

Outrage sparked in her eyes. "Think about it, Javar. Why wouldn't I tell you something like that? Because you were barely saying two words to me then, that's why. I had already burdened you enough. I didn't want to add to the stress in your life."

That hurt. Knocked the wind out of him. And the worst part was, Javar knew Whitney hadn't said that to make him feel like a lousy husband. She'd said that because it had been the truth. Angry with her for the death of his son, he had closed himself off emotionally. Like a fool, he had left her to suffer all her pain and guilt alone. He still felt angry, but now only with himself.

An apology would never make up for all the agony he had caused her. He could only hope it was a start. "Whitney—"

"Save it," she retorted, angrily brushing away her tears. "Nothing you say can change the past."

She spun around, ready climb the stairs. She halted, turning back to face him. "Why are you doing this to me?" Her eyes implored him to end her suffering. "Please, Javar, just give me a divorce. Please, just let me get on with my life."

* * *

Please, just let me get on with my life. The words haunted Javar as he thought about them for the millionth time as he sat hunched over the drafting table in his home office. He should be concentrating on his work, on the Li bid, but he couldn't.

Let her get on with her life ... Lord help him, he couldn't. Not yet. Not until they'd had a chance to work through their differences, resolve them.

Javar stood, stretched. Placing his hands on his hips, he walked to the large bay window and looked outside. The sudden movements of a robin frightened him, flying from the flowerpot on the window's edge. He watched the bird as it flew over the flower gardens, past the tennis and basketball courts to the left, finally stopping when it reached the pine trees that bordered the north side of his property. The landscape was beautiful—the gardener had seen to that. When Whitney was here years earlier, she had done a lot of the gardening herself, except the property was too vast to do it all.

He slowly let out a deep breath. He had all this property, yet he hardly used it. *When was the last time I used the pool, he wondered, or even took a walk in the backyard?* He'd done those things when Whitney was here, when J.J. was still alive.

His eyes settled on the basketball court. His mind wandered as he stared. Like it was yesterday, he remembered J.J. out on the basketball court, dribbling a ball as best he could. The image was so clear he imagined J.J. was actually out there, wearing his Chicago Bulls jersey. J.J. had loved the fact that his favorite player on the team shared his last name. When he told others that fact, his little eyes had widened with pride.

Javar shook his head, tossing the image aside. J.J. wasn't out there now; he never would be again. Javar's chest tightened painfully the way it always did when he thought of his son. Gone too soon. . . . He'd never have the chance to be a real father to J.J., the kind of father he had failed to be.

But he could be a real husband. If Whitney let him.

Javar strolled back to the drafting table. Looking down at the sketches, he shook his head. How could he come up with something appropriate for the Li proposal in less than two weeks? If he had the time to concentrate only on that, maybe, but he had Whitney to consider now. Whitney, who had always told him to take on a partner at his firm. If he did win the Li bid, he would be extremely busy with designs, budgeting, traveling to Arizona—even more busy than he presently was. As his firm's only principal, everything ultimately rested on his shoulders—meeting with clients, hiring interior designers. How could he prove to Whitney that their marriage mattered most if he continued to burn the candle at both ends? Maybe he should just forget the Li bid.

Oh, but he wanted to win it so badly. . . . He frowned. Maybe later, when he had more time to weigh the pros and cons, he would make a final decision about what he should do.

Right now, all he could think about was Whitney, and his startling revelation. She had received death threats after J.J. had died. Someone who held her responsible for his son's death.

Could it have been Stephanie? Cunning, faceless threats didn't seem to be her style. Then who? He scrunched his forehead as he thought, realizing there were probably several of his and Stephanie's family members who might have resorted to something that immature.

But there was one person whom he could easily exclude from that list, he realized, a smile touching his lips. The one person in his family who had accepted Whitney with open arms.

An idea hitting him, Javar grabbed his car keys and

headed out of the house. There was something he needed to do.

Whitney didn't realize she'd dozed off until the knocking on the bedroom door awoke her. She sat up, feeling somewhat groggy, and called, "Who is it?"

"Feel up for some company?" Javar asked.

Maybe it was the hurt look in his eyes this morning when she'd asked him to let her get on with her life, or maybe it was the nagging feeling that she was being unfair. But Whitney found she wanted to see Javar, to work out some sort of truce.

As she unlocked the door and turned the knob, she said, "Javar—", then halted when she saw he was not alone. The next instant, her eyes grew wide and excitement caused her heart to beat rapidly. She stood only mere seconds before stepping forward and throwing her arms around her surprise visitor. "Grandma Beryl!"

"Whitney!" Grandma Beryl held her in a tight embrace.

Javar said, "I'll be in my office."

Looking over Grandma Beryl's shoulder at Javar, Whitney slipped out of the older woman's arms. "Javar . . . thanks."

"No problem." His lips curled slightly in a grin. Then he was gone.

Whitney turned to Grandma Beryl, her grandmother-in-law. Dressed in a bright floral cotton dress that flowed around her ankles, Grandma Beryl was slim and gorgeous. She had a sense of style that many women lost as they grew older. Once a week Grandma Beryl made a trip to the hair salon, treating herself to a hot oil treatment and sometimes a touch-up of the raven color she dyed her hair. As a result, her shoulder-length tresses were thick and vibrant. Without a gray hair on her head, and with her smooth, almost wrinkle free milk chocolate complexion, Grandma Beryl didn't look a day over sixty-five.

Whitney took Grandma Beryl's hands in hers. "I am so glad to see you Grandma Beryl."

"Oh, Whitney. It has been much too long."

"I know." Whitney turned, leading Grandma Beryl to the cream-colored leather sofa. Grandma Beryl favored her left leg, due to troubles with arthritis. They both sat.

"What were you thinking, scaring us to death like that? Nearly getting yourself killed . . ." Grandma Beryl snorted. "And nobody even told me about it until you'd come home."

"Javar probably didn't want to worry you."

"I should have been there for you," Grandma Beryl said, emphasizing each word. "Hospitals are about as uplifting as the thought of being in a coffin. That must be why they didn't tell me. They must have thought the sight of you in that hospital bed would send me to my grave."

Whitney squeezed Grandma Beryl's hand. "Grandma Beryl, you're too strong to die."

Grandma Beryl chuckled. "And too bad. You know what they say. Only the good die young."

Whitney smile fondly as she looked at the mischievous gleam in Javar's grandmother's eye. She loved her so much. Despite the fact that blood didn't tie them, she and Grandma Beryl were as close as any blood relatives, even more so. "I see you haven't changed," Whitney said good-naturedly. "Still refusing to move into this house?"

"I do not need my grandson to take care of me. I am still absolutely able to take care of myself."

"We all know that. But this place is so big. There are so many rooms. . . ."

"It's not downtown."

For as long as Whitney had known Grandma Beryl, she had lived in a gorgeous condominium close to the Magnificent Mile. She preferred her privacy more than anything else, as she was a widow who liked to date.

It was then that Whitney noticed the huge ruby ring on Grandma Beryl's left hand. Whitney lifted her thin hand, examining the ring closely. The large ruby was oval-shaped, surrounded by a thin layer of diamonds. "Grandma Beryl, this is some ring! Planning on settling down soon?"

Grandma Beryl flashed Whitney a wry grin. "I am having too much fun to settle down, dear."

Whitney didn't doubt that. But she knew that after Vincent, Beryl's husband, had died of a heart attack at the age of sixty-five—right after he had retired—Beryl was devastated. She had gone on, but she'd closed off her heart to the possibility of deep romantic love. Having married at seventeen, Vincent had been the true love of her life.

Grandma Beryl shifted on the couch, crossing one leg over the other as she faced Whitney. She pinned her with a level stare. "You, on the other hand, do not look like you've been having any fun."

"I . . . well, I'm recuperating."

The stare grew more intense. "Recuperating has nothing to do with what I'm talking about. Life is hardly fun when you're not sharing your life with the man you love. When you've asked him for a divorce."

At Whitney's shocked expression, her grandmother added, "Yes, he told me. After I gave him the third degree. Told him that there's no reason for you to be apart."

"Grandma Beryl . . ."

"Don't Grandma Beryl me. I've been in love, you know. Was married forty-five years. And I can still remember what it's like to look at someone with love in your eyes. That's the way you looked at Javar five years ago. You still look at him that way now."

Whitney hadn't even had an opportunity to look at Javar during the brief time he'd been in the room. She told his grandmother that.

"I saw your reaction. It was immediate. And it was undeniable."

"What you saw was surprise," Whitney replied quickly. "Then gratitude. I was happy to see you."

"Mmm hmm." But Grandma Beryl was eyeing her skeptically.

What else could Whitney say? Grandma Beryl wouldn't understand. She was a romantic, and when she believed two people belonged together, her opinion couldn't be swayed. "When I'm all better, Javar and I will be getting a divorce."

Grandma Beryl pursed her lips, her expression saying she didn't believe a word Whitney said.

They sat together and talked for a long while, remembering old times, until the nurse came to examine Whitney. When Whitney had left Chicago almost two years ago, she'd tried to forget everything about her time with Javar. She'd called Grandma Beryl on occasion, but in her quest to shut out the bad in her life, she had ultimately shut out the good. Grandma Beryl was part of the good. From now on, they would stay in touch.

She was only divorcing Javar, after all.

Stephanie Lewis pushed the dining room chair back with such force it fell over and clattered against the hardwood floor. Food was the last thing on her mind.

Kevin, her older brother by a year, stood and placed a hand on her shoulder. "Steph, you've got to calm down."

"How would you feel if your dead son's father had the nerve to let your son's murderer live in his house?"

"Javar's a fool."

Stephanie grunted. She and her older brother hadn't always been close, but they'd formed a bond after J.J.'s death. They both hated Whitney and wanted her to pay for her crime. "Why didn't she just die in that car accident? I swear, that woman has nine lives."

Kevin turned Stephanie to face him, planting both hands on her shoulders. "Think of the bright side. At least we know where she is, right?"

"Right."

"And you know what they say. Don't get mad; get even."

Stephanie was silent for a moment. Then she frowned. "That place is like Fort Knox. I can't even get in there to spit in her face."

Kevin's eyebrows rose and he cocked his head to the side. "Don't be so sure, Stephanie. Where there's a will, there's a way."

Chapter Nine

"Hello?" Whitney held the receiver to her ear, waiting for a response. She only heard the sound of soft breathing. "Hello?"

Click. In the silence of the room, the dial tone filled her eardrum.

Irritated, she glanced at the clock radio. Three eleven A.M. Who on earth would be calling her at this hour? Only a select few knew any of Javar's three home numbers, and even less knew which line she was using.

She turned on the lamp and looked at the caller I.D. Private name, unknown number.

It was only a crank call. Or more likely, a wrong number. Nothing to worry about she decided as she lay back on the pillows and pulled the comforter around her neck. She closed her eyes, but sleep wouldn't come. Her nerves felt like they were trying to pop out of her skin.

Although Whitney hated relying on any type of drug, even aspirin, maybe taking a stress pill now wasn't such a bad idea. Maybe that would help her sleep. Not that it had done much good yet. She seemed to waver from groggy to wired, but never truly stress-free. At least her headache had lessened.

She sat up and hugged her knees to her chest. No amount of pills would help her get over the past. Only one thing now could possibly help her mental healing. And she couldn't avoid it any longer.

Whitney slipped out of the warm bed, her feet sinking into the plush carpet as they touched the ground. The house was silent, and she made no sound on the carpet, yet she tiptoed, not wanting to wake anyone.

Slowly Whitney opened the door to her bedroom, being careful not to make any sound. She paused only a moment before turning left and heading down the wide hallway.

Seconds seemed like hours, but Whitney was finally there. She stopped in front of the door, not sure if she had the strength to go on. Only once since the accident had she been in J.J.'s room, and then she had broken down and cried uncontrollably, overwhelmed by the guilt. How could she go in there now and face all the memories that she had tried to forget? But how could she not? The past would always haunt her if she didn't try to come to terms with it.

Her stomach fluttered with anxiety. It had been so long . . .

Slowly, Whitney reached out and grasped the brass door handle. She felt the onset of tears, but fought them. She had to do this. She had to go on. . . .

The first thing she noticed when she stepped inside the room was that everything was the same. J.J.'s posters, his stuffed animals, his model train set by the window. Whitney couldn't suppress a gasp. Her little J.J. Her darling, precious son.

Dead. Because of her.

No! her mind screamed. It was an accident. J.J.'s mother Stephanie and even members of Javar's family hated her because they thought she was guilty of a crime. The only crime she'd been guilty of was loving J.J. like her own son.

Yet Stephanie and her family, her mother and father-in-law, her sister-in-law, they all thought she should be in jail for killing J.J. Why didn't they realize that living with the memories of the accident, living with her own pain and guilt was worse than any jail could ever be? Although J.J.'s death was a senseless accident, she would always blame herself.

And so would Javar, Whitney thought, her stomach clenching as a sharp pain shot through her. How could he even think he wanted a reconciliation? Despite what he said now, he couldn't. Not after the way he had looked at her with such anger, such disgust, when J.J. had died. Not after he had insinuated that she had not taken the best care of J.J. simply because he hadn't been her flesh-and-blood son. The look of betrayal in Javar's cold eyes would always stay with Whitney, haunting her almost as much as the sight of J.J.'s immobile body on the side of the road.

Haunting her almost as much as her own privately suffered, profound guilt.

Wrapping her arms around her body, Whitney tried to fight off the chill that came with the memories. But it was a chill that started in her heart and worked its way outward, and she doubted she'd ever get over it. But she had to try.

Slowly, placing one foot in front of the other, Whitney moved into the room, toward J.J.'s car-shaped bed. The blinds were open, and the soft glow of the moonlight as well as the exterior houselights illuminated the room well enough that she didn't need to switch on a lamp. She lowered herself onto the bed, lifting J.J.'s favorite stuffed animal, his teddy bear Martin, into her arms. The animal he believed would protect him in the dark of the night.

If only he'd had Martin with him that day. . . . Whitney sighed wistfully, knowing that no stuffed animal could have saved Javar Junior. If only it hadn't been raining. If only she'd been able to control the car before it flipped over.

If onlys weren't going to bring J.J. back. Nothing was.

She didn't know she was crying until the salty taste of tears met her tongue. Holding Martin to her body tightly, she cried and cried until there were no more tears. Then she said a prayer, asking for the strength to go on with her life. But most of all, she prayed for the strength to forgive herself for being the one who had survived.

She shook her head, dismissing that thought. No, she didn't wish she were dead. In fact, she suddenly realized, what she probably felt most guilty for was being glad that she had survived. How could she so selfishly be happy for life when a five-year-old boy was dead? Yes, she decided, her stomach twisting with a newer, sicker, more poignant feeling of guilt. She was glad that she had survived. She was glad she wasn't cheated of her life the way J.J. had been. But God help her, if she had to live through that accident again, she would gladly exchange her life for J.J.'s. J.J. hadn't been driving the car. J.J. wasn't responsible for making sure he was buckled in.

The onus was on her. Only her.

As Whitney sat there on J.J.'s bed, with Martin in her arms, her eyelids grew heavy. The pain of the memories was more than emotional, it was physical, causing her head to pound and her chest to ache. Her body's need to heal, its need for peace, finally won out and lured her into a restless sleep. She dreamed. . . .

One hand on the steering wheel, she looked down at the boy beside her and smiled. He smiled back, his small dimples winking at her, and her heart expanded in her chest. How she loved him! He was so handsome, just like his father, except his young face was rounder. She loved him so much, as if he was her own flesh and blood. Since her marriage to his father, he'd been asking for a brother or a sister. Maybe they would give him one soon.

"How about some ice cream?" she asked. The sky was a clear blue and the day was perfect for such a treat.

"Yeah." He nodded enthusiastically. The next moment, he directed his gaze to the shore of Lake Michigan, pulling his T-shirt up over his chin.

She ran a hand over his hair, then looked out at the road before her. Suddenly, the sky turned black. Pitch-black. She couldn't see a thing in front of her. And then there was rain. Everywhere.

A scream.

Whitney's blood pumped wildly in her veins as she looked to the right. J.J. was gone.

She glanced at the road, saw a small body. Slammed on the brakes . . .

The scream tore into his consciousness, forcing him awake.

Whitney!

Javar threw off the covers and bolted out of bed. Through the door. Down the hall.

He burst through the door of Whitney's bedroom and in the darkness ran to her bed. It took him only a moment to realize that she wasn't there.

Where was she?

Again, she screamed, her voice a shrill and desperate sound, and Javar knew. Charging out of the room, he ran down the hall to J.J.'s room, the only other place Whitney could be. As he threw open the door to J.J.'s bedroom, panicked sobs filled the air. Immediately, Javar was at her side, drawing her into his arms.

"No!" she screamed, sounding hysterical. She squirmed, trying to free herself from his strong embrace. "I'm sorry. So sorry. Oh please, you have to believe me!"

"Whitney." He held her tightly, and when she didn't calm down, Javar framed her face with his hands. Despite his direct contact and the fact that he was staring into her eyes, she continued to fight to be free. "Whitney," he repeated, forcefully.

In the soft moonlight, he saw her face contort with grief, then confusion, and finally understanding. He had gotten through to her, drawn her back from the depths of pain. The sobs stopped but she froze, almost as if she didn't know what was happening.

Javar reached for the bedside lamp and turned it on. When he looked down at Whitney, she sat silently staring at him, seemingly dazed.

"W-what happened?" She asked.

"I was hoping you could tell me." Javar slipped an arm around her and rested his chin on her head. His body reacted to the intimacy, coming alive with heat. It had been so long since he had been beside Whitney like this, in a bed, even if it was his son's. He forced the wayward thought from his mind. "You were screaming."

"I . . . what am I doing here?"

Javar flashed her a puzzled look. "You . . . don't know?"

Glancing around, she seemed even more confused. She opened her mouth to speak, but then stopped.

"Whitney, you're in J.J.'s room."

After a long moment, she nodded. "I was . . . I was thinking . . . about him."

"What's going on?"

Both Javar and Whitney turned at the sound of Elizabeth's voice. She stood in the doorway, wrapped in a pink terry-cloth robe. Moving away from Whitney and sliding to the edge of the bed, Javar said, "Everything's okay."

Elizabeth averted her eyes, as though embarrassed that she had intruded on something. "I-I heard the scream. . . ."

Whitney merely stared at the nurse, clearly not sure what to say.

"What are you doing out of bed?"

"She doesn't seem to know how she got here," Javar explained.

"Do you have a history of sleepwalking?" Elizabeth asked as she strode toward Whitney with determined steps.

Shaking her head, Whitney replied, "No."

"Hmm." Elizabeth's brow wrinkled. Taking Whitney's wrist in her hand, she checked her pulse. "Your pulse is rather high. Did you take your pills earlier?"

Whitney stared up at the nurse, thinking that she reminded her of a drill sergeant. She suddenly felt like a young child who'd fed her broccoli to the dog under the table. "I . . . I didn't swallow them."

Elizabeth sighed. "Whitney, you must take those pills as prescribed. They'll help you relax, help you sleep, help you heal. Clearly, you're suffering from anxiety, so much so that you got up in the middle of the night and came into this room." She placed a hand on Whitney's back. "Come on. Let's go back to your room."

Javar was on his feet in an instant, wrapping an arm around Whitney's waist. The smell of her delicate floral shampoo flirted with his senses. Being close to her like this, even though she was healing, he wanted to run his fingers through the silky strands of her raven hair, lose himself in the smell and feel of her.

"Help her into the bed," the nurse instructed, pulling Javar from his fantasy. He did as the nurse said, leading Whitney to the bed and helping her under the covers. Elizabeth appeared with two pills in a cup and handed them to Whitney along with some water. "Here. Take these."

Whitney took the took small capsules from Elizabeth and popped them into her mouth, then downed them with a swig of water. There was no point arguing. Tonight's episode had left her frazzled, and she'd give anything for a decent night's sleep. She handed the glass back to the nurse and said, "Thanks."

"That should help you get through the rest of the night." Elizabeth looked at her with a stern expression, then sighed. "I'll check on you later."

After the nurse disappeared, Javar turned to face Whitney. She saw concern in his dark brown eyes as he took her hands in his. "Whitney, you've got to take your medicine. You know that."

"I . . . you know I don't like taking pills."

"This isn't about liking or not liking prescribed drugs. You need them now, whether you like it or not."

Whitney shrugged, then pulled her hands from Javar's. She shifted away from him on the bed. It wasn't what he said or the firm way in which he said it that bothered her. It was being so close to him like this. His musky smell, his sexiness, unnerved her. Made her remember the dreams and hopes she'd had as a young bride. "I . . . I was feeling better."

Javar frowned. "Whitney, you were almost killed in a car accident. And the only reason Dr. Adu-Bohene let you come home with me was because he trusted me to help you get well. That's why I hired Elizabeth, to help you get well. Whitney, you cannot skip your medication at this stage in your recovery."

"I know."

Javar looked down at Whitney, saw the sadness in her eyes. He was acting like a parent, not a husband. She needed his comfort, not a lecture.

He reached out and stroked her arm. "Do you remember your dream?"

Whitney shook her head. She did remember that she was dreaming about J.J., but she didn't want to tell Javar that. She wanted him to leave and let her rest. "I'm okay, Javar. You can go back to bed."

"Not until I know you're okay." He trailed his hand up her arm, over her shoulder, to her jaw.

The action was foreign yet painfully familiar. Javar was wearing only cotton pajama bottoms, exposing his brawny, sexy chest. He had only a sprinkling of dark, curly hair on his golden-brown chest that thickened at his belly button and went lower. It was a beautiful chest, a chest on which she could vividly remember raining kisses. A chest that had held her in a lover's embrace on numerous occasions.

She wanted to reach out and touch it now, felt the urge like a moth drawn to a flame. Dressed only in a silk nightie, things could easily escalate. All Javar would have to do was reach out and slip the material off her shoulders, over her breasts. . . .

The unexpected image caused Whitney to shudder. It also caused her to come to her senses. What she needed was for Javar to leave. Now.

"Javar, thanks for checking on me. I'm okay now."

"I found you in J.J.'s room, Whitney. And you have no idea how you got there."

His eyes held hers, told her he didn't believe her, wouldn't leave her until he knew that she was okay. "I," she began, then paused. "Look, I was thinking about J.J., and I just wanted to be close to him."

"Do you always have nightmares . . . about the accident?"

"Sometimes," Whitney admitted, her voice only a whisper. "But it's getting better. The dreams come less now."

"Is there anything I can do?" Javar asked, wishing there was, knowing there wasn't.

"No." Lying back on the pillows, Whitney half sighed, half yawned.

He wanted to say something else, but thought better of it. Now was not the time. Not only was she tired, there was the chance she might not believe his words were sincere. Folding his arms over his chest, he watched his wife a moment longer.

"I'll be fine," she assured him.

Taking that as his cue to leave, Javar rose from the bed. He shouldn't be leaving her bed. She shouldn't be in a guest room. They were husband and wife and she belonged with him in his bedroom, in the bed they had shared as a married couple.

"Good night, Javar."

Javar sat back down, planting both hands on either side of her body. He began to lean forward. Whitney sucked in a sharp breath, unsure what he was doing. Unsure she would be able to resist him if he advanced toward her.

To her surprise, he planted a soft, lingering kiss on her forehead. His warm lips on her cool skin caused a jolt of electricity to heat her blood. Goodness, he was still so sexy.

"Good night, Whitney," he whispered, his warm breath fanning her forehead. "I'll see you in the morning." Then he stood and sauntered to the door, his strong muscles moving beneath his sleek, golden brown back.

When he was gone, Whitney released her breath. Then, trying to put Javar out of her mind, she reached for the bedside lamp and turned it off.

Her brain said she was happy Javar was gone. Her heart said she was a liar.

Despite the fact that he'd worked a sixteen-hour day and had to be up early for another hectic day of investigative work, Derrick Lawson couldn't sleep. Whitney was on his mind. Had been for most of the day.

He was worried about her. How could he not be? She was staying with Javar, a man who had turned stone cold when she'd needed him the most. Javar might be a well-respected businessman in the community, but Derrick didn't trust him as far as he could throw him.

Javar would hurt her again, Derrick was sure.

Grumbling because there were only three hours left to sleep before his alarm went off, Derrick rolled out of his queen-sized bed since he couldn't sleep. It didn't matter that it was summer, the hardwood floor was cold on his bare feet. Slipping into the slippers his mother had given him for his last birthday, Derrick walked the short distance to the light switch and flicked it on.

Turning, he saw the framed five-by-seven picture of Whitney on his dresser. It was taken years ago, when she'd been a freshman at Northwestern University. That was a simpler time, before she had met Javar and fallen head-over-heels in love with him.

Derrick chuckled mirthlessly. He'd always hoped that Whitney would fall in love with *him,* but one look in her eyes after she'd met Javar and Derrick had known that he didn't stand a chance. Whitney's eyes had never lit up with that special spark when she'd looked at him. However, with Javar, that spark was there like a constant flame. She had loved him, and he'd hurt her. Abandoned her.

But a trip down memory lane reminiscing about the one girl he'd always loved was not why Derrick had gotten out of his bed this early in the morning. It was the unsettling feeling in his gut. The one that had him thinking constantly about Whitney's accident. Wondering . . .

Had it really been an accident? Or had someone deliberately run her off the road—tried to kill her? *Kill.* The word was so strong, yet he was very familiar with death—with murder. With the passions that could lead to deplorable crimes.

And that was exactly what was bothering him, as he began to give consideration to a theory he prayed was wrong. If Whitney's accident wasn't really an accident—if it had been a deliberate attempt to harm her—then Derrick could think of only one person who would go to such lengths. One person who had the motive to want to hurt her, and who now had the means.

Derrick prayed he was wrong. For if he was right, that meant that Whitney was in danger at Javar's house. Because Javar held her responsible for his son's death. And he may just want to see her dead in return.

Chapter Ten

As she did every morning since the accident, Eleanor Scherer sat at her small breakfast table with the morning newspaper before her. Her glasses perched on the bridge of her nose, she searched for any report of the accident she had witnessed. The morning after the car crash, she'd found a story that stated there had been a serious accident on North Lake Shore Drive late the previous evening, and that a young woman had been taken to the hospital with critical injuries. Then, Eleanor had felt terrible. She didn't know her, but that poor woman didn't deserve to be run off the road the way she had been. Eleanor had wanted to call the police and tell them what she knew, but something had stopped her.

She was afraid.

A chill swept over her as she remembered the fear she'd experienced that night. After the driver had run the woman off the road, he had slowed down. Now, she knew he'd been waiting for her to catch up to him. She had, and she'd been brave enough to look over at the car, attempting to see its driver. Fool she was, she had forgotten the one rule of the streets: Mind your business and nobody else's.

The car's windows had been tinted, and in the dark, Eleanor hadn't been able to see the driver. But she was sure he had seen her. She'd just been so shocked at what he had done that she'd stared, and she knew he had seen her. Every detail of her aging face. And no doubt, her license plate too.

Eleanor rose and made her way to the cupboard where she kept her pills. She would only take one. If Harry was still alive, he could help her make the right decision, but she was alone, and she was so very confused.

She could almost feel the effects of the Prozac immediately after she swallowed the pill that she knew would calm her nerves.

One more day, she decided. She'd wait one more day. If there wasn't a follow-up report stating that that poor woman had died, then she would forget about it. There was no need to go to the police if the woman was alive and well. No need at all.

"Carlos," Javar called as he walked quickly into the kitchen. When he didn't immediately see his butler, he called him again.

The door to the walk-in pantry opened and Carlos appeared, a bag of flour in his hands. His eyebrows rose as concern flashed on his face. "Yes, Mr. Jordan?"

"Carlos, are you aware that the alarm system was turned off? It appears to have been off the entire night."

Shrugging, Carlos said, "No, sir. When I retired to bed, the alarm system was activated."

"Well, how is it that I found the alarm deactivated this morning?"

Carlos ventured toward the kitchen's island, depositing the bag of flour on the granite counter. "Miss Templeton came early. Perhaps she forgot to reactivate it after she arrived."

Miss Templeton was Javar's housekeeper, who came in three times a week. Biting his inner cheek, Javar silently acknowledged that she could have forgotten to reactivate the alarm. It wouldn't be the first time either of them had forgotten to do so, so why did he feel uneasy about it this morning? His sixth sense was telling him something, but what?

"I suppose you're right," Javar finally conceded. When he'd discovered that the alarm had been deactivated, he'd done a check of all the rooms in the house, looking for anything of value that might be missing. Nothing of obvious value, like his art collection, had been taken. "I'm guilty of forgetting to activate the alarm myself sometimes, but while Whitney is recovering, I'd feel a lot better if the alarm were always on. Can you please check it consistently, Carlos?"

"Of course, sir. I'll speak with Miss Templeton as well, if you'd like."

"Please," Javar replied.

Carlos nodded. "Certainly." He paused. "What would you like for breakfast?"

"Actually, Carlos, I'm not very hungry. I'll just grab a cup of coffee."

As Javar was walking toward the coffeemaker, he noticed a black, silk scarf on the seat of one of the breakfast chairs. Forgetting the coffee, he walked to the chair and retrieved the scarf. With the initials A.J. embroidered in shiny red thread, the scarf was unmistakably his mother's.

Javar turned to Carlos. "Carlos, was my mother here?"

Pounding his open palm lightly on his forehead, Carlos said, "Yes, Mr. Jordan. I forgot to tell you. She dropped by while you were out yesterday, she and your sister, Michelle. She said she would call you later. She didn't?"

Javar fingered the delicate silk, wondering. His mother

and his sister. "No. She didn't call me last night. Did she say why they dropped by?"

"I believe they wanted to visit your wife, but she was sleeping. And since you weren't here, they left."

Innocent enough, Javar thought, knowing that with his mother and Michelle nothing was really innocent. Michelle had taken after their mother, knowing just how to control a situation to get what she wanted. Neither his mother nor Michelle had approved of Whitney as his wife, although Michelle had at first tried to give her a chance. Having discovered that Whitney's personality was so different from her own, Michelle later decided she didn't like her.

Sighing, Javar wondered how siblings, or even a parent and child, could be so completely different.

One restless night and Whitney felt like lead flowed through her veins. Her limbs were so heavy she could barely lift her body, and her head ached. Even worse, her stomach felt like it contained some vile concoction that needed to be regurgitated.

"You don't look well," Elizabeth was saying as she checked Whitney's pulse. "How do you feel?"

"Awful," Whitney moaned. "I feel nauseous."

"Taking your pills on an empty stomach can cause nausea. You should have some breakfast."

"Yes, that sounds great." Even bread and water sounded wonderful right about now.

"Open." Elizabeth stuck a high-tech digital thermometer in Whitney's mouth. "You look like you could use some more rest. Would you like me to have Carlos bring you some breakfast?"

Whitney shook her head. She'd spent too much time in this room as it was. Surely it would be more beneficial to her recovery if she went outside, enjoyed the fresh air and nature.

The thermometer beeped, signaling that the temperature had been computed. The nurse pulled it from beneath Whitney's tongue and checked the digital display. "Hmmm. Your temperature is a little higher than yesterday. You have a low-grade fever, indicating your body is fighting an infection. I'm just going to check your wound."

The nurse lifted the gauze that covered the gash on Whitney's forehead. "Oooh," she said, pursing her lips. "Well, now I know what's causing your fever. This cut is infected." She turned, moved to the nurse's stand, searching its contents. Moments later she produced a bottle of medication. "Are you allergic to penicillin?"

"No."

"Good." She opened the bottle and dropped a pill into her hand. "Take this."

Whitney groaned. "More drugs."

"I know this isn't fun, but soon enough you'll be completely healthy again."

"That day can't come too soon."

"I'm sure." Elizabeth cleaned Whitney's wound and rebandaged it, then handed Whitney a glass of water to drink with the pill. "Here you go."

Whitney mumbled her thanks, then swallowed the antibiotic. The day when she was healthy again wouldn't come too soon, indeed.

"Something smells *wonderful,*" Whitney almost sang as she walked into the kitchen. Bright sunlight spilled into the room, filling it with warmth. Already, Whitney felt revived.

Hearing her voice, Carlos looked up from the tray of biscuits he had just removed from the oven. The corners of his dark eyes crinkled as he smiled tenderly at her.

"Good morning, Mrs. Jordan."

Walking toward him, Whitney said, "Carlos, please call me Whitney. You know I prefer that."

"I'm sorry, Mrs—*Whitney*. The biscuits are fresh. Would you like some?"

"Please. Three." Whitney strolled to the fridge and opened it. After scanning its contents, she found the carton of eggs and took it out. She placed it on the gray granite counter, then opened a cupboard and took out a frying pan.

"Mrs. Jordan, what are you doing?"

Whitney couldn't hide her amusement at Carlos's shocked tone. She knew Javar paid him well, but she found it unnecessary to have him prepare something as simple as scrambled eggs for her when she was perfectly capable of doing that for herself.

Whitney turned to Carlos. "I'm making scrambled eggs."

"Oh no, Mrs. Jordan."

"Whitney."

"Whitney," Carlos repeated. "Please, sit down and relax. You are still sick."

"I'm fine," Whitney told him. At his concerned look, she reached out and squeezed his hand. "Honestly, Carlos. I'm quite capable of preparing eggs for myself. I appreciate your concern, though."

Whitney turned and walked to the ceranic-top stove, bringing the frying pan with her. She sensed Carlos's eyes on her, but she didn't turn around. He took his job seriously—too seriously sometimes. But she knew he only meant well.

Opening the cupboard above the stove, Whitney looked for some cooking oil. She found none. "Carlos," she began, "where's the oil?"

"You should be resting, Mrs. Jordan." When Whitney turned and flashed him a look that said she was not an invalid, he said, "In the pantry. But please, let me get it for you."

Carlos scampered off, and Whitney concentrated on the stove, turning on the element. She'd never get used to these new flat-surfaced stoves that lacked the coils. Sure, they were easy to clean, but without the old-fashioned elements she always feared she'd place her hand right on top of the darn thing and burn herself!

Her breath snagged then, and she froze for a moment. Once while helping her in the kitchen, J.J. had reached for the top of the stove, almost placing his hand atop the invisible element. She'd grabbed it just in time, saving him from burning himself horribly.

J.J. Would it ever get any easier?

A hand was on her back, helping her. "Mrs. Jordan, please. Let me prepare the eggs."

Inhaling a deep breath, Whitney waved him off. "I'm okay." She took the bottle of canola oil from him. "Thanks."

Whitney set about making her breakfast. The eggs sizzled as she cracked them and dropped them into the skillet. Originally, she had set out to make scrambled eggs, but now she opted for fried instead. It was faster, and right now, she needed to get something in her stomach as quickly as possible. Without any food in her stomach, she was queasy and light-headed.

When the eggs were done, she turned to see Carlos beside her with a plate and a glass of orange juice. She smiled at him. Bless him. He was a wonderful person who truly loved his job. On the plate were three biscuits, just as she'd requested.

Plate in one hand and the juice in the other, Whitney walked to the breakfast counter and slipped onto a stool, allowing herself a view of the spectacular rose gardens. After breakfast, she would go for a walk. Maybe even venture into the pool. She did love this house, and it saddened her that she would have to give up both Javar and this spectacular place. But as Luther Vandross had so eloquently said in one of his love ballads, "a house is not a home". Without the unconditional love Whitney had only dreamed of, this house would never be a home for her. It had never really been.

"Mind if I join you?"

At the sound of Javar's deep, sexy voice, Whitney shuddered. Why did he have to sneak up on her like that! Swallowing a piece of the buttery biscuit, Whitney turned and looked up at her estranged husband. He was wearing a simple white T-shirt with khaki shorts, but the shirt made him look so enticing you would think it was cut from the world's finest silk.

She lifted her eyes to his. "Good morning, Javar."

Easing himself down onto the stool beside her, Javar asked, "How are you feeling this morning?"

"Better . . . now that I've got some food in my stomach."

"No doubt." He smiled softly, and Whitney felt her stomach tighten. If things were different between her and Javar, this might be a time where she was compelled to reach out and stroke his face. He was smiling at her so lovingly now, as though they had never had the problems they'd had. But she held her hand where it was, letting the moment pass.

Javar said, "Why don't you join me on the patio?"

"Umm . . ." Whitney's mind scrambled for a suitable reason to turn him down. She could find none. He was only offering companionship, and she couldn't very well avoid him all the time while she was staying in his house. "Okay."

"Let me get that for you," he said, lifting her plate. Whitney took juice and followed Javar as he walked to the right, then out the patio doors. The moment they stepped outside, the heat enveloped her like a blanket of warmth. She paused, turning her face upward to enable the sun's rays to reach the entire surface of her face. Closing her eyes, she allowed herself to enjoy the moment.

"Whitney?"

Hearing the concern in Javar's voice, Whitney opened her eyes and faced him. "There's nothing like the sun to make one feel one hundred times better," she said, walking toward the wrought-iron patio table. A large cream-colored umbrella rested in the middle of the table, open and providing shade. She reached for a chair.

Javar placed his hand on hers, stopping her. Instantly, Whitney felt his warmth. She looked down at his large hand where it covered her smaller one, remembering the time she had looked forward to his touch. A time when things weren't strained between them. A time so different from now.

"Let me," Javar stated simply.

Nodding, Whitney slowly pulled her hand from beneath Javar's, telling herself that she didn't really like the way his hand had felt on hers. Her body didn't believe her, evidenced by the fact that her hand now tingled where Javar's had been. Slowly, that tingling sensation spread throughout her arm and to the rest of her body.

It was lust, she assured herself. That's all it was. It had been years since she had been touched by a man, especially one as attractive as Javar, and her body couldn't help responding to his warm touch.

"Sit," Javar said.

Whitney did, wondering why she hadn't noticed him pulling out the chair. The cool iron on her heated skin was exactly what she needed.

Javar pulled out a chair and sat next to her. "I didn't realize the rest of your body was bruised."

"Hmm?"

"Your legs," Javar explained. "I saw the bruises."

"Oh." Whitney glanced down at her white shorts, then back up at him. "I try not to think about it."

Nodding, Javar said, "Do they hurt? Your legs, I mean?" When he'd seen the purplish-blue bruising on her beautiful, slim legs, he almost gasped. Instead, he bit his inner cheek. He needed to be strong for his wife. Besides, he didn't want to make her uncomfortable by gawking at injuries she'd no doubt much rather forget.

"Everything still hurts, a little."

Javar supposed it would for a while. The emotional scars would take much longer to heal, if last night was any indication. Clearly, Whitney harbored guilt over J.J.'s death, and it was much more intense than he ever would have thought.

Whitney turned her attention to her food, and Javar watched her eat for several minutes. At least some things never changed. Whitney still had a voracious appetite, which was good. Eating was necessary to keep up her strength.

His eyes roamed the delicate features of her round face, the exotic-looking eyes, the high cheekbones, the full lips, the ever-so-slightly upturned nose. Her honey-colored complexion wasn't as pale as before, and the bruises were fading. Except for the cut on the left side of her forehead that was still bandaged, one wouldn't know that she'd been in a horrific car accident.

Emotions got caught in his throat, and he swallowed. Clearing his throat, he said, "So tell me what you've been up to in Louisiana."

Whitney finished chewing before turning her gaze to him. "The same thing I was doing here. Working at a youth center."

"Hmm." Javar's reply was curt.

When Whitney had lived in Chicago, Javar had never liked the fact that she worked at an inner-city youth center. He felt her job was dangerous, and among other concerns worried that someone might follow her home and try to attack her. Ironically, his wife's only threat of danger had come from a human invention, and later from someone close to him. He still could not believe that someone had been crazy enough to threaten her.

Whitney fiddled with the remaining eggs on her plate. "I love what I do. Especially working with the younger ones. Some of them have nobody in their lives to turn to, and they turn to me. I feel like I'm making a difference. Like I'm important to someone."

Javar doubted that Whitney's last comment was meant for him, but still his jaw flinched. She didn't have to say it. He knew. He hadn't made her feel important, even when things were good between them. Sure, the times they were together were amazing, but when it came down to it, he put his work first. And Whitney had never been able to accept his explanation that he was working hard to provide for her. On numerous occasions, she told him that she didn't care about money or a big house. She just wanted him.

He said softly, "I'm glad you're having a good time in Shreveport."

Her eyes flew to his. "That's not what I said. The last two years have hardly been a picnic, Javar. I've been trying to get on with my life, which isn't easy. But I do enjoy my work. In fact, it's what helped me get through the . . . the past two years."

"I didn't mean to imply—"

She paused, staring at him, as if trying to determine whether he was sincere. Finally, he saw her chest heave as she inhaled deeply. "I know."

"Tell me more."

As a smile touched her lips, cute dimples winked at him. "Some people don't like working in that kind of environment. They find it depressing. So many of the young people come from troubled families. They have brothers who've been murdered, sisters who are crack addicts. I see it as a challenge. An opportunity to help influence lives in a positive way.

"Take Terrence, for example. He's only fourteen, but most people would be willing to give up on him. He's got a fiery temper, a bad attitude, but that's all just a facade. Deep down, he's a hurt child who needs some guidance. He saw his father gunned down before his eyes, and his mother ended up turning tricks to support a drug habit. She died. Now, he lives with his grandmother. I've connected with him. When I first met him, he was cold, distant, running with a bad crowd. Now, he's not as cold, not as angry. With my help, he's discovered that his aspirations to be an artist aren't unrealistic. He's still fighting the temptation of gangs, but Javar, I swear, it makes me feel so good to see him find some self confidence. Realize that he's a worthy human being with something to contribute to the world."

As Whitney spoke, she was animated. Her eyes were bright, alive, and she exuded such a sense of commitment as she spoke about a young man whom others would rather forget. Just seeing her talk about what she loved made Javar realize that she truly was dedicated to helping troubled youths, to making a difference. That job was as important to her as his architecture was to him. And much more noble.

"I think what you do is truly wonderful, Whitney. It's great that there are people like you out there who are willing to dedicate their lives to helping people. Sometimes we take for granted that everyone has had the same start in life, and therefore can achieve the same things."

"It's such a great feeling when I can help them learn the meaning of self-worth."

Placing her chin on her hand, Whitney sighed happily. "What about you, Javar. How's your work going?"

"Busy. Really busy. I'm trying to land a bid for a shopping complex in Arizona."

Whitney sensed a "but" in his tone. She said it for him.

"But . . . I've been too busy. And now with your accident . . . my mind's preoccupied. I've got so many other things on my plate."

Shaking her head, Whitney gazed at Javar. "Have you taken on another associate, or made one of your present ones a partner?"

"No."

"Javar. My goodness, do you want to work yourself to death? You're only one person, after all. How much do you think you can do? How creative can you be when you're burned out?''

She was right, he knew. That was why he hadn't been able to come up with something dynamic for the Li bid. He already had too much to do, too much responsibility on his shoulders. But he always met his goals. ''I guess I threw myself into my work to take my mind off everything.''

''That's not the way to do it.''

''And running away was?''

''I didn't run away. You forced me to leave.''

''I never told you to go. . . .''

''Not in so many words. But you gave me no choice.''

Javar said, ''If our marriage was important to you, you would have stayed and tried to work things out.''

''Really?'' Whitney asked, pushing her chair back on the concrete and rising. ''If our marriage was important to *me*? I was the only one trying to keep our marriage together!''

Javar rose, met her gaze with hard eyes. ''Why don't you just admit that you were unhappy and looking for a way out? You said yourself that I was married to my job, not you. And then when J.J. died, you found that way out. . . .''

Angry, Whitney slammed both palms on the table. ''How dare you!''

''I needed time to grieve, Whitney. You didn't want to accept that.''

''And what about me? For God's sake, Javar, I was grieving too. Why couldn't you accept that?''

Unable to deny that accusation, Javar stood, silent.

''Why don't you admit that you still blame me for the accident. An accident where *I* could have been killed!''

He hesitated only a second before saying, ''No, I—''

''Puh-lease!'' In that fraction of a second when he had hesitated, Whitney had her answer. God, she was incredibly stupid to have believed otherwise. To let herself hope. The only reason he had her here and was ''taking care'' of her was out of pity. Or maybe just to make her life miserable. She pivoted on her heel and was about to stalk off, then stopped. Slowly, she turned back to Javar. "If you wanted to make me suffer for killing your son . . ." Her voice broke, and she wasn't sure she could go on. Swallowing her rage, she did. "You're doing a very good job, Javar. I'm more miserable than I've ever been!"

As she turned and started to run, he hastened after her, grabbing her arm. He pinned her with a pained gaze. "Maybe you're right, Whitney. Maybe there is no point in trying to work things out when we're obviously making each other miserable." Though he said it as a statement, it came out as a question.

Her bottom lip quivered as she looked up at him, into the eyes that she had once regarded with fondness. If he wanted her to reassure him that they had a chance, he would wait forever. A reconciliation was not in their future.

Pulling her arm from him, Whitney turned and hurried down the steps. He called her name, once, twice, but she didn't turn around. Propelling her legs as fast as they could carry her, she didn't stop moving until she reached the beach.

Chapter Eleven

"Whitney!" Javar called again. She didn't turn. Instead, she hobbled toward the beach, even though she seemed to be in pain.

Javar watched as Whitney ran down the path toward the beach, wanting to follow her but knowing that he shouldn't. How had a lovely breakfast together turned into such a disaster?

He ran a hand over his head. Man, she was stubborn. Almost two years away from her and he'd forgotten how determined she could be. Why couldn't she just listen? Beneath her vulnerability was fiery anger. Anger directed at him that prevented her from even listening to anything he had to say.

But what had he said? All the wrong things. He hadn't meant to sound selfish in his grief; he understood that Whitney had suffered too. But, at least he was making an effort.

Javar sighed. He hated to admit it, but he had to accept the fact that Whitney was right. How would they ever work things out if they couldn't even speak civilly to one another?

The not-too-distant ring of the telephone interrupted his thoughts. He would let it ring. Speaking with anyone now was the last thing he wanted to do. Hopefully Carlos would think he and Whitney were still together and not disturb them.

The phone stopped, then immediately started ringing again. Where was Carlos? Maybe it was someone from work trying to reach him. Grumbling, Javar ran toward the patio doors and the kitchen.

Once inside, he grabbed the receiver from its cradle on the wall. "Yes?" he couldn't help barking.

"Whoa. That's no way to greet your sister."

Running a hand over his hair, Javar said, "Oh. Oh hi, Michelle."

"I don't think I like that any better. You certainly are in a funky mood."

"Yeah, I guess. I've got a lot on my mind."

"I missed you in church yesterday. We all did." Her voice was smooth and sweet. "Javar, I'm worried about you."

Nosy was more like it, but Javar bit his tongue. "Well, sis, I'm fine."

"If you're okay, then why are you at home today? Javar, in all the years you've had your business, I don't think you've ever missed going to the office, even when you should have stayed home."

Clearly, his dear sister was fishing for information. Or confirmation of what she already knew. He said, "I'll be working at home for a while."

"Working at home?" She made it sound like a prison sentence. "Why?"

Michelle was good. Smooth. To someone who didn't know her, she might actually seem concerned as opposed to manipulative. "Michelle, you must know that Whitney is here. That's why I've been home. I want to be here as she recovers."

"Oh, that's right," Michelle said, sounding as though she truly had forgotten. Javar knew better. "I heard about the accident. How awful."

"Yeah, it was. Thank God she's alive, and she'll make a full recovery."

"Oh, that's good to hear." She paused. "So, what exactly is happening with you and Whitney? I mean, are you getting back together?"

"We're talking." Javar's tone was guarded. "That's all."

"Hmm. I hear she wants a divorce."

Stunned, Javar asked, "Where did you hear that?"

"That doesn't matter. Is it true?"

Javar replied, "Like I said, we're talking."

"Well, if it's true, then I think you should take it and run. That girl was nothing but a gold digger."

Michelle had never really liked Whitney, Javar knew. Now, he wondered. Wondered about the death threats Whitney said she had received. Wondered if Michelle was capable of such cowardly acts.

No. He couldn't see it.

But . . . Michelle had been particularly vicious once in high school, but she was also younger then and more immature. Still, she had known what she was doing when she sought to sabotage the reputation of a classmate, all because she had wanted the girl's man. After spreading rumors to the effect that the girl had slept with a married man and aborted his baby, that girl lost her boyfriend and numerous friends. People hadn't cared whether or not the rumors were true. They were only interested in having something to talk about, something to divert attention from their own boring lives.

". . . ruined your life," Michelle was saying when Javar tuned in again. "You deserved much better."

Rolling his eyes to the ceiling, Javar said, "Michelle, I've got to go."

"Wait!" she cried. "Uh, I need to talk to you about something."

"Talk then," Javar replied curtly.

"Not on the phone. I need to see you in person. Tonight."

Javar's lips twisted, skeptical. "Can't this wait?"

"No," Michelle replied quickly. Her voice softened. "It can't. It's about, um . . . the renovations. Uh, you remember. The addition to the house that we're thinking of. Curtis and I would really like to get started as soon as possible, before the summer's over. Unless you'd like us to find another architect." She chuckled.

"You know you won't have to do that." He suspected there was more to this sudden visit, but didn't say so. "All right. I'll be by at seven."

"Make it six."

Whitney wasn't sure how long after she had arrived at the beach that her heart stopped racing. Over and over, the ugly scene with Javar had played out in her mind until she'd finally made a conscious effort to forget it. The only thing thinking about it had accomplished was worsening her headache.

Now, Whitney sat on the back end of *Lady Love's* tramp, trying to relax. The rhythmic swooshing sound of the waves as they lapped at the shore had a calming, almost hypnotic effect. There was a slight breeze off the water, cooling her body from the heat of the day. It also cooled her anger.

Javar . . . A mirthless chuckle fell from her lips as his name floated around in her mind. Sure he loved her. Sure he forgave her for the accident. And yesterday a cow jumped over the moon!

But why did it matter if he didn't love or forgive her? She didn't want a reconciliation. However, she had loved him once, and being here, being near him, reminded her of all she had lost.

Whitney shifted on the tramp, stretching a big toe so that it touched the water. Instantly, she recoiled her foot, the frigid water a shock to her system. Instead, she lay back, letting her feet dangle, and closed her eyes.

Just because she wanted a divorce didn't mean she and Javar couldn't be friends. She had her own demons to deal with, so did he, but maybe—hopefully—they could learn to put their ill feelings aside. After all, they had loved each other once. Maybe in time they could have a great relationship as friends.

The shrill cries then sudden departure of a flock of seagulls drew Whitney's attention to the left and the thick cluster of tall pine trees that bordered Javar's property. Concentrating on listening, she heard rustling movements, but that was probably the breeze.

Wasn't it?

Like the birds had done, Whitney suddenly wanted to flee. Despite the sun's heat, she felt her skin prickle with the onset of goose bumps.

She scrambled off the tramp, almost tripping as her feet hit the sand. Footsteps. Oh God, she heard footsteps! Yet she couldn't see anyone as she frantically looked around.

Stop acting crazy. You can't hear footsteps on the sand!

That thought scared her even more. Anywhere in the thick of trees someone could be waiting . . . Watching . . .

She tripped. Gasped. Dug her fingers into the sand and pushed herself to her feet. Then started running. Somehow, she knew her life depended on it. The path to the house was only steps away, and if she could reach . . .

A scream tore from her throat, her heart pounding in her chest like a frantic boxer. That next moment she felt like a complete fool. It was only a squirrel that had darted out in front of her. A harmless squirrel, for goodness sake! Not some big, bad person who was out to harm her.

Still, Whitney felt like eyes were watching her, shooting daggers at her back.

As she hurried up the bush-lined path to the house, she

glanced backward several times. Nothing. Only the sense that she should be afraid.

And she was.

Michelle and her husband lived in the mature, well-established Chicago suburb of Evanston. Slowing his Dodge Viper to a crawl, Javar hit his indicator and turned left into the circular driveway. The landscape was a vibrant green, complemented by an array of colorful flowers. Set amid mature maple and pine trees, the Country French home was quiet and serene on the outside, but Javar mentally prepared himself for a battle inside.

Javar parked his car and killed the engine. Moments later, he was at his sister's front door. Just as he raised his hand to ring the doorbell, the door swung open.

"Hey, Javar," Michelle said, a wide smile on her narrow, cinnamon-complected face. Stepping forward, she hugged him. "Come in, come in."

"Hey, sis." Looking down at her, she seemed genuinely happy to see him. Maybe he was wrong to assume her motive to get him over here was anything other than what she'd said. "You're looking great."

Dressed in a simple pink, form-fitting summer dress, Michelle looked top-notch. After having two children, she'd gained unwanted pounds. Immediately after giving birth to her daughter a year ago, Michelle had started a strict diet and exercise plan—complete with a physical trainer—that had helped her regain her trim figure. She hadn't breast-fed as she found it primitive, and not having to nurse a baby had allowed her to concentrate on working out.

"Thanks," Michelle said, running her perfectly manicured hands over her hips.

"Uncle Javar!" came a young cry, and as Javar looked up, he saw his nephew, Michael, running down the curved staircase at full steam.

Bending to meet him as his little feet hit the white porcelain floor, Javar scooped him up into his arms. "Hey, Michael! You're getting big, man."

"I know," he said succinctly.

"You know . . . ? Well I hope you never get too big to be my favorite nephew."

"I'm your only nephew."

Tilting his head, Javar stared at Michael with narrowed eyes. Michael was four now, a year younger than J.J. had been when he died. At the time, Michael had only been two, and too young to have known J.J. Every time he saw Michael, held him, Javar thought of his son and wondered. Wondered what he'd look like today, how he and his younger cousin would get along.

"Uncle Javar, did you hear me?" Michael asked, cupping Javar's face firmly.

"Hmm?"

"I said I'm your only nephew."

"You are so smart, you know that, Michael?"

"I know."

Chuckling, Javar set Michael down, patting him affectionately on the back. He rose and faced Michelle. "Where's Sarah?"

"Sleeping," Michelle replied. "Finally." Turning to Michael, she said, "Why don't you go to your room and play for a while?"

"Uncle Javar, will you come with me? I want to show you my new police car."

"No," Michelle said sternly. "Your uncle and I need to talk." She placed a hand on his little shoulder, gently nudging him. "Go on."

A pout pulling his lips downward, Michael slowly began to walk away.

"I'll come see your car in a few minutes," Javar called to him.

Michael turned and flashed him a bright smile, then ran off.

Michelle watched her son run away, then smiling, shook her head. "Some days, I swear."

"He's a good kid," Javar said, remembering J.J.'s own enthusiasm and energy at that age.

Linking arms with him, Michelle said, "Let's go to the living room. We can talk there."

She led him to the right, out of the two-story foyer, down the short hallway, and into the large, brightly lit living room. Shaped in a semicircle, the part that was circular was one great window. The view was beautiful, facing a wooded ravine.

Javar sank into the teal-green leather sofa, releasing a sigh. "Where's Curtis?"

"Hello, Javar."

At the familiar voice his stomach knotted, and Javar whipped his head around. In the entranceway of the living room stood his mother. She was elegantly dressed in a beige flowing pantsuit. If she was here, instead of Curtis, then that meant Michelle and his mother were up to something. Something he was sure he wouldn't like.

Javar stood and greeted his mother, although what he felt like doing was reaching out and strangling Michelle. Why had she lied to him, lured him here under false pretenses? He turned to Michelle. "You don't want to discuss any renovations, do you?"

Michelle's expression was serious as she said, "No."

"So why lie? If you wanted me here to talk about something else, why didn't you say so?"

His sister merely folded her arms over her chest and shrugged.

"I asked her to set this up, Javar," his mother said, her voice deep, authoritative. "We need to talk."

Suddenly feeling ambushed, Javar moved to the window, away from his mother and sister. He gazed outside, into the shadows of the trees. "I don't appreciate being manipulated." He heard soft footfalls on the hardwood floor. His mother. He didn't turn around.

Angela Jordan said, "Would you have come here if she told you we wanted to discuss Whitney?"

Not a chance, Javar thought. Neither his mother nor his sister had anything good to say about his wife. Why stay here and listen to their opinions? Turning, he said, "I'm leaving."

Angela reached out and gripped his arm with the speed of a bullet. "Javar—"

"Why should I stay?"

"Because." It was Michelle who had spoken. "This is family business."

"It's *my* business." Javar couldn't help raising his voice. "Not yours, nor yours," he added, looking at his mother and his sister in turn.

"You'll want to hear what we have to say." Angela's brown eyes held his in a steady, uncompromising gaze.

Javar didn't like her tone. He didn't like the fact that she didn't respect his choices. But if she wanted to get in his face, he'd make sure she regretted it.

Michelle placed a palm on his back. It felt cold, even through his cotton shirt. "Sit, please." When Javar glared at her, she added, "My God, Javar. We are not the enemy!"

Against his better judgment, Javar dragged his feet across the floor, depositing himself on the love seat. He wasn't about to sit beside either them.

Angela and Michelle took a seat on the sofa. Clearing her throat, Angela spoke first. "Stephanie called me. She told me what happened."

Javar rolled his eyes. He could only imagine what Stephanie had to say.

"Goodness, Javar," Angela said, her tone letting him know that she was disgusted. "What were you thinking? Manhandling her?"

"She threatened my wife. I threw her out."

"You've changed, Javar," Michelle said. "Ever since you met Whitney . . ."

He grasped the love seat's arms, ready to heave himself off the chair. "I think I've heard enough."

"Wait," Angela said sternly. "There's something you should know."

Javar released his grip on the chair's arms, silently agreeing to stay. For the moment. "And what is that?"

Angela and Michelle shared a concerned glance, then slowly, Angela reached into her purse. She withdrew a medium-sized manila envelope.

"You think you love her, Javar," his mother began, "but you don't even know her." Angela rose and approached him, placing the envelope on his lap. "We had her investigated."

"You what?" Incredulous, Javar sprang to his feet, letting the envelope fall to the floor.

"She's a gold digger, Javar. You should thank us for getting the proof now before you got further involved with her," his mother said as she bent to retrieve the envelope.

Glancing down, Javar saw several scattered photos. Color and black-and-white photos of Whitney with some man.

Michelle appeared beside Angela, helping her scoop up the last of the pictures. Picking up the last one, Michelle forced it into Javar's hands. "You think she loved you? You think you were so special to her? Well, get over it. She never loved you. After she killed your son, she went on to the next man. *Men*, probably. See this guy here?" Michelle indicated the picture in his hands.

Although Javar didn't want to, he looked down at the glossy photo. In it, Whitney sat beside a thin black man, attractive nonetheless, his arm intimately draped around her shoulder. They were both smiling at him. They seemed happy.

Javar tore his gaze away, meeting Michelle's chocolate colored eyes. "It's only a picture."

"Is it? Javar, this guy was a millionaire. Coincidence? I don't think so."

His heart pounding, Javar glanced down at the picture

in his hand. Whitney and that man had been lovers? No, he didn't believe that. Is that why she wanted a divorce? But she'd told him there was no one else in her life.

"Like Michelle said, Javar, we're not the enemy." Angela gave him the rest of the pictures, as well as a folded piece of paper. "That's the investigator's report. Read it."

His throat was so dry, Javar didn't think he could speak. But after a moment he found his voice. "It's not what you think."

"Oh really?" Angela scoffed, her face contorted with skepticism. "If she wasn't sleeping with him, then why did he leave her money in his will?"

"He's dead?"

"Yes, and he left her two hundred and fifty thousand dollars."

His gut clenched. Ached. Why hadn't Whitney mentioned this to him?

Michelle touched his arm softly. "Don't you see? This is a pattern for her. Rich men . . . milking them for their money. That's all you were to her, Javar. A rich man who could give her the kind of life she wanted."

"And now that you know, you don't have to feel guilty about divorcing her," his mother added.

Javar inhaled a steadying breath. "That's my decision to make."

"What?" Angela stared up at him in stunned disbelief.

"You heard me."

"My God," Michelle uttered, her expression as confused as her mother's. "What is wrong with you? Haven't you heard—"

"I will not be bullied into making any decision." Javar spoke slowly and clearly so that they would not mistake his words.

"So . . . she's still going to be living at your house?"

"She's recovering from an accident. I can't kick her out on the street."

Angela replied, "She has her mother. She has two hundred and fifty thousand in the bank, for goodness' sake!"

Javar had heard enough. It was all a lie. He didn't know how his mother had done it, how she had gotten the pictures, who'd done the phony report. But if he was making a mistake with Whitney, then it was his mistake to make.

He brushed past his mother, stalked to the entryway of the living room. He heard his mother's and sister's hushed, angry voices, but that didn't deter him.

Michelle spoke when he reached the hallway. "Javar, if you let that murderer stay at your house, then you're no longer welcome here. I won't let you see Michael or Sarah."

Javar hesitated. He was about to turn and respond. But he couldn't make himself do it. He couldn't, wouldn't, allow himself to be manipulated. "Please explain to Michael that I had to leave," he called over his shoulder.

Javar proceeded, hurrying down the hallway to the front door, the pictures and letter scrunched in his fist.

Javar still wasn't home. Since their argument, Whitney hadn't seen nor spoken to him, but through her bedroom window she had seen his red Viper pulling out of the driveway. Now, it was almost midnight, and he wasn't home yet.

Without Javar at home, the house was extremely quiet. Almost eerily so. At least when they'd been newlyweds, even when Javar had spent long hours at the office, J.J.'s little voice had filled the house with laughter. Now, there was an emptiness, almost as if the house lacked a soul.

Whitney flipped through the television channels, stopping when she found a rerun of a comedy show. After watching for several minutes, she turned off the television and placed the remote control on the glass coffee table.

Television wasn't going to distract her from the fight they'd had earlier and the fact that she was worried.

Not worried, she decided. Javar was a grown man who could take care of himself. But she was concerned. Earlier in their marriage, when they argued Javar would leave, either going for a long drive or going to the office. And after J.J.'s death, he had turned not only to long hours at the office, but also to alcohol. As far as she could tell, the alcohol had only been a temporary crutch, but she hoped that while he was angry with her now he didn't do anything crazy.

The phone was ringing, Whitney realized. The main line. Jumping off the sofa in her bedroom, Whitney ran to the door and threw it open. The closest phone was in Javar's room, so she turned right, heading to the south wing and the master suite. She opened Javar's bedroom door and hurried inside.

The machine picked up before she could answer. Stopping, she stood and listened. What if Javar had gotten himself into some trouble and someone was calling?

A woman's voice filled the air. "Javar, hi. It's Melody." Pause, then, "We need to talk. Call me, tonight if you want. I'll be up till about three."

A mix of emotions overcame Whitney: confusion, anger, jealousy. Melody, Javar's administrative assistant who had a definite thing for him. She doubted this was a business-related call. Javar had told her that he had not been involved with anyone since their separation. If that was the truth, then why was Melody calling him at almost midnight?

Strangely rattled, Whitney crossed her arms over her chest. As she walked back to her bedroom, she told herself she didn't want to know. It didn't matter. Was none of her business.

Man, her head was hurting her! When she reached her room she headed straight for the pills she had to take, this time longing for them. She dropped one for pain and two for stress into her mouth. Swallowed them.

Prayed they would dull the ache in her heart.

*   *   *

It was amazing what you could accomplish when you redirected your energy. Blocked creatively for days, Javar now knew exactly what to do for the Li proposal, and was doing it. Creative genius was flowing from his brain right to his fingers, and from there right onto paper. The sketches were rough, of course, but could be re-done. Right now, all he wanted to do was get his ideas down on paper and perfect them later.

After working for hours at his office, Javar was finally satisfied. He knew he could land this bid. And the sketch he'd just completed was no doubt one of his best. Innovative, modern, with a touch of old classic designs.

All this energy, passion that needed to be released, just from the argument with his mother and sister.

Not just that argument, a voice said. The voice was his own internal one, he realized, although it had seemed to come from somewhere else.

His eyes moved to the chair in his office where he'd placed his jacket . . . and the pictures. The pictures of Whitney and another man. Another rich man.

His heart began beating furiously again. The two hundred and fifty thousand, the story that his wife had seduced some rich man . . . that he could discount. Could if it weren't for the photos. Despite his resolve, he had flipped through the various shots the private investigator had taken.

The pictures were clearly taken on different occasions, as both Whitney and the man wore at least three different outfits. The photos spoke a truth he couldn't deny. But how much of the story was true?

Would Whitney have married this man if he hadn't died?

Moving to the floor-to-ceiling windows, Javar tried to push the thoughts of Whitney and her friend out of his mind. What Whitney had done in Louisiana was none of his business.

Then why did he feel like jumping in his car and driving home, where he could finally get to the truth?

Grabbing the pictures, his jacket, and his car keys, that's exactly what he did.

She was dreaming. Dreaming that someone was in her room, wrapping thick hands around her neck. Pressing . . .

Gasping, Whitney's eyes flew open, and to her horror she realized she wasn't dreaming. Someone was over her, hands on her neck. A bellaclava covered her attacker's head, preventing her from seeing his face.

A surge of adrenaline shooting through her body, Whitney grabbed at the attacker's hands. She tugged, scratched.

Managed to scream.

Her attacker paused, as though startled and not sure what to do. As he glanced over his shoulder toward the bedroom door, Whitney took the opportunity to grab at his face.

He was too quick for her, knocking her hand away. The next instant he rushed out of the room.

Knowing she shouldn't but unable to stop herself, Whitney jumped from the bed and hurried into the hallway, following the perpetrator. She screamed again, a loud, desperate scream that could wake the dead.

As she followed the intruder down the staircase, she silently wondered, *Where is Javar?*

Chapter Twelve

Javar heard Whitney's scream as he entered the house
from the garage. Weariness seized him and his feet moved
faster, propelling him to the front of the house. As he ran
through an archway into the foyer, he heard heavy footfalls
as someone raced down the stairs. A figure in black whizzed
by, heading for the front door.

"Javar!"

He heard the fear in his wife's voice without having to
turn around. Good God, some creep had attacked
Whitney!

Anger burned in his veins, refueling him. That man
would live to regret he had ever attacked his wife! He
charged after the intruder, down the front steps and out
onto the concrete sidewalk. With each step, he gained on
the man. Finally, he extended his body, reaching for the
intruder's arm. His fingers closed around the cottony fab-
ric of the man's long-sleeved shirt.

The man kept going across the concrete driveway to the
lawn, pulling his arm free from Javar's grasp. Javar couldn't

let him get away. Pumping his arms to accelerate his speed, Javar quickly gained on the intruder. Closer . . . closer . . .

Javar lunged forward, tackling the man from behind. They both fell onto the ground with a loud thud. Javar held the man as he squirmed, but the man dragged himself forward, kicking the legs that Javar held.

The man got the better of Javar as his thick boot landed squarely on Javar's chin.

Recoiling in pain, Javar eased his hold on the man a little, but it was enough to give the man an avenue for escape. The intruder rose to his feet, once again taking off into the darkness.

Javar got up, ready to take off once again when he heard Whitney yell, "No, Javar! It's not worth it!"

His chest heaving from ragged breaths, Javar glanced at Whitney, saw her running toward him, then back at the silhouette of the intruder. He wanted to go after the jerk, but he didn't want to leave Whitney alone. And the man had too much of a head start now.

"Oh, my God, Javar!" Whitney had stopped her mad dash and was now standing before him, her face contorted with fear and concern. Reaching up, she touched his face with her long, delicate fingers. She probed, softly massaged. "Honey, are you okay?"

Javar knew it was a slip of the tongue, a word tossed out carelessly considering the situation, but he couldn't prevent the immediate reaction he felt. His loins suddenly burned, ached for his wife. And the way she was touching him was not helping matters. Her fingers softly caressed his skin, awoke a longing in him he had once thought dead. Man, it had been so long since a woman had touched him.

Not just any woman. This woman.

But there was so much between them, so many problems, so many bitter feelings. Drawing in a ragged breath, Javar captured Whitney's hand in his, pulled it away from his face. "I'm okay."

WE INVITE YOU TO JOIN THE ONLY BOOK CLUB THAT DELIVERS HEARTFELT ROMANCE FEATURING AFRICAN AMERICAN HEROES AND HEROINES IN STORIES THAT ARE RICH IN PASSION AND CULTURAL SPICE...

And Your First 4 Books Are FREE!

Arabesque is the newest contemporary romance line offered by Pinnacle Books. Arabesque has been so successful that our readers have asked us about direct home delivery. We responded to your requests. You can start receiving four bestselling Arabesque novels a month delivered right to your door. Subscribe now and you'll get:

- ✦ 4 FREE Arabesque romances as our introductory gift—a value of almost $20! (pay only $1 to help cover postage & handling)
- ✦ 4 BRAND-NEW Arabesque romances delivered to your doorstep each month thereafter (usually arriving before they're available in bookstores!)
- ✦ 20% off each title—a savings of almost $4.00 each month
- ✦ Just $1.50 for shipping and handling
- ✦ A FREE monthly newsletter, *Zebra/Pinnacle Romance News* that features author profiles, book previews and more
- ✦ No risks or obligations...in other words, you can cancel whenever you wish with no questions asked

So subscribe to Arabesque today and see why these books are winning awards and readers' hearts.

After you've enjoyed our FREE gift of 4 Arabesques, you'll begin to receive monthly shipments of the newest Arabesque titles. Each shipment will be yours to examine for 10 days. If you decide to keep the books, you'll pay the preferred subscriber's price of just $4.00 per title. That's $16 for all 4 books with a nominal charge of $1.50 for shipping and handling. And if you want us to stop sending books, just say the word...it's that simple.

See why reviewers are raving about ARABESQUE and order your FREE books today!

WE HAVE 4 FREE BOOKS FOR YOU!

(If the certificate is missing below, write to: Zebra Home Subscription Service, Inc., 120 Brighton Road, P.O. Box 5214, Clifton, New Jersey 07015-5214)

FREE BOOK CERTIFICATE

Yes! Please send me 4 *Arabesque* Contemporary Romances without cost or obligation, billing me just $1 to help cover postage and handling. I understand that each month, I will be able to preview 4 brand-new *Arabesque* Contemporary Romances FREE for 10 days. Then, if I decide to keep them, I will pay the money-saving preferred subscriber's price of just $16.00 for all 4...that's a savings of almost $4 off the publisher's price with a $1.50 charge for shipping and handling. I may return any shipment within 10 days and owe nothing, and I may cancel this subscription at any time. My 4 FREE books will be mine to keep in any case.

Name _____

Address _____ Apt. _____

City _____ State _____ Zip _____

Telephone ( ) _____

Signature _____ AP0798
(If under 18, parent or guardian must sign.)

Terms and prices subject to change. Orders subject to acceptance by Zebra Home Subscription Service, Inc. . Zebra Home Subscription Service, Inc. reserves the right to reject or cancel any subscription.

"Javar, there's moisture on your face. I think you're bleeding."

"I'm okay," he repeated forcefully, immediately regretting his tone. Sadness flashed in Whitney's brown eyes, and in the pale moonlight, he could see the shiny moisture brimming beneath her lids. He thought of only one thing he could say to mask his attitude. "I'm sorry, I'm just mad. Did he hurt you?"

Whitney shook her head, but it looked more like a nervous twitch. God, her whole body was shaking. She didn't look ready to answer any questions.

Still, she spoke. "He . . . was . . . in my room. . . ."

Javar swept her into his arms, pressed her soft body against his. Releasing a moan, she sagged against him, wrapped her arms around his waist and held him tight.

"Oh, Javar."

An electric current shot through his body, but this time it wasn't a sexual response. It was the response of someone whose heart felt warm because he was needed. The response of someone who realized that despite a lot of pain in his relationship, he was able to offer comfort, and that comfort was being accepted.

"I was sleeping . . ." Whitney murmured.

"Shh." Javar kissed her forehead, let his lips linger. "Let's go inside."

Whitney nodded, continuing to hold Javar's strong body as he moved slowly, walking across the lawn toward the house. Strength radiated from him, went from his body directly into her pores. Filled her with warmth. He was offering comfort, and she readily accepted.

Thank God he came home when he did. If he hadn't . . .

She didn't want to think about what might have happened if Javar hadn't shown up when he did. Right now, all she could think about was being in Javar's arms and how good it felt to be both offering comfort and receiving comfort. How good it felt just to hold each other after all this time.

*   *   *

"How did this happen?" Javar demanded, staring at Carlos. "Tell me how someone got in here without tripping the alarm."

The middle-aged man shrugged his shoulders, the dark circles under his eyes evidence of his fatigue. Somehow, he had slept through all the commotion. "I don't know, sir."

"Was the alarm set?"

"Yes. I checked it before I retired for the evening."

Javar slammed his palm against the wall in the foyer where the security box was. "Well, it's clearly not set now. Damn. Does this mean someone forgot to activate it, or that the creep who broke in here knew the code?"

Again, Carlos shrugged, considering the options. "Perhaps Miss Monroe forgot to activate it."

"Did she say where she was going?"

"No," Carlos replied. "She said nothing to me."

"Hmm," Javar hummed absently. The nurse was another of his concerns. She wasn't in her room. In fact, she was nowhere to be found. Why would she have gone out without letting anyone know she was leaving? He had hired her as a twenty-four hour nurse. What if Whitney had had a relapse in the middle of the night and rang for her?

Walking back and forth, Javar paced the black marble floor. Something wasn't right. If the nurse had accidentally forgotten to activate the alarm tonight when she went out, it was still too much of a coincidence that this would be the night an intruder just *happened* to break in and find he didn't have to disable an alarm.

Javar paced to the alarm system, stopping to examine it again. That only told him what he already knew. The box was intact, so the intruder clearly had figured out the code.

Or had someone told him the code?

Javar cast a sidelong glance at Carlos, his brain working

overtime. Carlos's eyebrows rose and he shifted uncomfortably beneath Javar's probing gaze, as if sensing the direction of his thoughts.

Carlos said, "Surely you don't think this was deliberate?"

"I don't know what to think, Carlos. All I know is that someone attacked my wife—in her bed—and that that person gained access to this house without activating the alarm. Now, that was either a lucky break for this guy, or he knew the code."

"I don't know, sir."

Javar's expression softened as he stared at his butler. For the past seven years he had known Carlos, trusted him. Whatever had happened here tonight, he knew that Carlos was not involved.

"Of course you don't know, Carlos," Javar said, then heaved a long sigh. "Thanks for helping me look around. Please, go back to bed."

"Do you want me to call the police now?" Carlos asked.

Javar shook his head. "No. Not tonight. Whitney's not up to any questioning."

Nodding, Carlos walked away, toward his room on the main level.

Wild, crazy ideas whirling in his mind, Javar headed to the kitchen. He found Whitney sitting at the breakfast table, her hands wrapped around a mug of hot tea. Her eyes lowered, she looked like she was praying.

Maybe she was.

Her eyes rose to meet his as she heard his footsteps. "Did you find out anything?"

Shaking his head, Javar replied, "Nothing." He didn't want to worry her with his concerns. Not yet. "Do you know where Elizabeth went?" he asked. He found it highly suspicious that tonight of all nights, she was nowhere to be found.

"No. I saw her around ten-thirty, and that was the last time. She gave me my medication. She didn't mention anything to me about going out.'' Whitney raised an eyebrow curiously. "Why?''

Javar shrugged, then leaned a hip against the kitchen's island. Changing the subject he said, "You haven't had much of your tea.''

"I . . . I don't feel like it.''

Javar took a few steps toward Whitney. "Drink it. It'll help settle your nerves.''

A timid smile lifted Whitney's lips. "You sound like Elizabeth.''

Just one smile, but it made so much of a difference to her whole demeanor. Every part of her exuded such warmth when she smiled. Even when he knew that under the circumstances, she didn't want to be smiling.

As though she heard his inner thoughts, Whitney's smile faded. She said, "You don't think this was a random attack, do you?''

She knew him so well, Javar thought. Knew that he was keeping his true thoughts from her. Still, he wasn't ready to admit his suspicions. Instead he asked, "What do you think?''

"I . . .'' Whitney's voice trailed off, and she gripped her mug harder. "I don't think it was random.''

It was what he was thinking, but hadn't wanted to voice. It would be so much easier if the attack *had* been random. "Why do you think that? Because of the threats you told me about?''

"Partly.'' Whitney released her grip on the mug, and with a forefinger traced the outline of the rim. "But there's more. Earlier today, when I was at the beach, I thought . . . felt like someone was watching me.''

"Right here?'' Fear snaked down Javar's spine. "On this property?''

Whitney nodded. "I thought I was overreacting. You know, with all the medicine I've been taking. That maybe I wasn't thinking straight.''

A hand on his jaw, Javar walked toward the counter by

the stove. He stood a moment silently, then banged a fist on the gray granite counter. Turning to face Whitney, he asked, "Whitney, do you have any idea who might be doing this?"

Bringing her mug to her lips, Whitney took a long sip of the hot herbal tea. As far as she was concerned, the list of suspects was lengthy. She started with the most obvious. "Stephanie." She paused a moment, then added, "Unless you've made some enemies at work. Gotten a bid that someone else wanted and now they're trying to get to you through me."

"That's a possibility," Javar admitted. "Although I really doubt it."

Whitney doubted it too. She glanced down at her tea, then returned her eyes to Javar's dark gaze. "I don't know what to think, Javar."

Gnawing on his lower lip, Javar walked toward Whitney. He stood behind her chair and placed two strong hands on her shoulders.

Whitney shuddered. And not because she was cold, or scared. Because as Javar touched her, she had to admit to herself that she wanted him. Wanted his warmth, his strength, his affection.

"Let's go to bed," he said softly, his deep voice washing over her like a gentle breeze.

He didn't mean it *that* way she tried to convince herself when her body reacted to Javar's words, her heart beating erratically at the erotic thought. He couldn't. He must mean their respective beds. But God help her, Whitney found herself hoping he had meant they'd share one bed. His bed.

"C'mon." He patted her shoulder, then helped ease her chair back.

Whitney stood, instinctively reaching for him, placing an arm around his waist. She felt the stirrings of desire deep in her belly, and it spread lower.

They walked silently up the spiral staircase. When they

reached her bedroom, Javar stopped. So did Whitney's heart. As Javar pulled out of her embrace, she looked up at him. "Javar . . ." Her voice trailed off, unable to express the words in her heart.

"Whitney?"

"I . . ."

She was shaking again. Earlier, she had seemed strong, but Javar now realized that she had been putting on a brave face. She was scared. Glancing down at her hands he saw that they were trembling. Until now, the thought that someone actually meant to hurt Whitney had seemed unreal somehow, incomprehensible. Now, however, the severity of the situation was all too real.

Someone had broken into his house. Someone had invaded Whitney's room. Someone had tried to kill her.

"Javar . . ." She was clenching and unclenching her robe. "I . . . don't want to be . . . alone."

She didn't need to say another word. Pulling her close, Javar nuzzled his nose in her raven hair, inhaling her flowery scent. Again, he felt his loins ignite with a desire too long denied, but he fought to keep the reaction under control. Whitney didn't want sex, he told himself. She wanted his comfort.

Moments later, they were at his bedroom. Casting a quick glance at Whitney, he opened the double doors. She seemed suddenly cautious, tense, staring into the room from wide eyes.

"It's okay, I won't bite," Javar said, attempting humor.

Whitney's eyes flew to his, as though shocked to think she looked unnerved. She flashed him a shy smile, then slowly ventured into the room, staring around with interest.

Javar was still wearing the T-shirt and shorts he had worn all day. "I'm going to change. Make yourself comfortable."

Whitney watched as Javar walked across the plush rose-colored carpet to his dresser. He opened a drawer and withdrew pajamas, then disappeared into the large ensuite bathroom. A memory hit her, a memory of another time, and she shivered. She recalled the gigantic Jacuzzi, how on occasion they would fill it with bubbles and frolic in there together. How frolicking would lead to passionate lovemaking.

Whitney tried to shake off the image. She turned, directing her gaze to the large gas fireplace and then the sitting area. A black leather sofa and matching love seat sat atop the plush carpet. A black entertainment center rested against the wall, complete with a giant screen television and a CD player with numerous selections beneath.

Whitney shifted her gaze toward the king-sized bed. The iron posts at the head and foot of the bed were black, matching the color scheme in the room. The furniture was the same as when she'd lived here, but he had changed the accessories in the room. In fact, any proof that she had once shared this room with him was gone. There were no pictures of the two of them, none of the dainty statuettes she had bought. Nothing. Her touch was evident in the rest of the house, but not here, where she had spent every night with Javar.

There was a lump in Whitney's throat, and she swallowed it. Tried to. It wouldn't go away.

At that moment, Javar exited the bathroom. Their eyes met and held. Maybe it was the stress of the accident, or even tonight, or maybe it was the realization that she wanted things to work out for them but feared they never would, but Whitney suddenly felt winded. Overwhelmingly sad. Her desire for Javar fizzled, giving way to doubt. One night with him would not erase the gap between them that was as wide as the Grand Canyon.

"I'll take the sofa," Javar said.

No, Whitney wanted to say, but only stood there.

"Whitney?"

"Whatever you want," she finally said, her heart pounding in her chest. She was a coward, afraid to ask for what she wanted.

Her head lowered, she walked toward the bed. As Javar's hand wrapped around her upper arm, she halted, gasping.

He looked down at her from heavy lids. "Don't you want me to sleep on the sofa?"

Whitney swallowed. All she had to do was tell him what she wanted. All she had to do was say no. It was that easy. . . .

"Hmm?" he prodded, his hand tightening.

She looked up at him, into his dark eyes. Something sparked in their depths, something powerful, something electrifying. Suddenly, the doubts were gone again, and there was only need. The need to be held, to be touched, to be loved.

Turning to him, Whitney pressed her body against Javar's. She answered him now the only way she could, by showing him what she wanted, all the while praying he would not reject her.

She slipped her hands beneath the open pajama top, ran her fingers up over his chest. Her fingertips stopped over his heart, and she could feel its frantic beat. It matched her own.

Whitney's hands ventured upward, finally resting at his nape. She heard the sharp intake of breath, felt it as she pressed her breasts against his chest, but wasn't sure if it came from Javar or from her.

"Whitney . . ." His voice was deep, captivating.

His eyes drew hers to his like a magnet, pulling, energizing. Tilting her head back, she merely stared at him, wanting his strength, wondering if he would offer it.

He did. Wrapping his hands around her small waist, Javar pulled her closer. As he held her tightly, he lowered his head, his lips ever so slowly approaching hers.

Whitney's lips parted, waiting. The pull between them was so strong, she wouldn't be able to stop herself if she tried.

Javar's lips met hers, tentative at first, teasing. Softly he kissed her mouth, the top lip, the bottom lip, the corners.

Whitney's eyelids fluttered shut and she moaned, digging her fingers into the curly hair at his nape.

"Whitney," Javar murmured, before claiming her lips urgently. His tongue played over the flesh of her mouth, slipping inside, forcing its way past her teeth, connecting with her own. Hot was the only thought in Whitney's head. His tongue was hot. His body was hot. She was hot.

She arched against him, pressing her curves into his solid muscles. Heat pooled in her center, spreading to the rest of her body, making her delirious with longing. It had been so long. Too long.

Javar's hands were suddenly inside her silk robe, delicately running over her back, her buttocks. Back up to her shoulders. Gently nudging the robe off her body. Letting it fall to the floor. The material fell in a heap around her feet.

Pressing his fingertips into the soft flesh of her back, a groan rumbled in Javar's chest. Everything about Whitney was sweet temptation. Her soft lips, her smooth flesh, the way she had her arms wrapped around his neck as if she would never let him go.

He tore his lips from hers, looking into her eyes. They were dark, glistening pools of desire. In no uncertain terms, the passion in her eyes told him not to stop.

He didn't. Moving his lips over Whitney's face, Javar kissed her forehead, the bandage that hid her cut, each eyelid, the tip of her nose, her cheeks, her lips. With every part of his being, he drank in her sweetness. The desire he felt for her now was only equaled by their wedding night, the first time they had ever made love.

When he flicked his tongue over her earlobe, Whitney shuddered, digging her nails into his shoulder blades. Javar's body went up in flames. He scooped Whitney into his arms, carrying her to the massive bed.

It was time he reclaimed his wife. There were no questions now, no concerns. There was only him and his wife and the all-consuming need for her that had to be released.

As he laid her body atop the comforter, he gazed into her eyes. He had to be sure she was sure. "Whitney . . ."

She cupped his face with her hands, drew his lips to hers. Again, a moan escaped her lips as she kissed him, told him in no uncertain terms what he needed to know.

He eased his body down beside her then captured her lips in a soft, sensual kiss. God, he had been so lonely without his wife. God, how he needed her now.

Reaching out, he slipped a fingertip beneath the spaghetti strap of her silky white nightie. Gently, he fiddled with the material, dragging it down, then back up, then down again. Whitney dropped her head back, moaned, invited. Javar accepted her invitation, pulling the nightgown off her shoulder and exposing one breast. He drew in a sharp breath as he looked at her, drank in the sight of her beauty. His hand slipped lower and he cupped her fullness, relishing the feel of the hardened tip against the palm of his hand. As Whitney arched against his hand, her head hanging backward, her teeth sinking into her bottom lip, Javar lost all control. He replaced his hand with his mouth. Nearly died from the pleasure.

"Oh, Javar . . ."

Whitney pulled at his clothes, dragging his pajama top urgently from his body. She wanted to feel his chest against her breasts. She wanted to be skin to skin. Heart to heart.

How she had gone so long without loving Javar, she didn't know. She only knew that she wanted this special moment to last forever. In her heart, there was no yesterday, no tomorrow, only now.

When their bodies finally joined, their coupling was slow, gentle, beautiful. Like two lost souls finding each other and savoring every inch of each other reverently. They clung to each other, giving, receiving. Together they reached that special place of spellbinding passion and earth shattering pleasure.

Afterward, Javar pulled Whitney's body against his, wrapped his arms around her possessively, like he used to do on the other occasions when they had made love. She covered his hands with hers. Together, they lay silently.

The moment was so familiar, it was haunting. It was as if no time had passed since they'd last been together. Yet it had.

As Whitney drifted off to sleep in the comfort of Javar's arms, she couldn't help wishing tomorrow wouldn't come. But it would. And with it would also come reality.

Chapter Thirteen

It was too soon to be pregnant, Whitney told herself as she sat on the floor beside the toilet in her ensuite bathroom. But man, did she ever feel sick. One minute her stomach would lurch and she would run from the bed to the bathroom, only for her stomach to settle as soon as she got there. If she could only get whatever it was out of her system, she knew she would feel better. It was the back and forth, teeter-tottering that she couldn't handle.

Finally, it was once again apparent that she was not going to throw up. Groaning, Whitney rose to her feet and walked to the white marble sink with brass fixtures, where she splashed her face with cold water, then cupped her hands and captured some of the liquid. She drank several handfuls, but that did nothing to ease the nasty feeling in the pit of her stomach.

She turned from the sink and dried her hands and face on a towel. The only thing to do now was to go back to bed.

Her bed. Shortly after six a.m., she had snuck out of Javar's bed and returned to her own room. Having awoken from a pleasurable sleep to find herself in his arms, she realized the major mistake she had made.

How had she let things get so out of hand last night?

Because she'd wanted comfort, closeness. Because Javar offered her those things when she had needed them. That was all, she told herself. As she walked back to her bed and crawled under the covers, she told herself that what had happened last night between her and Javar would never happen again.

In his sleep-induced state, Javar reached for his wife. Reached, and felt air where her body should have been. His hand stretched over the cotton sheets as he continued to search for her warm body.

His eyes popped open as soon as the realization hit him. Whitney wasn't in his bed.

Looking around the room, he quickly surmised that she wasn't there either. And there were no sounds coming from the ensuite, which meant that Whitney wasn't in the bathroom.

Sometime during the night she'd gotten up and left him.

Rolling over onto his back, Javar groaned. Last night had been . . . incredible. And he was a fool. He'd allowed himself to believe that when Whitney had come to his room last night—to his bed—that that had been the beginning of a reconciliation. Yes, there were things that had to be worked out, and to be honest, they weren't going to be easy. Still, he hadn't expected to awake to an empty bed.

Javar groaned. He shouldn't have gone against his better judgment last night. He shouldn't have fallen into bed with Whitney. But his yearning for her had been too strong.

Slipping a hand behind his head, Javar wondered if making love had brought them closer, or only added to the distance between them.

* * *

When Whitney heard the soft rapping on her door, she froze. God knew, she wasn't ready to face Javar. Wasn't ready to deal with the grave mistake she'd made last night.

The door began to open. Whitney grabbed her pillow and dragged it over her face. If she had to, she'd play dead. She had nothing to say to him.

"Whitney?" a voice called softly. Elizabeth.

Slowly, Whitney moved in the bed, feigning someone awaking from sleep. She pulled the pillow away from her face and looked up at Elizabeth from narrowed lids.

"Good morning, Whitney." The nurse's smile was pure saccharine. "It's time for your medicine."

Whitney sat up for the nurse and they went through their morning routine. When she plucked the thermometer from beneath her tongue, Elizabeth said, "Good news. Your temperature is back to normal. That means your infection is healing."

The nurse lifted the bandage from her forehead, then said, "Oh yes. That's healing nicely now." Moments later, she rebandaged Whitney's forehead with fresh gauze and tape. "Shouldn't be too much longer before you're good as new."

Whitney asked, "Are you sure about that? I feel awful. Really, really nauseous."

"Hmm." Elizabeth's face contorted with concern. "I can only suggest that you make sure you eat. Taking these medications can be harsh on your—"

"Elizabeth." The voice was unmistakably hard, barely containing it's anger. Whitney's eyes darted to the bedroom door. There Javar stood, his hands planted firmly on his hips, a scowl distorting his handsome features.

Clearly startled, the nurse's eyes bulged as though frightened. Turning to face him, she replied, "Yes, Mr. Jordan?"

"I need to speak with you," Javar said sharply. He was

going to get to the bottom of last night's incident, and Elizabeth's part in it, if any. "Out here, please."

Wiping her palms on her pale green pant outfit, Elizabeth walked briskly toward him, her expression wary. Behind her, Whitney watched him curiously.

When the nurse stepped into the hallway, Javar reached for the brass handle of the bedroom door and closed it. Then, folding his arms over his chest, he turned to face Elizabeth. He got right to the point. "Where were you last night?"

Her eyebrows rose and fell. "Last night?" she repeated, as though she couldn't believe the question.

"Yes, last night," Javar replied, irritation evident in his voice. "Last night, when you should have been here, taking care of my wife."

She withered under his hard gaze. "I was . . . out. At my . . . boyfriend's."

"Why didn't you mention that you were going to be gone for the night?"

"I . . . Mr. Jordan, I apologize. I made sure that Whitney had her medication last night, and then . . ." She shrugged, as if the rest was self-explanatory.

"I'm paying you to be here, Elizabeth. Twenty-four hours a day unless it is arranged otherwise."

"Did something happen last night? Did Whitney need my—"

"Yes, something happened last night, Elizabeth," Javar answered, his voice rising an octave. "While you were out, Whitney was attacked by some creep who broke into the house, right in her bedroom."

"My God," Elizabeth exclaimed, bringing a hand to her heart.

Javar continued. "The alarm didn't even go off. Probably because you forgot to reactivate it when you rushed out."

Elizabeth's mouth fell open at the allegation, but she closed it promptly. Her eyes narrowed pensively, as though in thought, and after a few moments, she shook her head. "I reactivated the alarm when I left. I'm sure of it."

Javar was about to ask her if she knew anything about the break-in, but thought better of it. All of a sudden, the idea seemed ridiculous. He was grasping at straws if he believed the nurse he'd hired from an agency, whose credentials were topnotch, was somehow involved in the attack on his wife.

Frustrated, he blew out a ragged breath, letting his shoulders sag. "I'm sorry if I came down hard on you, Elizabeth but I'm sure you can understand my concern. My wife was attacked last night, *in this house,* and the alarm didn't go off. There was no forced entry from what we can tell. I know criminals are more sophisticated these days, but . . ." He let the statement dangle in the air.

"Top-of-the-line security systems can't even guarantee one's safety," Elizabeth said, shaking her head. "Gosh, I'm so sorry. What did the police say?"

"Nothing. Yet. It was so late when everything happened last night, and Whitney was so shaken up. . . . I decided to let her rest and call the police today."

Rest . . . yeah, right, a voice teased from somewhere in his subconscious.

Javar bristled at the intrusive voice. The direction of his thoughts quickly went to last night, to the image of Whitney's closed eyes as she cried out his name. His hands dropped to the front of his groin as he felt the first stirrings of desire. The last thing he needed right now was to embarrass himself in front of Elizabeth.

He said, "Actually, I'll call them now." Turning on his heel, Javar made a hasty retreat to his bedroom.

"Sorry," Whitney mumbled when her elbow hit Javar's arm as she brushed past him on her way to the dishwasher. The large kitchen suddenly seemed too small for the both of them. She hadn't come downstairs until ten, thinking that for sure Javar would have already had his morning coffee and read the *The Chicago Tribune*. Instead, he was only now making an appearance in the kitchen. She took that as her cue to leave.

"Whitney."

"Hmm?" She didn't even look up as she opened the dishwasher and placed her plate in the rack.

Javar sighed audibly. "Is this how it's going to be now?" he asked. "You rushing out of a room as soon as I enter?"

Rising, she found his nutmeg gaze scrutinizing her. "What are you talking about?" she asked, pretending she didn't know. "I've finished my breakfast. No point—"

Javar was grinning wryly. "Sure." He walked toward her. "Look, about last night—"

"Gosh, I'm feeling pretty tired," Whitney said, cutting him off. She was not ready for this conversation. Probably never would be.

"So you're not up to talking to the police yet?" Javar asked.

"The police?" Whitney asked, before realizing what Javar had obviously been referring to when he'd said "last night." Heat spread across her face, and she was thankful her darker complexion prevented Javar from seeing her blush. "Oh, yes. The police. Uh, sure. Yeah, we should call them now."

"You're not tired?"

Whitney shook her head. "Uh, yeah. But they should be notified now. After all, the break-in happened last night."

Pressing his lips together tightly, Javar tried not to chuckle. Whitney was trying to avoid him, all right. If she didn't look so cute when flustered, he might just want to press her for some answers. But he'd let her sweat. At least until after the police were contacted.

Turning, he walked to the kitchen phone. He lifted the receiver from its cradle and placed it to his ear.

"Wait," Whitney said. When he turned to face her, he

saw her walking toward him. "Call Derrick. Detective Lawson."

"Why?" Javar asked, a sudden surge of jealousy causing his stomach to twist into a knot. "We're in Kenilworth. Derrick works for the Chicago P.D."

"I know. But, well, I trust Derrick. I'd just feel better calling him first, at least."

The mention of Derrick, her insistence that he call him, had Javar remembering his visit with his mother and his sister last night. Had him remembering the pictures of Whitney and that man in Louisiana.

He swallowed. Tried to suppress the memory. Tried to ignore the tightening in his chest.

One night of great sex. That's all he and his wife had shared.

"Javar?" She was looking at him with a puzzled expression. "Are you going to call Derrick?"

Javar nodded tightly. "Sure. What's the number?"

Long after Derrick had arrived at the Jordan home, he finally took a seat across from Whitney in the living room. With Javar, he had searched the seven thousand square foot house from top to bottom. Now, he sat on the antique-styled sofa, a frustrated frown playing on his lips.

"You didn't find anything, did you?" Whitney asked, already knowing what his answer would be.

Derrick shook his head. "No sign of forced entry in the least. With a house this large, there are often places that an intruder can gain access, but he or she would usually leave some sign of that. Or at least trip the alarm. In this case, it looks as if this guy was invited in through the front door and even took off his shoes."

"He had shoes on. At least I think he did," Whitney said.

"I'm sure he did," Derrick said. "He just left no trace

of them. Not even a smudge of dirt on the stairs. Nothing for us to go on."

Javar, who was leaning an elbow against the fireplace mantel, pinched the bridge of his nose with a thumb and forefinger, clearly frustrated. "In other words, this looks like a professional job."

"The guy knew what he was doing," Derrick conceded.

Javar asked, "So what now?"

"Well, I'm here as a friend," Derrick explained. "Kenilworth is way out of my jurisdiction."

"So we should call the Kenilworth P.D.?" Whitney asked.

Derrick's shrug was noncommittal. "If you do call them now, they're going to wonder why you've waited as long as you have. Technically, since you were attacked, Whitney, what happened last night wasn't a break and enter. It was a home invasion. Cops get a bit testy when people wait hours to call them, for no apparent reason."

Crossing to the sofa where Whitney sat, Javar took a seat beside her. "Whitney was too shaken up to talk to the police."

But not too shaken up to make love, Whitney thought, suddenly wondering about her warped priorities.

"They could have come in, started dusting for prints and so forth. Now, they'll say the evidence has been tampered with."

"But there wasn't any," Whitney protested. "You said so yourself."

Derrick shrugged. "I can't advise you not to report this crime. I'm only giving you my opinion."

Javar said, "So basically you're saying that not only will it be a waste of time, but the police won't be too impressed with us for having waited so long to call them."

Pursing his lips, Derrick nodded.

Although she wasn't looking directly at him, Whitney could tell Javar was angry. Angry at his helplessness. Inhaling a deep breath, Whitney turned to face him. "Let's just forget it. There's nothing we can do about it now."

Derrick asked, "Did either of you get a look at this guy? Maybe there have been similar crimes in the area—"

"I doubt it," Javar said sourly. "And no, we didn't get a look at him because his face was covered."

Whitney rose from the sofa, slapping her hands against her thighs. "I just want to forget this ever happened. There's nothing that can be done now, and the more we talk about it . . ."

Javar rose to meet Whitney, placing his hands on her shoulders. She stiffened at his touch, at this simple gesture that many a married couple shared. But they weren't really married. Only in name, and that was soon to be resolved.

He must have sensed her unease, because he pulled his hands away from her and walked to the bay window. A pang of guilt tugged at her heart as she watched him, thinking once again how her need for comfort last night had caused a greater rift between the two of them.

The phone rang, jarring her from her thoughts. Javar quickly turned from the window, saying, "I'll take it in the kitchen."

When Javar was clearly out of earshot, Derrick stood and approached Whitney. Concern marred his handsome features, as no doubt, it did hers.

"Whitney," Derrick began softly. "I've got to tell you, I have a bad feeling about this."

The curious slant of his eyes, the firm set of his mouth and the skeptical tone in his voice all told Whitney that Derrick was talking about more than the misfortune of last night's occurrence. Arching a brow, she met his eyes with curiosity in her own. "I don't follow you. . . ."

Derrick glanced over his shoulder, then back at her. "Whitney, I think it's time you faced some things."

Alarm caused her stomach to lurch. In response, she wrapped her arms around her belly. "What kind of things are you talking about?"

"How have things been here with Javar?"

Her face grew warm as she remembered last night. Until

then, things had been pretty straightforward. She was staying here only until she was completely healed, and then she would get a divorce and move on with her life. Last night complicated the situation, but her plan was still the same. She finally answered, "Tense."

Derrick nodded, as though he expected that answer. "I have to tell you, Whitney. I wonder about Javar's true motives."

Intrigued, she asked, "What do you mean?"

"I mean," Derrick continued, pausing for effect, "I wonder if he's saying one thing but means another."

"You've lost me."

Derrick placed a hand on his hip, glancing around again. He stepped toward Whitney, closing almost all the distance between them. "The accident . . . I haven't had a chance to tell you, Whitney, but it's looking less and less like an accident. More and more like a hit-and-run."

Gasping, Whitney threw a hand to her mouth. "What are you saying? That someone deliberately hit me, then took off?"

"I can't say whether or not it was deliberate, but Forensics has found traces of black paint on your car. That indicates contact with another car. But now, in light of the attack on you last night, I have to wonder if the hit-and-run wasn't random."

"You mean, like someone's stalking me?" The very thought terrified her, chilled her to the bone. But if she were to be completely honest with herself, she had to admit that she knew coming back to Chicago might be dangerous for her. She was a hated woman here. All because of another accident on another Chicago road two years ago. Clearly, someone wanted her out of the way permanently.

"Not just someone," Derrick replied. "Someone who has a personal vendetta against you."

"Like Stephanie Lewis," Whitney said softly, wondering if Javar's ex-girlfriend would have gone as far as she had threatened.

"Actually, I was thinking maybe Javar."

"Javar!" Whitney exclaimed.

Derrick threw a nervous glance around the room, then placed a hand on Whitney's arm. He lowered his voice as he said, "Yes, Javar. Think about it. He has a motive for wanting you dead."

"That's crazy!"

"Is it?" Derrick challenged with the raising of an eyebrow. "You were behind the wheel in the accident that took his son's life. After that, he wanted nothing to do with you. Now, you return to Chicago and all of a sudden he wants to play husband? I don't buy it."

"Javar wouldn't want me dead," Whitney replied, confident of that fact. He may never forgive her, but he wasn't a killer.

"How can you be so sure? If you ask me, you being here in his house is just a convenient way of keeping an eye on you. You're vulnerable here, and he knows that."

Shaking her head, Whitney said, "No." She turned from Derrick and moved to the window, her thoughts whirling around like a tornado in her brain. Stephanie, yes. Other members of Javar's family, she could see that. Javar, never.

She heard the shuffling of Derrick's clothes as he moved up behind her. "Whitney, I'm sure this is hard to believe, but think of these facts. Who encouraged you not to call the police last night?"

Whitney spun around, tilting her chin upward to meet Derrick's gaze head-on. "Javar was worried about me. He didn't want to put me through the stress of answering questions in the middle of the night."

"How convenient," Derrick said, not bothering to hide his cynicism. "A little too convenient, if you ask me."

"Javar wasn't even here when the guy broke in. He came just as he was taking off. Javar chased him, tried to tackle him. . . ."

"But he let him get away. Again, convenient."

"Why are you doing this?" Whitney asked, incredulous.

"Because I care about you, Whitney. Trust me, my cop instincts are telling me that something is wrong with this whole picture, and his name is Javar."

Her chest was so tight, it was hard to breathe. She felt like she was suffocating. She felt like she was going to be ill. Suddenly, her legs were as weak as jelly and her knees buckled.

Derrick reached for her and caught her before she fell. "Whitney?"

The moment of weakness passed, and she inhaled a deep, steadying breath. She pulled away from Derrick and walked to the armchair, where she took a seat. She asked, "Are you finished?"

Derrick seemed determined to make her believe his accusation. Squatting on the floor before her, he took both of her hands in his, staring at her with a worried expression. "I know this is upsetting, Whitney. But think about it. It makes sense."

"What makes sense?"

At the sound of Javar's voice, Whitney threw her gaze to the living room entrance. Derrick quickly rose to his six foot plus height. Gleaming onyx peeked out at Whitney and Derrick from narrowed eyelids, the intensity of the glare causing a chill to pass over Whitney.

"What makes sense?" Javar asked again.

"That the intruder probably won't strike twice at the same place," Derrick said, his own eyes uncompromising as he walked toward Javar. "Don't you agree?"

Whitney watched, waited. Suddenly, Javar's response to Derrick's question was extremely important to her. Her gut wrenched with guilt for even considering that Derrick might be right in his accusation.

"You're probably right," Javar said, but his voice lacked conviction.

Whitney commented weakly, "Derrick doesn't want me to worry."

Derrick turned then, flashed her a look that said he was

worried about her. Whitney rose from the armchair and approached the two men. "Derrick, thanks so much for coming over here. I know you must be busy."

Derrick hesitated, seeming almost reluctant to leave. But after a few seconds, his lips curled into a smile. "Any time you need me, Whitney, you know where I am."

"Thank you. I'll see you out."

Placing a hand on his upper arm, Whitney led Derrick out of the living room and down the hallway to the foyer. A quick glance over her shoulder told her Javar was there, watching them intently.

Derrick noticed as well. He planted a chaste kiss on Whitney's forehead, said a quick good-bye, then exited, taking the front steps two at a time to his white Honda.

"He really cares about you," Javar said as Whitney closed the door.

"Yes," Whitney said, nodding. "He's one of my oldest friends."

Javar held his retort in check, not wanting to let his jealousy get the best of him. Man, when had he started feeling so insecure? *Since Whitney told me that she wanted a divorce,* he answered himself silently.

"I'm feeling tired," Whitney said, turning on her heel and heading for the stairs.

"Wait." Javar reached out and placed a hand on her arm. Her eyes widened as she looked up at him. She was either startled, or scared. He couldn't tell which.

"Javar . . . please."

Javar pinned her with a level stare. "Whitney, you can't avoid me forever. We need to talk."

"There's nothing to talk about."

"Not even last night?"

"Last night was . . ." she hesitated, "a reaction to the stress of the situation."

Sarcasm flashed in Javar's eyes as he stared down at her. "A reaction?"

"Yes," Whitney said quickly, thinking desperately to

come up with more words. "I was afraid. I needed someone."

"Just someone?" Disbelief resonated in his voice.

Squaring her jaw, Whitney said, "I needed someone. You were there."

"Why do I find that so hard to believe?"

Whitney pulled her arm free, then started up the stairs. Javar followed her, darting in front of her path, blocking her avenue of escape. She could always retreat, but he would be there again, preventing her from getting away.

"Why are you doing this, Javar?" Whitney asked, heaving a frustrated sigh. "Last night doesn't change anything." But as she said the words, her heart was pounding wildly in her chest. Being so near to him, she felt the powerful pull to reach out and touch him. Biting her inner cheek, she fought the urge. Fought to keep her thoughts focused. Last night had been a distraction. Albeit an unforgettable one.

The muscle flinched in Javar's jaw. "Damn it, Whitney. Why are you being so cold? You made promises to me when we got married—"

"And you broke them, Javar. Every one of them. Like 'for better or worse'. Remember that vow?" She felt her eyes mist, and she paused, forcing the tears back. "I made myself clear in the beginning. I want a divorce. Stop this pressure. I'm not going to cave in."

"Fine."

"Thank you."

Javar moved out of her way, and Whitney started up the stairs. Nervous energy caused his hands to jitter as he watched her ascend quickly, desperate to get away from him. All reason fled his brain and he blurted out, "Guess Derrick will be there to help pick up the pieces."

Anger sparked in her eyes as Whitney turned to face him. Retracing her steps, she marched toward him, a hand outstretched. "This has nothing to do with Derrick. I already told you that."

"It's pretty obvious he has a thing for you. The fact that he doesn't like me makes things less complicated. For him at least."

"I'm sure Melody feels the same way," Whitney retorted, regretting the words as soon as they left her mouth. It was just that Javar was making her so angry with his holier-than-thou attitude, she couldn't help stooping to pettiness.

"Melody—"

"Called here last night," Whitney completed. "Oh, around midnight. A little too late for a business call, I'd say."

"Melody is my employee."

"I'm sure."

"Okay. That's it." Wrapping his fingers around her wrist, Javar led Whitney down the hall. If they were ever going to have a chance at a future, they had to clear the air on all the issues. But they would do it in private, not in the foyer where his butler, his housekeeper, or the nurse could walk by at any moment.

"Javar!" Whitney cried, trying to wring her arm free from his strong grip. "Stop this stupid Tarzan act, will you!"

Despite her protests, Javar led Whitney to his first-floor office. He didn't let her go until she was safely in the room. Turning, he locked the door behind them.

Whitney marched toward him, both hands firmly placed on the curve of her hips. "Let me out of here."

Javar looked down at his wife with uncompromising eyes. "Not until we've had it out, Whitney. And I mean everything."

Chapter Fourteen

Whitney growled. Spun around and paced to the desk. Then she turned toward him again, her chest heaving with each angry breath. She spat out, "This is ridiculous."

"I meant what I said. We're going to clear the air once and for all. So go ahead. Ask me what you want to ask me. Whatever you want to know. I'll answer you honestly. Then let's put it behind us forever."

"This isn't going to save our relationship."

"Maybe not. But at least we can make some sort of truce and try to be friends."

Whitney walked to the mahogany desk and propped a hip against it. "I have nothing to say."

"Fine. I do." From the back pocket of his slacks, Javar produced the picture of Whitney and that man, his stomach clenching as he did. For some reason, he'd slipped the picture into his pocket this morning. Silently, he reminded himself that he really had no claim to Whitney, not if he didn't have her heart. Still, he wanted an answer. Flashing the picture before her face he asked, "Who is this?"

"Where did you get that?"

"That's not important. But I want to hear from you who he was, what he meant to you."

She flashed him a distasteful look. "I owe you no explanations."

"Were you involved with him?"

Through narrowed eyes, Whitney asked, "Did you have me investigated? Is that it?"

Javar sighed, suddenly overwhelmed with shame. He hadn't personally had her investigated, but by throwing this in her face, it was as if he had hired the detective himself.

"You did," Whitney stated, disbelief clouding her beautiful face. "God, Javar. Why?"

"I didn't," Javar told her, his tone softening. "But my mother, and my sister—"

Whitney huffed. "I'll bet. What did they tell you? That I was sleeping with him?"

Javar didn't deny the truth. He nodded. "Were you?"

"Javar! God, I've already told you the truth. I won't repeat myself."

"Whitney, they told me that this guy left you two hundred and fifty thousand dollars in his will."

Her chin held high, Whitney held his gaze. Her eyes said she wasn't about to dignify him with a response. But then her eyes lowered to the ground and she took a deep breath. When she lifted her eyes to his again, they portrayed such sadness that guilt gnawed at his conscience. Her shoulders sagged, and her eyes glistened with unshed tears. She said softly, "He was a friend. A very dear one."

"I gathered that much." Somehow he prevented his feelings of guilt from infiltrating his voice. "Did he leave you all that money?"

Whitney brushed at a tear that spilled onto her cheek. "His name was Leroy. He had AIDS. His entire family disowned him when they found out. We connected, but not in the way you think. We both worked at that youth center. We both had lost a lot. He wasn't about to leave his money to a family that disowned him because they didn't like the lifestyle he led." She chuckled mirthlessly. "Maybe they would have reacted differently if they had known that he'd received a chunk of money from his deceased lover."

"So he left the money to you because he had nobody else to leave it to?" Javar guessed.

"He didn't leave it to me. He made me executor of his will, but he left his money to the center. To the inner-city children he loved so much."

If it was possible to shrink away and disappear, Javar would have. As it was, he felt about two inches tall. Deep in his heart, he knew that this story was twisted—to make Whitney look like a scheming, conniving gold digger. Now he had the proof. God, he felt like an idiot for ever listening to his family's lies.

"I'm sorry," Javar said, knowing he sounded lame. But he *was* sorry. Sorry for being such a fool.

"And you wonder why I want a divorce," she whispered before moving from the desk and walking to the window.

Javar said nothing. What could he say to that? What he wanted to do was reach out and touch her, make her believe that they had a chance if they could get past all the obstacles keeping them apart.

"You don't even trust me." Turning, she looked at him pointedly. "Why would you want to stay married to me?"

Running a hand over his head, Javar groaned. "I do trust you. It's just that—"

"That you don't believe a word I say. Great basis for a marriage." Last night he had made love to her. Today, he was acting like she had betrayed him and was unworthy of his trust. For his family, everything boiled down to the fact that she had come from the Chicago projects and not from money. In Angela Jordan's eyes, that made Whitney a gold digger in the first degree. Forget love. To the Angela Jordans of the world, the Whitney Jordans of the world didn't understand the meaning of the word.

Whitney's head began to swirl again, making her weak. Last night's attack, Derrick's suspicions, Javar's lack of trust were all too much to deal with right now. Moving from the window, she strode purposefully to the door. But she didn't make it. On the way she suddenly felt too dizzy and she stopped mid-stride, falling to the floor as darkness overcame her.

"You stupid fool," the voice hissed. "What on earth is wrong with you?"

"She woke up," the second voice replied. "She screamed. I couldn't take any chances, so I got out of there. Then he came in. . . ."

"I want no excuses. You've been paid to do a job. *Very* well, in fact. You *will* do it."

"I plan on it, but it's not as easy as I thought it would be. Do you still want it to look like an accident?"

"At this point, I just want her dead." Pause, then, "Any way you can do it."

Javar took a break from pacing the carpet when he heard the door to Whitney's room open. As the nurse stepped into the hallway, he reached her in two long strides. He asked, "Is she going to be okay?"

Elizabeth looked up at him, flashing a sheepish grin. "Yes. Her body is reacting to the fact that she's overexerted herself, and that she's stressed. I injected her with a sedative, something stronger than the stress pill, but it will help her get the sleep she needs."

"Thank you." From the moment she'd fallen into a heap on his office floor, Javar was worried. What had he been thinking, pressuring her to answer his questions? She had enough stress to deal with and he had only succeeded in making matters worse for her.

He took a step toward the door, but Elizabeth darted

in front of him, stopping him from going any further. "Mr. Jordan, the best thing you can do for your wife is to let her rest. Believe me, she'll be out for hours. This is the perfect time to take care of some business, if you need to. You can see Whitney later, when she wakes up."

Elizabeth was right, he knew it. He couldn't help Whitney now. If she even woke up and found him in her room, she might get more stressed out. That thought caused a knot to form in his chest, restricting his lung capacity. He was her husband, yet he had caused her more stress than probably anybody else who had claimed to love her.

"Trust me," the nurse added.

Javar nodded. The nurse was right. This was the time to take care of some business.

Marching to his bedroom to grab his car keys, Javar knew exactly what he was going to do first.

Stepping into Island Breeze was like was like stepping out of the United States and onto a quaint Caribbean island. Located in downtown Chicago, Island Breeze was one of the few authentic Jamaican restaurants in the city.

The upbeat sounds of reggae music played over the speaker system. Fake palm trees, complete with sand at their bases, were placed sporadically around the restaurant, giving the place a definite island feel. The spicy smell of jerk chicken and curried goat filled Javar's nose as waitresses clad in floral sarongs and bright tube tops hurried by with various Jamaican dishes loaded on trays.

He would bring Whitney here if it wasn't for the fact that Stephanie Lewis was one of the restaurant's managers.

Presently he stood, hands in the pockets of his khaki slacks, his eyes scanning the crowd. The assistant manager had promised to call Stephanie for him, and he now stood waiting for her to make an appearance.

When he saw her round a corner, he turned his back. The last thing he wanted her to do now was run from him.

And he didn't want to cause a scene by going in there and dragging her out. But he would, if necessary. If she refused to talk to him.

Seconds later, he turned. She was steps away from him. When she recognized him, her eyes grew wide, startled, but she didn't turn and run. Instead, she continued toward him. "Javar. What are you doing here?"

His voice was deceptively calm as he said, "Stephanie, do you think I could see you outside for a moment?"

"I've got a restaurant to run. . . ."

"This won't take long."

Stealing a glance over her shoulder, she said, "Okay."

As she took Javar's arm, leading him to the glass enclosed foyer, Javar couldn't help thinking that he was surprised at Stephanie's cooperation.

She leaned against the wood paneling. "Okay, what's so important that you came to my workplace to talk to me?"

"Like I said, I'm going to make this quick. Did you have anything to do with the attack on my wife last night?"

Her mouth fell open, incredulous. "What?"

"You heard me. Not too long ago, you threatened Whitney, right in my home. Now, she's been attacked by someone who clearly meant to do her serious harm. I want to know if you had anything to do with that."

"Get a life, Javar. My world does not revolve around your precious Whitney."

He didn't really expect her to answer. But he wanted to show her that he meant business. If she had anything to do with the attack on Whitney's life, she would pay.

"Listen to me, Stephanie. And listen good. I don't want to see you anywhere near my house. I don't want to see your brothers anywhere near my house. I don't want to hear from my mother how I 'manhandled' you today. I want you to stay the hell out of my life, and stay away from Whitney. Because if you don't, you'll have to answer to me. So if you had anything to do with what happened last night, forget about trying again. Got it?"

Stephanie's eyes glared pure hatred. But beneath the anger he could tell she was afraid. Which was exactly what he wanted.

"Got it?" he asked again, his voice rising.

"Go to hell," she snapped.

It was about as good as he was going to get, he knew, but at least he had the answer he wanted in her eyes. She wasn't stupid enough to mess with him when she knew he meant business.

Her lips twisted in a sour pout, she said, "I heard you."

"Good." He glowered at her, making sure his message was clear.

Then, without another word, he turned and walked away, all the while feeling the heat of Stephanie's indignant gaze burning a hole in the back of his head.

Somewhere, there was a phone ringing. Somewhere far off, out of her reach. She wished someone would answer it.

Whitney bolted upright, fighting with the cotton sheets that seemed to entrap her. Finally, she struggled out of their grip and reached for the phone beside her bed.

"Hello," she said, her voice sounding as groggy as her mind.

"Whitney?" That was her mother's voice.

"Mom," Whitney said in reply. Sitting up, she placed the phone in her lap.

"My God, you sound horrible. What's happening over there? I thought you were supposed to be getting better. . . ."

"Hi, Mom. I was just sleeping. Gosh, what did that nurse give me?"

"I don't know. But you don't sound well at all."

The grogginess was starting to fade, but it still hovered in her mind, making her less alert. "I'm okay," she lied, remembering last night and the fact that she hadn't told her mother what happened. Telling her mother would only worry her beyond belief, and Whitney wasn't about to do that to her. "What's up with you? I called you a couple of times but you were nowhere to be found."

Her mother chuckled softly. "I'm taking the advice you've been giving me for years. I've been spending some time with Robert."

Whitney squealed, delighted. "And . . . ?"

"And, it's been . . . nice. He's a sweet, sweet man. He knows the meaning of the word *gentleman,* that's for sure."

Whitney smiled into the receiver, matching the one she knew was on her mother's face. "Good. I'm glad to hear it."

Her mother's tone grew somber. "I'm sorry I haven't been to see you, but you know how I feel about Javar."

"I know. And don't worry. I'll be out of here soon, and back with you."

"Are things okay over there? Really?"

Whitney lied, "Mmm hmm. As good as they can be, considering everything."

"I don't like the way Javar is making you stay there. Like some kind of prisoner."

Think about it, Whitney. Javar has the motive. . . . The words seeped into her thoughts, making her shudder. Derrick couldn't be right, could he?

"I just hope Javar isn't trying to pressure you into getting back together with him," Whitney's mother was saying. "After the way he treated you, really."

The phone line beeped. "Mom, hold on a sec, okay? That's the other line." Whitney clicked over. "Hello?"

The sound of slow, heavy breathing filled her ear.

"Hello," Whitney repeated.

More breathing, along with unidentifiable muffled sounds in the background. Maybe street sounds. Perhaps a club.

"Who is this?" Whitney said, her voice rising with anger.

She hated cowardly, spineless people who had to hide behind faceless threats and other immature mind games.

Click. The dial tone resonated in her ear. Because her mother was on the line, the caller I.D. did not display the second caller's number. As she clicked back over to her mother, Whitney's mind worked overtime. Was that a crank call, or something more sinister? Something like a warning that whoever wanted to hurt her wasn't finished yet?

"Who was it?" her mother asked, interrupting her thoughts.

"Wrong number," Whitney replied absently, hoping that was the truth.

"Well, honey, I won't keep you. You sound like you could use some more rest, and I want to make sure you recover quickly, so you can finally get on with your life."

"No, you don't have to go."

"Yes, honey, I do," her mother replied, a hint of playfulness in her tone. "Robert is taking me out tonight. And I want to make sure that I look my best. You know how it is."

"You'll look beautiful, as usual," Whitney told her, meaning every word. At forty-eight, her mother was gorgeous, and looked about ten years younger. She'd been without a man for too long, since her father had left her eight years ago for a younger woman. It had been a devastating event in her mother's life, but she had gone on. Her strength was remarkable, and Whitney only hoped that she could be half as strong as her mother in the coming years without Javar.

If she was doing the right thing, why did that thought hurt so much? There was a nasty lump in her throat, just thinking about the prospect of finally ending her marriage. It wasn't going to be easy, she suddenly realized. Maybe it would be the hardest thing in her life. But it was something she had to do. She couldn't live a lie anymore.

". . . okay, honey?" her mother was saying.

"Hmm? Oh, well have fun."

Her mother hesitated a moment before she asked, "Whitney, are you sure you're okay?" Concern was evident in her voice.

"Yeah. I'm okay. Go on. Go get ready. Have a great time."

"Okay, honey," Carmen said. "Look, if you need anything . . ."

"I know, Mom. Love you."

"I love you too."

Whitney replaced the receiver and sat quietly for several minutes. The crank call had unnerved her, more than she wanted to admit. Or was it the fact that Derrick's suspicions still floated around in her mind, confusing her?

"Stop this," she said aloud. Just earlier today, she'd gotten angry with Javar for his lack of trust. She could not, would not, distrust him now.

Javar sat in his parked car, his cell phone at his ear. He listened to the rings of his mother's mobile phone, and after the fourth one, a recorded message came on. Angela Jordan's voice was smooth and cheerful as she instructed the caller to leave a message.

Javar did. He said, "Mother, Javar here. This is just a quick message. I know the truth about the pictures and the money. But then, you probably do too. Anyway, I want you to stop this plan of yours to sabotage Whitney. You're not going to influence me one way or another. I know you care about me, but you've got to let this go."

He flipped his phone closed, praying his mother would not only hear his message, but that she would really listen.

"What's wrong, Stephanie?" a pretty, dark-skinned waitress asked.

"Nothing," Stephanie snapped. "Don't you have work to do?"

The waitress recoiled as if physically stung, taking a few steps backward before she turned and hurried out of the kitchen.

Stephanie watched her go. Watched others come. All the while, she was seething. She needed an outlet for her anger. Javar couldn't come to her place of business and treat her like a bag of dirt. She couldn't let him get away with that.

Forget the restaurant. Turning, she marched to her office, her thick heels clicking on the orange tile floor. She slammed the office door shut, locked it, then dropped into the swivel chair. She grabbed the sleek black receiver of the phone and placed it at her ear, then began punching in the digits to her home.

The phone rang . . . and rang. *Why wasn't anybody around when she needed them?*

With her finger, she broke the connection, resting the receiver against her forehead. Maybe she could reach Kevin on his cell phone. Hopefully, he wasn't in the middle of a delivery.

She punched in the digits to Kevin's phone. After four rings, his answering service picked up. Angry, she dropped the receiver in its cradle and stood. What now? She was going to go crazy if she couldn't vent. And her brothers were the only ones who understood her feelings and agreed with everything she said. She could count on them.

She would try Keith's pager. He worked as a custodian at Northwestern and couldn't be reached by phone. But if he had his pager on him, he could go to the nearest phone and return her call.

Stephanie paged him, leaving the number to the restaurant instead of a voice message. That way, her brother would know immediately that it was her who had called.

Less than two minutes later, the office phone rang. Stephanie grabbed the receiver. Anxiously, she said, "Keith?"

"Steph, it's me. What's going on?"

"Javar, that punk, was here today. Getting in my face

and *threatening* me. I swear at one point I thought he was going to hit me, right here where I work!''

"Okay, Steph. Calm down. Where is he now?''

"He's gone now, probably back to Whitney. That's why he was here. To tell me to make sure we stay away from his precious Whitney. The woman who murdered my son. Hell, what if he comes back?''

"Don't worry, Steph. Javar won't hurt you. Kevin and I will make sure of that.'' He paused, then said, "We waited too long to deal with him, but we will now. And when we're done, he'll know never to mess with you again.''

As Stephanie replaced the receiver, a smile tugged at the corners of her mouth. For the first time since Javar had made his surprise appearance, she released a long, satisfied breath.

No way, Javar couldn't treat her like a bag of dirt. He would see who had the last laugh.

Chapter Fifteen

His heart racing, Javar ran from Whitney's bedroom down the spiral staircase to the first floor. Where was she?

A quick run through the first-floor rooms and he discovered that she wasn't in any of them. He didn't like this. The nurse had said that Whitney would sleep for several hours. God, had that sedative rendered her helpless against a second attack?

Retracing his footsteps, he ran back to the foyer and through the archway that led to the kitchen. Rays of sunlight brightened the kitchen, but Javar hardly noticed. His nape prickled with fear as he realized nobody was around.

He scurried to the floor-to-ceiling windows and looked out at the vast backyard. He caught movement out of the corner of his eye, and he looked to the south. Carlos was walking alongside the rosebushes toward the house.

Javar ran outside, down the concrete steps and onto the grass. He called, "Carlos!"

Seeing him, Carlos quickened his pace. "Mr. Jordan, is something wrong?"

"Yes," Javar answered, slightly out of breath from both

worry and from having run through the entire house. "Whitney . . . I can't find her. She was supposed to be sleeping. . . ."

Relief softened Carlos's features. He replied, "She's at the beach, sir."

"The beach?"

"Yes. She was heading there only a few moments ago."

"Thanks." Javar turned, heading to the concrete path that led to the beach. After what Whitney had told him yesterday, why would she even consider going to the beach alone?

He saw her sitting on *Lady Love,* with her back facing him and her feet dangling over the side. She wore black jeans that were rolled up to her knees and a pink tank top. Supporting her body with outstretched hands behind her, Whitney seemed not to have a care in the world.

Relief flooded him, allowing his heartbeat to return to normal. Whitney had always been strong-willed, and it didn't surprise him that despite her fears yesterday, she was out here at the beach again. Still, he wished she would keep a low profile until this whole mess with the attacker was resolved. Like Whitney, he suspected Stephanie, but until there was concrete proof, he couldn't be sure that she was the one who was actually behind the attack.

While he made no sound on the sand, Whitney must have sensed his presence for she suddenly whipped her head around, a startled expression stretched across her features. When she saw him, she visibly relaxed but said nothing, instead turning back and staring out at Lake Michigan.

A jolt of electricity attacked his stomach, spiraling through the rest of Javar's body. Whitney was a vision of loveliness. Even in jeans and a tank top, she was irresistible. Her smooth, honey-brown back flirted with him from beneath the material of her top, inviting him to taste of its sweetness again. And he wanted to. Like a moth drawn to a flame, Javar was drawn to Whitney, knowing he might get burned but not caring if he did.

She'd said sex for them last night had been a reaction to her distress. Well, reaction or no reaction, he wanted more of what she had to offer. She was like a drug, intoxicating, tempting.

The lake was calm today, gently lapping at the shore. No wonder Whitney was drawn here. It was peaceful, serene, calming. This was his property, yet he hardly made it out here. But then, he hadn't wanted to. *Lady Love* sat on his private beach, and just coming down here reminded him that Whitney wasn't in his life.

But she was here now. On *Lady Love*.

Javar slipped out of his shoes and socks, leaving them in the sand as he continued toward Whitney. When he stepped into the water, it was cold, and he quickly jumped backward onto the sand.

Whitney giggled. Looking up at him, she said, "Weren't expecting that, were you?"

A warm sensation washing over him at the sight of her smile, Javar smiled back. "No, I guess I wasn't."

An awkward silence fell between them, and Javar looked out at the water, watching as the gentle waves rolled toward the shore. He wished his life could be as rhythmic, normal, predictable even. Chaos and excitement were overrated.

He ventured into the water again, rounding the back of the boat to get at the tramp where Whitney sat. He slipped onto the boat beside her.

She didn't turn, but said, "It's so peaceful out here. That's what I love about it. So beautiful."

"It is," Javar agreed, staring out at the waves. With the sun shining brilliantly on the lake, it looked like it was sprinkled with gold.

"How often do you get out here?" Whitney asked. She turned and faced him then. "Hmm? How often do you come down to this piece of heaven and just relax? Enjoy the beauty of nature that God has blessed us with?"

I would, if you were here, Javar said to himself. But he said, "Not very often."

"That's what I thought." She stretched a toe into the water, swirling it around. "When are you going to stop working so hard?"

"I have to work hard."

"You don't have to work as hard as you do. You can take on a partner. Maybe two. Your company is thriving. You've already proven to your mother that you're a success."

"This isn't about my mother."

Whitney flashed him a wry grin, saying she knew better. She knew that Angela Jordan hadn't approved of her son's desire to be an architect, as opposed to a doctor like his parents. But he had stood his ground and shown them that he could make a life for himself on his own, even paying back all of the start up capital they had given him. Whitney admired Javar's fierce independence. But she wondered if that same independence hadn't left him incapable of giving and receiving love. Certainly, in their relationship, that had been the case.

Whitney said, "At the rate you're going, you're going to be dead of a heart attack before forty."

Javar shook his head, a smile playing on the corner of his lips. "I don't plan on dying anytime soon. You should be happy, I've actually taken a few days off. Since . . . your accident."

"I know. I also know that it must be hard for you. Staying away from work when it's so important to you."

"You're important to me too."

His piercing gaze penetrated her through to the core of her being, and despite the heat, Whitney shivered. He wanted her, his eyes said, as clearly as if he had voiced the words. The crazy thing was, she wanted him too. There were residual feelings in her heart for this man, and she needed to get them out of her system before she went on. Maybe more nights like last night would give her enough physical satisfaction that she could walk away and keep her heart intact. . . .

Goodness, she was crazy. She should be mad at Javar right now, but for some reason she felt strangely euphoric and couldn't be angry if she tried.

Looking at Javar, she sighed inwardly. She felt the pull to stay and give their marriage another chance just as strongly as she felt the pull to go and get on with her life. She wondered if it was this hard for other couples who broke up. What tomorrow would hold, she couldn't be sure. The only thing she did know for sure was that Javar had had nothing to do with the attack on her life. In his gaze she saw a hint of sadness mixed with warmth, but not hatred. And he would have to hate her to want her dead.

"About before," Javar said, interrupting her thoughts. "I'm sorry."

"I'm sorry too." And she was. For the events that had transpired to keep them apart. For the rift that was probably too wide to close between them. But Javar was right. They should at least try to be friends.

"Feel like going for a sail?" Javar asked.

The other times they had sailed on this catamaran, they had ended up in each other's arms, teasing each other with words of love. A couple of times, they had even made love on the boat's tramp under the moonlight. If she went out there with Javar now, she would lose all perspective. Lose all control, was more like it, she thought wryly.

"I really shouldn't," she finally replied, noticing the disappointment that flashed in Javar's eyes. "I need to . . . go in and . . . take my medication."

It seemed to pain him to do so, but Javar said, "Okay."

Javar stepped down into the water and stood before Whitney. "Let me help you."

He didn't wait for a response as he reached for her waist and scooped her up. His strong hands pressed into her back as she wrapped her own hands around his neck.

The energy that passed between them was tangible and undeniable. She was still attracted to her husband.

God help her.

Carrying her past the water, Javar deposited her on the sand. But even as her feet touched the ground, she still kept her hands around his neck, her eyes locked with his. Her heartbeat accelerated as his warm breath fanned her forehead. She was weak now, too weak to resist him if he wanted to take her.

Looking down at her, Javar dragged his bottom lip into his mouth. Conflicting emotions warred on his face and Whitney held her breath, waiting, wanting.

Javar's Adam's apple rose and fell as he swallowed. Taking her hands from around his neck he said, "You better go."

It was like getting doused with a cold glass of water. Her desire fizzled as quickly as someone flicking off a light switch, and reason took over. "Yes," she replied softly. "Are you coming?"

"Actually, I'd like to stay here a while longer. Think."

"Okay." Turning toward the house, Whitney started off.

"Whitney?"

She turned, the familiar heat of longing starting to burn in the pit of her belly. "Yes?"

"How about dinner tonight? Here, at the house." He smiled weakly. "I'll cook."

It was at moments like this that she was most vulnerable. When Javar's full lips curled in a sincere, sexy smile. When she saw that he was being thoughtful of her feelings. During these times, it was so easy to remember why she had first fallen in love with him.

A sheepish smile playing on her lips, Whitney said, "Sure." But even as she said the words, she knew that she was walking into dangerous territory.

"Great," Javar replied, his lips growing into a wide smile. "Let's make it eight o'clock. In the dining room."

* * *

Nothing. Derrick slammed the file against his cluttered oak desk, then fell into the chair behind it. Absolutely nothing.

Bringing a palm to his face, he squeezed his forehead, as if that could force all the answers he needed into his brain. "Think," he said aloud. "Damn it, think!"

Derrick spun the chair around to face the desk and flipped the file open. Running his finger over the text of the pages, he scanned the contents for what must have been the hundredth time. The strongest evidence right now was the finding of black paint on Whitney's rental car. But without any idea *which* black car that came from, it was like looking for a needle in a haystack.

Then, there was Whitney's account of the accident, of the bright lights in her rearview mirror. But she couldn't identify even the type of car, so again, that information was useless.

Oh, there'd been witnesses. All of whom had been interviewed, but their accounts of the accident scene didn't hold water. Most had come to the scene after the fact and hadn't actually witnessed the accident, despite their helpful suggestions as to what must have happened.

He needed to get the proof soon. It existed, and he would find it.

He had to. Whitney's life depended on it.

Whitney shouldn't feel nervous about dinner with her husband, but she did. Standing before the mirror in her bathroom, her stomach fluttered as if it had a thousand trapped butterflies inside desperate to be freed.

Bracing her hands against the white marble counter, Whitney let her head fall forward. Why did the thought of spending an evening with Javar have her so stressed? She raised her head, staring at her reflection in the mirror.

She knew the answer to her question. At least her heart did. Despite everything, she was falling for Javar again. Against her better judgment, she was tempted to give their relationship another chance.

Javar was trying, she knew. He was making more of an effort than she was. But did he really and truly forgive her for the accident? Could she ever forgive him for the way he had treated her after J.J. had died?

Whitney sighed. They had meant so much to each other once. And after last night . . .

"Last night was only sex," Whitney muttered to her reflection, but the peculiar gleam in her eyes told her she was lying.

Okay, so she was attracted to Javar. So the sex between them was fabulous. That wasn't enough to base a future on.

But it's a great start, the voice in her head told her. The voice that loved playing devil's advocate.

Till death do us part . . . That was part of the vow she had taken. If Javar wanted to make a genuine effort at repairing their marriage, could she really say no?

Eleanor Scherer drew in a deep, steadying breath as she climbed the steps of the police station. A bout of nervousness caused her stomach to tighten. Even now, she wasn't sure she was doing the right thing. When a surreptitious glance over her shoulder proved nobody was watching her, she continued.

Last night had been the worst. After the newspaper had failed to give her the answers she so craved, she'd been wracked with guilt. Finally, when she had fallen asleep, she dreamed of Harry, her dear, sweet, deceased husband.

He always knew the right thing to do. Harry, who was so courageous. Much more so than she. In a dream, he had come to her and told her to do the right thing.

And that's what she was doing now.

She hesitated when she saw all the hustle and bustle within the police station. Whispering a silent prayer, she forged ahead to the reception desk.

"I have some information," she blurted out to the receptionist behind the desk. "About that accident last week. It wasn't really an accident. Someone tried to kill that poor lady."

Chapter Sixteen

Whitney stepped through the French doors into the mammoth dining room, immediately noting the dimmed lights and the two red candles burning at either end of the large mahogany dining table.

Flashing her a wickedly sexy, charming smile, Javar rose from the chair where he was seated and moved to the sideboard where a portable CD player lay. Moments later, the soft, seductive sounds of Johnny Gill filled the air.

Whitney's heart went wild. Her mind said she should turn and flee. Yet her feet remained firmly planted where they were, on the sparkling cherry wood floor.

Dressed in all black, with the first few buttons of his loose fitting silk shirt undone, Javar looked so sexy. Whitney couldn't help remembering other romantic evenings they had shared. More specifically, she remembered the time shortly after they'd been married when they were in this same dining room, and Javar had seduced her with his eyes. Instead of dinner, they'd feasted on each other, making love on the large dining table, and eventually in the bedroom. She couldn't look at the mahogany table

without remembering the wonderful passion they had
shared there.

She tore her gaze from the dining table and looked at
Javar. His nutmeg eyes had darkened to onyx, heated desire
evident in their depths. Slowly, determination in his steps,
Javar approached her.

Whitney's eyes took in the length of him. His long, lean
body; the sprinkling of black curls at the opening of his
silk shirt. He was still so incredibly handsome, so incredibly
sexy. So irresistible.

When he was mere inches away from her, a shiver of
desire snaked down her spine. With the bittersweet feeling,
sanity crept back into Whitney's brain. Sexy or not, she
couldn't do this. She couldn't stay here and get caught up
in the past. She turned on her heel, determined to leave.

Javar grabbed her arm, and Whitney stopped. The feel
of his long, strong fingers wrapped around her slender
forearm caused her skin to tingle, and she remembered
too easily the way he used to hold her when loving her.
Remembered how wonderful last night had been. Knew
she wanted to experience that again.

She felt his head nearing hers, felt the heat of his breath
on the side of her face. Her knees almost buckled on the
spot.

His face stopped moving when his mouth reached her
ear. With a deep, sexy voice he murmured, "Don't go."

It figured, the moment he was about to leave the office
and go home that his private line would ring. Grumbling,
Derrick doubled back and searched for the phone among
the files on his desk. When he found it, he lifted the
receiver and brought it to his ear. "District Two, Detective
Lawson speaking."

As he listened to the police officer on the other end of
the line, Derrick's eyes grew wide with excitement. "You're
sure? Wednesday, June twenty-sixth?"

"That's what she says," the officer from District Four replied.

"And you believe her? She doesn't seem like a flake?"

"It's hard to tell. But I'd say she knows something."

Derrick allowed himself to smile. This could be the break he was waiting for. "Where is she now?"

"She's sitting in an interview room. Seems real scared. I don't know how long she'll wait."

"I'm on my way." Hanging up the phone, Derrick grabbed his blazer.

Then, he ran.

A tremor of desire rocked Whitney's body as the sweet sound of Javar's voice vibrated in her ear. Memories of last night invaded her mind, exciting her. Sex had always been wonderful for them and she could easily fall into his arms again, if only for the comfort she knew loving him would bring. And the excitement. And the passion. God, she was tired of being so lonely.

She swallowed. Part of her wanted to run. She had left Javar, after all, and she'd had a good reason. She was afraid. So afraid of being hurt again. Because she had to admit that he had the power to do that, to break her heart, and she didn't know if she could deal with that kind of pain again. Last night could be explained away, but if she fell into her husband's arms right now, that could mean disaster.

But still her feet did not move.

"Dinner's in the oven."

He may as well have been speaking Chinese, her brain wasn't processing his words. She couldn't think, only feel. Looking up at him from what must have been dreamy eyes, Whitney stammered, "D-d-dinner?"

"Mmm hmm. I made barbecue chicken." But his eyes said, "Let's skip dinner. You're all I want."

"Oh, ch-chicken. That's what that, uh, smell is." God,

she sounded pathetic! You'd think she and Javar had never been lovers the way her longing for him was now consuming her entire being.

"Take a seat," Javar told her. "I'll get the plates."

He backed away slowly, pinning her with a heated gaze and a beguiling smile. Her heart fluttered; her breath snagged in her throat. God, her mouth even watered, and she doubted it had anything to do with the spicy aroma of barbecue chicken!

When he finally disappeared, Whitney released the breath she'd been holding. She whimpered. How dare Javar—Johnny Gill! He knew how much she loved his smooth love melodies.

If she didn't know better, she'd say that Javar was setting her up to be seduced. Worse still, she hoped he was.

"Okay, dinner is served."

Whitney's head spun around at the sound of her husband's voice. As he carried the two plates of food into the dining room, she ventured toward the table, not wanting him to know just how frazzled she was. If he could seem unaffected by the sexual energy fizzling in the air, then she could at least pretend not to be affected by it either.

Javar placed one plate at the head of the table, and the other to its immediate right. The table could easily seat fourteen, but even Whitney conceded that the opposite end of the table would be too far away for an intimate dinner. Because that's exactly what this was.

"Let me get your chair," Javar said, gently brushing a hand over her shoulder as he moved behind her.

The gentle touch made her shudder. She drew in a slow, deep breath in an effort to quell her desire, but it was no use.

Javar pulled out her chair, and she sat. Her senses were extra-sensitive, for even as he pushed her chair beneath the table and his shirt lightly touched her skin, she found that utterly erotic.

It was Johnny Gill, singing about losing self-control, that had her losing all hers.

She concentrated on the food, trying to put Javar's alluring musky smell out of her mind. The chicken . . . looked like chicken, she mused. She concentrated harder. It looked like barbecue chicken, accompanied by rice pilaf and steamed broccoli.

Javar reached across the table and took her hand in his. She knew what was next. Whenever they dined together like this, he liked to hold her hand while saying grace. Closing her eyes, she bowed her head.

"Lord, we thank you for this food and pray that you bless it and make it good to our bodies. We also thank you for the gift of life . . . and love. Amen."

"Amen," Whitney whispered. Slowly she opened her eyes, noting that Javar still held her hand.

But it was only for a moment. He slipped his hand away, and immediately, Whitney's felt cold where it had only a second ago been warm.

Again, Javar seemed unaffected. Lifting the bottle of wine from the chilled carafe, he filled her wine glass with the rose colored liquid first, then his own. Zinfandel. Her favorite.

Javar lifted his crystal glass and twirled the stem between his fingers. Following his lead, Whitney lifted hers. His eyes held hers as he said, "To finding peace, and happiness."

He touched his glass to hers, clinking crystal against crystal. A soft *ping* sounded in the air. Even when he brought the delicate crystal to his lips and took a sip, his eyes never left hers.

Finally, he picked up the silver fork beside his plate and scooped up some rice.

Whitney couldn't seem to get her brain to let her do the same. It was working hard enough to keep her nerves under control.

Javar seemed to notice her reluctance, and his eyebrows drew together in a questioning look. "You're not hungry?"

"Hmm? Oh, yes. It just . . . looks so wonderful." *Okay, enough of being this pathetic,* she told herself. Picking up her fork, she spiked a piece of broccoli. She brought it to her mouth, popped it inside, then began chewing.

See? It's not that hard, her inner voice said.

The meal was actually very good. Excellent, in fact. The combination of spices Javar had used on the chicken had resulted in a tangy, spicy flavor that was simply delicious.

"You sure you didn't have Carlos help you with this meal?" she asked, playfully.

"No way. Hey, you know that I can cook. Or have you forgotten?"

She shook her head. "No, I haven't forgotten. Your culinary skills are still excellent, I see. This is a terrific meal."

"Thanks." His eyes crinkled as he smiled. "Wait until you see what I have for dessert."

"Oh, you have to tell me!" Whitney exclaimed. She loved dessert. She loved food, period. And Javar knew that.

Humor danced in Javar's eyes at Whitney's response. "You'll find out soon," was all he said.

They fell into silence as they ate the rest of the meal, Johnny Gill followed by Barry White provided the mood music. Everything was so romantic, so like the way Javar had been when they were first dating. Maybe that's why she had felt so nervous about tonight. If things didn't go well, there probably wouldn't be any other nights like this. There probably wouldn't be anymore chances to make a go of their relationship.

And suddenly, she wanted that chance.

Javar told Whitney to stay seated when she offered to help him get dessert. Maybe the few glasses of wine she drank were clouding her sanity, but she found herself looking forward to what would come after dessert.

A little while later, he returned with a bowl of vanilla ice cream topped with cherries jubilee. "I admit I didn't make this," Javar said.

"It looks delicious," Whitney said.

"Here." Javar dipped a spoon into the bowl and captured some of the dessert. He held it in front of Whitney, but when she opened her mouth and moved her head forward, he pulled the spoon away.

He chuckled as Whitney's eyes grew wide. Then, slowly, he brought it to her mouth and pulled it away again.

"Javar! Stop teasing me!"

She was smiling as she said the words, and Javar felt a blanket of warmth wrap around his heart. He loved this woman. Had always loved her, even though he'd lost sight of that. But if he had learned anything, it was that love wasn't always enough.

Javar pushed the irksome thought from his mind, concentrating instead on feeding Whitney. This time, he allowed her tongue to flick out and taste the dessert before he slipped the spoon into her mouth.

"Mmm." Whitney both moaned and giggled, closing her eyes as she savored the flavor of the ice cream. Some of the melted dessert trickled down the side of her chin, and she brushed it away with a finger.

Javar couldn't help reaching out and touching the smooth skin of her chin, helping to wipe off the ice cream. Their fingers collided. The giggling stopped. So did Whitney's finger, beneath Javar's.

She looked so beautiful, he wanted to lean forward, press his lips against hers, taste the dessert on her mouth. He held his desire in check and spoon-fed her again.

"How is it?" Javar asked, though he didn't need to, given her earlier response.

"Absolutely heavenly," she replied, her voice husky. She took the spoon from him, dipped it into the dessert, then lifted it to his mouth. Like he had with her, she pulled the spoon back just before it could enter his mouth, teasing him. Bringing the spoon closer, she rotated it around his mouth, slowly, seductively. Javar couldn't help laughing, and Whitney did too when he surprised her by seizing the spoon in his mouth.

They continued the playful routine until the last spoonful. But instead of putting the dessert into her mouth, Javar trailed the spoon around the outline of her lips, leaving a path of melted ice cream as he did.

Whitney knew what was coming next. Wanted it. Leaning forward, she brought her lips to meet Javar's. When their mouths were a mere fraction of an inch from each other, he hesitated. Pulled back.

"Whitney," he said, his voice barely above a whisper. "I—I've missed you so much. You have no idea."

Whitney placed a palm on his cheek, relishing its warmth. "I do, Javar."

"This . . . tonight . . . it's not about sex. And it's not about old feelings. It's about . . ."

"Finding peace and happiness and love," Whitney said, completing his thought.

Javar nodded. "Whitney, I promise I'll change. Work less, whatever it takes. Just say you want me as much as I want you right now. That you're willing to try."

Whitney's heart stopped. Oh, she wanted to say yes. Wanted to so badly. But the thought scared her.

But she was also tired of being lonely. And without Javar, she certainly was lonely. Without Javar, she didn't know if she'd ever find the happiness she so craved.

She moved her fingers down the side of his jaw, over his chin, and finally to his lips. "I'm willing to try, Javar. But . . . I can't make any promises."

"No promises," he agreed. With a hand, he held her own against his mouth, kissed her fingers. His mouth felt cool against her fingers, and they tingled from his touch. The sensation spread down her arm and to the rest of her body.

Her eyelids heavy, Whitney looked up at Javar from lowered lids. Javar's eyes were clouded with desire. Slipping a hand behind her neck, he swept her hair aside, then braced the back of her head with his hand. Slowly, he drew her closer to him, closer, until their lips finally met in a sweet, sensual, glorious kiss.

His lips were cool and he tasted of vanilla, but he also tasted of something else. On his lips, she tasted passion and temptation, and as if she had waited for this moment all her life, she moaned into his mouth.

Passion ignited. Temptation consumed them like a burning inferno. Scraping his chair back, Javar rose, his lips still connected with hers. He wrapped muscular arms around her back, pressed her against him as if he couldn't get enough of her.

Javar's tongue urged her lips apart and slipped into her mouth, dancing with her own. Here, now, she wanted him, with Barry White crooning in the background. But what if Carlos or Elizabeth walked in and found them?

Javar must have read her thoughts because he broke the kiss and said, "Let's go to the bedroom."

The walk upstairs hand-in-hand seemed like it would never end. The hunger for her husband was overwhelming in its intensity, and it shook her to the core of her being. Never had she wanted anything as much as she wanted her husband right now.

He stopped outside the master suite, enveloped her in an embrace. Kissed her neck, her lips. Javar's muscular chest pressed against her soft breasts, and Whitney's nipples hardened in response. He fiddled with the door handle behind him, and the moment it opened, he swept her inside.

Javar's tongue delved into Whitney's mouth with urgency as his hands found the zipper at the back of her black dress and drew it all the way down. She pressed her buttocks into his hands, and he cupped them, squeezed them. Slipped his hand beneath her dress and felt the lacy trim of her panties.

Whitney wanted to feel him, too, and after undoing a few buttons she slid her hands beneath his silk shirt, run-

ning them over his chest, through the sprinkling of curls
on his brawny flesh. She found a small, taut nipple and
squeezed, then leaned forward and flicked a tongue over
it.

Javar moaned, a deep rumbling in his chest. Gripping
her by the shoulders, Javar pulled Whitney up to meet his
lips. He nipped, sucked, trailed his tongue to her earlobe.

When his tongue found one of her most sensitive spots,
Whitney whimpered. After their lengthy separation, they
still knew how to please each other, how to turn each other
on. In his arms, she felt right. Felt like she belonged. Felt
like she had come home.

They came together like desperate lovers, lovers who
had been denied too long. Their passion was like a thirst
that couldn't be quenched. They clung to each other as
they loved wildly, not wanting to let go of the new bond they
had found. Together, they moved in a sensuous rhythm all
their own, one that brought them to a height as great as
the stars.

And when they had loved until they could physically love
no more, they lay breathless in each other's arms. Words
weren't necessary to make what they had shared any more
special. So there were none.

Javar's slick body snuggled against hers, Whitney fell
asleep, a feeling of contentment wrapped around her heart
like a blanket of warmth.

Chapter Seventeen

Javar awoke with a start. Glancing beside him, the rumpled but flat sheets told him that his worst fear had come true.

Whitney was gone.

Javar rolled onto his back, heaving a long-suffering sigh. He wouldn't go after her. Not this time. If, after last night, she didn't want to be with him this morning, if she wasn't ready to attempt a reconciliation, then he didn't know what else he could do. He had given her everything last night, heart and soul.

A soft, lingering moan interrupted his thoughts. Lifting his head, Javar strained to identify its source. Silence rewarded his efforts, and he wondered if he had imagined the sound. But seconds later, he heard it again.

It was coming from the ensuite bathroom.

Whitney.

He threw off the covers and sprang from the bed, charging into the bathroom. There he found Whitney huddled on the floor beside the toilet. In one quick stride he was at her side on the floor. One touch on her clammy skin and it was obvious she was trembling.

His heart ached for the pain she was clearly suffering. "Whitney . . . sweetie."

She looked up at him, her eyes round and gleaming with tears. "Javar, I feel awful." She coughed, then quickly poised herself over the toilet. The coughing ceased. She slapped the toilet seat and slid back onto the white marble floor. "I wish I could just puke and get it over with!" Soft sobs fell from her lips. "It hurts. Oh God, it hurts."

Javar rose and darted to the sink. He turned on the brass cold-water faucet, then grabbed a hand towel and slipped it beneath the cool water. In moments he was back at Whitney's side again, pressing the damp towel against her forehead, over her face.

It happened then. Whitney's chest heaved as she succumbed to a coughing fit. Bracing her hands on the toilet, she leaned over the bowl and vomited. And vomited again.

With one hand, Javar rubbed her back and with the other kept the wet towel against her face.

"Why is this happening?" Whitney asked. "I'm supposed to be getting better."

Javar jumped to his feet. "Let me call the nurse."

"No," Whitney said, a hint of panic in her voice. "Don't leave me."

"Okay," Javar conceded, lowering himself once again. "What do you want me to do?"

"Help me . . . help me back to bed."

Wrapping an arm around her, Javar lifted Whitney from the floor. He helped her to the bedroom, where he laid her on the bed.

He said, "Stay here. I'm getting Elizabeth."

Whitney clutched her stomach and moaned in response.

Minutes later, Elizabeth was there, handing Whitney a glass of water. "Drink this," she said.

Whitney moaned, as if it was too painful to sit up. Javar lowered himself onto the bed beside her and helped her up. "C'mon, Whitney. Drink this. It'll make you feel better." To the nurse, he said, "Why is she in so much pain?"

"It has nothing to do with the accident," the nurse replied, her tone confident. "This kind of violent reaction indicates to me that her body is reacting to something she ingested. She could have a case of food poisoning. What did she eat last night?"

"I ate the same thing she did, and I'm fine," Javar replied, his tone dismissive.

"Indulge me," Elizabeth said.

Javar cast a sidelong glance at Whitney, who was lying back on a pillow, moaning softly. His stomach churned at the sight of her, and the air gushed out of his lungs. Turning back to the nurse, he said, "We had barbecue chicken, rice, uh, some broccoli. A little wine . . ."

"Wine. There we go."

Javar's brow wrinkled as he stared at Elizabeth quizzically. "What? I don't get it."

Elizabeth strolled toward Whitney, stopping when she reached the bed. Looking down at her, Elizabeth asked, "Whitney, did you take your medication last night?"

Whitney's eyes fluttered open. "Yes," she replied, her voice almost a whisper. "Sometime . . . in the night."

Elizabeth sighed and faced Javar. "Mixing medications with alcohol can cause this kind of reaction."

A wave of guilt washed over Javar. This was his fault. "Well, what now?"

"Has she vomited?" Elizabeth asked.

"Yes," Javar replied.

"Well, that's the best start. She has to get the toxic mix out of her system. Other than that, lots of water. Maybe some hot tea will help her feel better."

"Okay. I'll make her some. Stay with her, please."

Javar felt like kicking himself when he went downstairs. How could he have been so stupid? His only concern had been of creating the perfect romantic evening. It was just that Whitney had seemed so much stronger, he'd forgotten about the fact that she was still taking medication.

He was so flustered from seeing her in such anguish that he could hardly find the teapot, let alone boil hot water. But finally he did. He prepared a pot of mint tea. When he was a child, that's what his mother used to give him for an upset stomach.

Minutes later, he was back upstairs, the tea and a mug on a tray. But as he entered his bedroom, Elizabeth shushed him.

"She's sleeping," she said. "Thankfully."

"Okay." He blew out a relieved breath. "Good. That's good." Javar walked to the sitting area in his room and placed the tray on the coffee table. He continued to the large window, cocking a hip against the ledge. Outside, the sun was shining brilliantly in a cloudless sky, but Javar couldn't appreciate the moment.

He dragged a hand over his face, stretching the skin as he did. "I was going to go in to work, but now . . ." He fell silent.

Elizabeth sauntered over to him and placed a delicate hand on his arm. "Go," she urged. This isn't serious. Whitney will be fine. You go to work."

"But Whitney's in pain. . . ."

"She's sleeping, and trust me, she'll feel a lot better when she wakes up. I'll be here with her, like you're paying me to be."

Her closemouthed smile was sincere, and looking at her upturned lips, Javar felt a modicum of relief. "I feel so helpless. Like there's nothing I can do for her."

"You're doing plenty. But if you want to do something else, why don't you help me transfer the equipment from her room to this one. I don't want to disturb her sleep."

Javar nodded absently, still deep in thought. Finally, he met the nurse's gaze. "Okay. Okay."

After he had helped transport the blood pressure machine and medicine tray, Javar eased himself onto the bed beside Whitney. Lifting her hand to his mouth, he pressed his lips against her soft, warm flesh.

The nurse had assured him that Whitney would be fine, but he couldn't shake the feeling of foreboding. Like a premonition that told him he might lose her.

Maybe that was because every time he saw his wife in pain, he remembered his guilt. And that guilt made him fear losing her, the way he had lost his son. Initially, he hadn't wanted J.J.—hadn't welcomed the news that Stephanie was pregnant. Involved with his work, he hadn't been excited about the prospect of becoming a father. And he hadn't wanted to be tied to Stephanie for the next eighteen years, minimum. If anyone was a gold digger, it was Stephanie. She hadn't wanted J.J., only the money Javar could give her. Stephanie had made that clear when Javar had refused to marry her, and to spite him, she'd dropped J.J. on his doorstep, giving him custody.

He had loved his son, while resenting Stephanie. And now, J.J. was gone. Whitney didn't understand that the reason he had been so angry after the accident was because he couldn't come to terms with *his* guilt, not hers. Sure, he'd initially blamed her, but when he'd had time to cool down, the residual blame had been for himself. That's why it was hard talking about the accident, even now, because the burden of guilt was still there, like a lump lodged in his heart.

Now . . . he couldn't lose Whitney. But he'd turned his back on her after the accident, almost the way he'd turned his back on J.J. before he was born. Would he lose her, too, as further punishment for his faults? He silently prayed that that would not happen.

The nurse was there then. "Javar, you should go. Let her rest."

Solemn, Javar rose. A worried expression marring his features, he turned and faced Elizabeth. "Are you sure she'll be okay?"

"Javar . . ."

He turned and faced Whitney the moment he heard his name fall from her lips. Her eyes still closed, she shifted on the bed, seemingly getting comfortable.

"Javar . . ." she repeated, and this time her lips twitched with a smile.

Thank you, God. He realized now that he hadn't wanted to leave her until he'd had a sign, something to give him some hope. Now, he had the sign he needed.

"Mr. Jordan," Elizabeth said, a bright smile gracing her lips. "Whitney will be just fine."

What was the point in coming to the police station to make a statement if you weren't going to make yourself available for questioning? Derrick wondered as he held the receiver to his ear. Ever since he had arrived at District Four last night and found that the witness had left, Derrick had been trying to reach her. After unsuccessful attempts last night, he decided that he would call her first thing in the morning. Yet Eleanor Scherer, a possible witness to Whitney's hit-and-run, wasn't home.

Still holding the receiver to his ear, Derrick grabbed his mug of lukewarm coffee, downed it in three gulps. As he replaced the mug on his desk, his patience paid off. The phone on the other end of the receiver stopped ringing, and an elderly woman's breathless voice said, "Hello."

Derrick sat forward, placing his elbows on the edge of his desk. "Hello. I'm trying to reach Eleanor Scherer."

"This is Eleanor Scherer."

Derrick silently mouthed, *Yes!* To her, he said, "This is Detective Lawson of the Chicago Police Department. I understand you came by the station yesterday."

"Oh yes. Yes, I did."

"You witnessed a car accident on the evening of Wednesday, June twenty-sixth. Is that correct?"

"Mmm hmm. Yes. It was awful, what happened to that poor woman. Is she all right?"

Derrick nodded, although it was only for the receiver's benefit. "Yes, Ms. Scherer. Thankfully, she's going to be fine."

Eleanor exhaled a gush of air into the receiver, sounding relieved. "I was so worried. After what happened that night . . ." Her voice trailed off.

"I know." Derrick paused, then continued. "Ms. Scherer, I would really like to get together with you to speak about what you saw."

"Well, okay. I don't know if I'll be of much help, but I felt I should come forward. Tell you what I saw."

"Believe me, I'm glad you did." Soon enough, he would figure out if she was one of the flakes or if she was actually a credible witness. But for now, she was his only hope. "Can you come to District Two this morning? You can give me your statement. . . ."

"Certainly, Detective. What time?"

"How about eleven o'clock?"

"Okay. I'll be there."

"And you know the directions to the station?"

Eleanor chuckled. "Oh yes. Chicago's my hometown. I was born and raised here."

As Derrick ended the call, he allowed himself to hope. Eleanor Scherer *would* be the witness he had longed to find. Whitney's life depended on it.

Javar's Italian dress shoes sank into the soft gray carpet as he stepped off the elevator on the thirtieth floor. A large brass sign that read "Jordan & Associates" hung on the cream-colored wall, beneath which an arrow pointed to the right. Javar turned in that direction, toward the several feet of smoked glass that led to his company's offices. The double doors were propped open, and Hilary Robbins, the company's receptionist, sat at a large oak desk. Dressed in a simple but elegant pale blue dress, the mocha-complected woman looked impeccable.

She smiled up at Javar as he approached her desk. "Hello, Mr. Jordan. Great to see you."

"Morning, Hilary," he said, returning her smile. He didn't slow his stride as he rounded the corner, and walked down a long hallway that led to his office at the opposite end of the floor. There was an extra pep in his step, that was certain. And it all had to do with Whitney. Now that he knew she was going to be okay, he allowed himself to remember the incredible night they had shared. The night was much more than great lovemaking. Last night symbolized a new beginning for them.

A few of the draftspersons seemed surprised to see him, but pleasantly so. He nodded and said hello to everyone he passed, feeling somewhat foreign in his own company. He'd been away from work less than a week, yet it seemed like years.

He quickened his pace, anxious to get to his office and sort through his notes before heading to the boardroom for the ten o'clock meeting with his associates and project architects. As he neared the mahogany doors of his office, he saw Melody standing at the corner of her desk, a black man in baggy jeans and a loose fleece shirt partially obstructing his view of her face. Intrigued, Javar's forehead furrowed. Casually dressed, the man didn't look like the type who usually frequented his office. He and Melody were huddled so closely together, as though sharing some secret, that Javar became curious. Was this man a friend of Melody's?

Melody's eyes were lowered, fixed on some spot on the ground, so she didn't notice Javar approaching. But the moment she lifted her gaze and saw him, her eyes grew wide, clearly startled. Then her hand was on her visitor's chest, pushing him away as she said something to him in a hushed tone.

The young man retreated, turning his head as he did. Cold, hard eyes met Javar's, but only for a moment. The man quickly averted his gaze then shuffled past Javar.

Javar's neck swiveled with the man's movements, watching him as he walked away. Narrowing his eyes, a peculiar feeling snaked down his spine.

"Good morning—"

"Who was that?" Javar asked, spinning around to face Melody.

His administrative assistant looked like a deer caught in a car's headlights with that bug-eyed, somewhat dazed look.

Javar was even more curious at the reaction. His forehead furrowed as he looked her. "Melody?"

"I'm sorry. Uh, he's a . . . a friend. Um, he dropped by to say hi."

Something wasn't right about the way Melody was acting. Javar eyed her with curiosity for a few moments longer, but when she turned and started shuffling papers on her desk, a voice told him not to press her. Not yet, at least. Maybe the man was a new boyfriend and she was flustered only because she didn't expect to be caught taking a few minutes from her work to talk to him.

Javar cleared his throat. "Did everyone receive the message about the meeting?"

"Yes." Melody moved around to her black leather chair, standing before it. "I sent memos to everyone and I was told they would all be there. Except of course Andrew Feldman, who is in Minneapolis."

"Great."

"Oh," Melody said, waving a hand in front of her as if to magically stop him from walking away. "Your brother called."

Javar arched a brow. "Khamil?"

Melody cracked her first smile of the morning. "He's your only brother, isn't he?"

"What did he say?"

Melody sat. "He asked when you were going to be in New York, so I told him the dates. Then he said for you to call him."

"Yeah, I'll give him a call," Javar said, more to himself than to Melody. "Any other messages?"

Melody passed him a stack of pink message slips a couple of inches thick. "Only these. Oh, and Althea Harmon called. A few times." She raised an inquisitive eyebrow, her eyes imploring Javar to offer her an explanation.

He didn't, because he owed her none. "Thanks, Melody."

As he started off, Melody asked, "How's Whitney?"

For an instant, Javar was startled. Then he remembered that the last time he had called the office he'd told Melody about Whitney's accident—including the fact that she was staying with him—because she'd asked several questions. . . .

"My wife is recovering nicely," Javar replied, tossing in a smile for good measure.

Melody's smile was clearly forced.

If he didn't have a successful business here, Javar might consider packing it in and moving with Whitney to another state. Start fresh. Maybe that would give them the advantage they needed.

No, he decided as he stepped into his office. What he and Whitney needed was time. Time to sort through their problems and build a strong marriage that would withstand any external pressure. Somewhere along the line, they had lost sight of that. But last night, they had recaptured some of the love they'd once shared.

"Enough about last night," he said aloud, lowering himself into his soft leather chair. He was here to work, and work he would.

Javar spent time going through his phone messages, returning the urgent calls and leaving the others for later. Along with the agenda for this morning's meeting, he went over his schedule. The trip to New York next week was something he couldn't put off. He needed to present the interior design team he had hired to the Domning Corporation, the client for whom he was designing a ten-story hotel just outside of Manhattan. He anticipated no problems, but still, this trip could not be avoided. It would only be a day. *Maybe Whitney could come with me,* he thought, a smile lifting the corners of his mouth.

After he finished with his urgent business, including having Melody confirm his travel reservations, Javar headed to the boardroom for the meeting. As he neared the opened double doors, he heard voices.

". . . hear she's had a breakdown. That this second accident sent her over the edge. . . ." That was Kathleen Morrison's voice, one of his project architects.

"Poor thing." That voice belonged to Peter West, Javar's chief draftsperson.

"Apparently, that's why he's got her there. Who knows how long she'll be *recovering,* if she ever completely does."

"Wonder why he's calling this sudden meeting?"

These were people Javar worked with, people he had known to be utmost professionals. Yet they were stooping to rumors and gossip. Whitney's name hadn't been mentioned, but he wasn't stupid. That's who they were talking about. Javar wondered where this spiteful gossip had originated. Melody?

"I can only hope—"

Clearing his throat, Javar stepped into the large boardroom and made his presence known. Kathleen stopped mid-sentence, her face flushed with embarrassment when she saw that Javar was standing in the doorway. Peter flashed a smile at Javar, but the guilty look in his eyes could not be camouflaged.

"Morning, everyone," Javar said, his tone exuberant. He moved to the mahogany boardroom table, taking his place at its head.

Curious eyes from other staff members, and even his associates bored into him as he opened his leather folder and slipped a pen from his tan Armani blazer. Though he felt like throttling Kathleen and Peter for gossiping, he smiled instead. He wanted to get this meeting over with as soon as possible so he could get back to what was really important: Whitney.

At least Richard Sanders, the newest project architect he had hired, had been sitting at the table going over a file instead of participating in gossip. Clearly, Richard had his priorities straight—like being loyal to the boss.

Javar looked around the table. All his project architects were present: Robert Dick, Alex Carlisle, Diane Williams, Kathleen Morrison, Richard Sanders. Peter West sat quietly at the far end of the table. Jerry Price, his junior associate, occupied the second seat down from Javar on the right. The only two missing from this meeting were Harvey Grescoe and Duncan Malloy, his senior associates.

Flicking his wrist forward, Javar eyed the time on his Rolex. Two minutes after ten. He pushed his chair back and was about to rise when the two senior associates came hurrying into the room.

"Sorry," Harvey mumbled as he closed the doors.

Javar tapped his Mont Blanc pen on the table as the two men sat down on either side of him. When they were seated, he opened the meeting. "Good morning, everyone. I know a lot of you have questions about my absence, and I'd like end the speculation by taking a moment to answer those." Lowering her head, Kathleen averted her eyes. Peter was concentrating on the folder before him. Javar continued, "By now, you all must know that my wife was in a car accident a week ago. Well, I'm happy to report that her injuries were not serious and she is now recovering nicely. I've been home with her, supervising her care, but should be back to work full-time next week. To those of you who sent cards and flowers, my wife and I thank you.

"Now, onto company business." Javar looked down at his notes. First, he wanted to know how the final inspection of Simmons's House, a quaint bed-and-breakfast that had been completed a year earlier, had gone. "Alex, how was your trip to Springfield?"

Alex replied, "Simmons's House is doing very well.

Everything is up and running smoothly. The property is in topnotch shape from the shingles on the roof to the plumbing. And the Simmonses are very happy. So far, the bed-and-breakfast is doing extremely well."

"Great," Javar said. It pleased him when his clients were happy, and when the loose ends of a deal were finally tied into a nice bow. He turned his attention to Kathleen. "What's happening with the proposal for the industrial mall in Oak Park?"

"I've narrowed the contenders down to five construction companies," Kathleen explained. "Maybe later, you can look over the list and their packages. . . ."

"Yes, I'll do that." As sole principal, it was Javar who made the final decisions as to which companies they hired.

"I have some news," Harvey announced, and Javar's eyes went to him. "In your absence, I hired an interior designer for the motel in Gary, Indiana. Janine Kelley and her firm."

Javar nodded. "I know her work. It's impressive."

They spoke a while longer about more company business. Peter West and his technicians had successfully completed the blueprints for the Manning Group, a company that had hired Jordan & Associates to design a low-level apartment complex in St. Louis. Jerry Price had finished the miniature model of a strip mall for another client, and both the model and the budget were ready to be presented to the client, who would be flying into Chicago in a week.

Javar closed the meeting, scheduling a second one for that afternoon with his associates so that they could go over more intricate business matters. Everyone filed out of the room, heading back to their respective jobs. Everyone except Richard Sanders.

"Mr. Jordan . . ."

Javar turned and looked into Richard's face. "Yes, Richard?"

"I've come up with a proposed budget for the Li bid. Do you have time to go over it?"

The Li bid. Running a hand over his hair, Javar groaned inwardly. He was still debating forgetting the whole thing, given the time commitments he already had. If he submitted his proposal, if he landed the bid . . . Would that leave any time for Whitney?

There was a solution, Javar realized. There had always been a solution. However, he hadn't wanted to consider it before. But if he was going to make an honest effort at saving their relationship, now was the time.

"Give me the proposed budget," Javar told Richard. "I'll go over it and let you know what I think."

In his mind, he was thinking of the stunned faces of his associates when he made his surprise announcement this afternoon.

When Whitney awoke, she was momentarily startled to find herself in Javar's bed. But only briefly as memories of last night quickly flooded her, making her lips curl. Javar . . . last night . . . everything had been incredible.

"Whitney."

The nurse's voice shocked her, and Whitney whipped her head to the right. Elizabeth dropped a novel and rose from the sofa in the sitting area, a bright smile on her face as she walked toward her.

Whitney's mind scrambled to find a reason for the nurse's presence. After a moment, it did. She remembered being as sick as a dog this morning.

"How are you feeling, Whitney?"

She sat up, gathering part of the down comforter in a bundle on her lap. "I'm a lot better, thank you."

"That's good."

"Where's Javar?"

"He's at work," Elizabeth replied. "I'm not sure when he'll be back."

"Hmm." She felt a strange pull in her stomach. She had

been awake only a few minutes, and already she wondered when Javar would be home.

"Can I get you anything? Some soup?"

Whitney looked up at Elizabeth and smiled. "Soup sounds great." Glancing at the digital clock beside the bed, Whitney exclaimed, "Holy!" It was after two in the afternoon. "I slept that long?"

Crossing her arms over her chest, Elizabeth chuckled. "Clearly your body needed the rest. I'll go get some soup. Is chicken-noodle okay?"

Whitney nodded, and Elizabeth scurried off.

When the nurse was gone, Whitney threw the comforter off her body and got out of the bed. Thank God she felt better; this morning she didn't know if she would survive. All right, she conceded, that was an exaggeration, but still, she'd felt so sick that she was surprised she now was out of bed and walking around.

She moved to the window and looked outside at the front lawn. It was a gorgeous summer day. A light breeze flirted with the leaves of the maple trees and, even though the windows were closed, she could hear the joyful songs of the sparrows among the trees' branches. She wished Javar were here, that they could do something together on this beautiful day. Maybe even take *Lady Love* for a sail.

Whitney stretched, and her stomach fluttered from a residual bout of nausea. A thought invaded her brain for the second time in two days, the thought that maybe she was pregnant. Whitney quickly dismissed that thought. It was absurd . . . wasn't it?

The nurse returned with the food and a smile. On the tray was a large bowl of chicken-noodle soup, beside which was a spoon and a package of crackers. The nurse brought the tray to the sitting area where Whitney was, and Whitney quickly took a seat on the black leather sofa, sinking into its softness, accepting the tray from Elizabeth.

"Thanks," Whitney said, reaching for the spoon.

"Do you need anything else?"

Dipping the spoon into the delicious smelling broth, Whitney replied, "No, I'm fine. Thanks a lot."

"Okay. I'll be downstairs if you need me." Elizabeth walked a few steps, then stopped suddenly and turned around. "Oh, let me get your antibiotic. The infection may be gone, but you have to finish the prescription as a precaution."

"Of course."

It was when Elizabeth handed her the pill cup that the thought hit her. Whitney bristled at the implication, fear crawling down her spine. No, it couldn't be.

"Whitney . . . your water."

Whitney's head flew up. She saw Elizabeth holding a glass of water. "Uh . . . no. I mean, I'll take it with the soup. I don't want to mix hot and cold."

Elizabeth stood above her, waiting.

"The soup's a bit too hot," Whitney explained. "I'll take the pill in a few minutes." At Elizabeth's skeptical look, Whitney added, "I promise."

When Elizabeth left the room, Whitney dropped the yellow-and-white capsule into her hand, staring down at it as her brain worked overtime. Then, she went to the nurse's stand and opened the other two bottles that contained the painkiller and the capsule for stress. She thought hard.

Last night, after she had taken the stress medication and painkiller, she had awoken feeling wretched. She had also awoken feeling nauseous the morning before—after having taken these pills.

Since the accident, she hadn't felt one hundred percent. The pills were to aid her in her recovery, but now that she thought about it, she couldn't be sure whether the pills had helped her at all.

A weird, numbing sensation swept over Whitney, causing her legs to wobble. She stepped backward until her legs hit the mattress, and it was then that her knees buckled. She fell onto the king-sized bed. Suddenly, she was horrified.

Was somebody trying to *kill* her?

"No," she said aloud, rising. The antibiotic in hand, she marched back to the sitting area and her soup. She was expecting too much too soon. Despite the fact that the accident hadn't been life threatening, she was hardly as healthy as she had been before. She had to expect bouts of nausea, headaches, and any other type of temporary discomfort until she recovered completely.

Deciding that it was the stress of the accident that had her conjuring such crazy ideas, Whitney tilted her head back, opened her mouth, and dropped the pill inside.

She couldn't believe that Derrick was right. There was no way that Javar wanted her dead.

Chapter Eighteen

"What?" Duncan Malloy asked, his eyes wide with shock.

"You're kidding," Harvey Grescoe added, seconding Duncan's surprise.

Harvey and Duncan both sat on the opposite side of Javar's desk. Javar crossed one leg over the other as he sat in the swivel chair in his office, then eyed each one in turn squarely. "I couldn't be more serious."

"But . . ." Duncan began. "Why now?"

A smile played at the corners of Javar's mouth. "Everything's okay on the home front, if that's what you're asking. I've just . . . had a sudden change of heart."

Harvey swallowed, apparently speechless.

"Well?" Javar said. "Does your reaction mean neither of you is interested in a partnership?"

"Of course I'm interested," Harvey replied. "I've been interested in a partnership for a long time. You know that. It's just that I'm . . . surprised. This seems sudden."

"It's something I've been considering for a long time. And since I couldn't narrow my choice down to one of you, I decided to offer you both a chance at a partnership, and see who'd be interested." He shifted his gaze to Duncan. "Duncan?"

"I'm definitely interested, but I'd like to think about it."

Javar nodded. "That's fine. I don't expect an answer today." He inhaled deeply. This hadn't been as hard as he had anticipated. And instead of dreading the thought of taking on a partner or two, Javar now felt a sense of relief. He had worked with both Harvey and Duncan for years. He valued their talent as well as their friendship. And it was time he rewarded them with the offer of a partnership in Jordan & Associates.

Minutes later, Javar rose and saw both men to the door.

"Thanks again, Javar," Duncan said. "I'll let you know."

"I look forward to your decision," Javar said.

As Duncan stepped into the hallway, Harvey lingered. When Duncan was out of earshot, Harvey turned to Javar and said, "Better get ready to change the company signs. I don't need anymore time. I accept your offer of a partnership. Whenever you want to go over the details, I'm ready."

Javar and Harvey shook hands, then agreed to wait for Duncan's decision before discussing the actual business of the partnership.

When Harvey was gone, Javar walked back to his desk, a wry smile lifting his lips. He hadn't thought about the company name, and thus the signs. No longer would the signs and stationery read Jordan & Associates. They would read Jordan, Grescoe & Associates, or Jordan, Grescoe, Malloy & Associates. Yikes. His baby would no longer be only his.

But despite the thought, Javar smiled. Whitney would definitely approve.

"C'mon, Whitney," Derrick said into the receiver. "Pick up."

"Hello?" It was the butler, Carlos, who answered the phone.

"Carlos," Derrick said. "This is Derrick Lawson calling again. Is Whitney awake yet?"

"Yes, she's awake, Mr. Lawson. But she's not here."

"Not there?" Derrick's stomach fluttered. "Where is she?"

"She stepped out. She may be down by the beach."

Derrick blew out an irritated breath. "All right," he said, his mind contemplating what to do. "Look, can you tell her that I called? That she should call me as soon as she gets in?"

"Certainly, Mr. Lawson," Carlos said.

Derrick broke the connection, then sat silently for a moment. In his moment of repose, the door to his office burst open.

"Lawson," a male voice said in an urgent tone.

Derrick spun around and faced Detective Kurt Mulvany. His face was contorted with both anxiety and excitement. Instantly, Derrick was on his feet, knowing that something was wrong.

"Lawson, remember Whitfield?"

Derrick nodded. How could he forget Whitfield? He was one of the biggest drug dealers in the Chicago area, but he somehow always evaded the law. "What about Evan Whitfield?"

"Just got a call from an informant. Says he knows where Whitfield hides his stash and can lead us to him. The captain is sending us both out on this one. C'mon. We've got to move now."

Adrenaline surged through Derrick's veins as he grabbed his light blazer and followed Kurt out of the office. Both men—every cop in the city of Chicago, in fact—had wanted to nail Whitfield for a very long time.

Duty called now, which meant that Derrick wouldn't be able to talk to Whitney until much, much later.

                              *   *   *

Curtis Nichols paced the beige tile floor in the garden
room of his home, listening to the hollow sounds of his
wife Michelle and his mother-in-law Angela's laughter. He,
Michelle, their son, Michael and his parents-in-law had just
finished dinner. The dinner had been a reunion of sorts,
as Marcus had just returned from a week's conference in
Miami for plastic surgeons.

It should have been a cheerful event, and yes, there was
laughter. However, not even the laughter and smiles could
cover the sour atmosphere.

As if he sensed Curtis's thoughts, Michael came running
into the room. He wrapped an arm around his father's
leg.

"Where's Uncle Javar?" Michael asked, surprising the
adults in the room. "Why isn't he here too?"

Michelle's laughter stopped cold. Her eyes grew wide.
As she held her daughter on her lap, Sarah's small hand
grabbed at Michelle's lips but Michelle didn't seem to
notice. "Michael," Michelle began, "I already told you
Uncle Javar couldn't make it tonight. He's busy."

"But why?" Michael demanded. "He always comes
over." When Michelle said nothing, Michael looked up at
Curtis.

Curtis shrugged. Before bending to lift his son, he cast
a perturbed glance at Michelle. She had gone too far when
she gave Javar that stupid ultimatum. The fact that Javar
wasn't here now, when he usually would have been, wasn't
lost on his young son. And the circumstances under which
Javar was not here was what made this evening seem so
fake.

Curtis could not, however, tell Michael that his mother
had ordered his uncle to stay away unless he did what she
wanted. Instead, he said to Michael, "You know your uncle
can be very busy sometimes. I'm sure he would be here if
he could be."

"But I never got to show him my new police car last time. I want him to see it."

"I know," Curtis said, hugging his son close. Over Michael's shoulder, he glowered at Michelle, who was watching him intently. "But why don't we call him a little later, see if he can come by sometime soon?"

"Okay," Michael agreed. Curtis returned his son to the floor and watched as he ran out of the room.

Walking toward Michelle, Curtis said, "Do you see what you're doing? It's not right, you keeping Javar away from our son. Michael's the one who's suffering."

"What's going on?" Marcus asked, his forehead wrinkled as he looked from his wife to his daughter to his son-in-law.

Curtis arched a brow, challenging Michelle to tell her father the story.

Michelle rolled her eyes to the ceiling and frowned. "I . . ." she began. "I told Javar that as long as Whitney is staying at his place, not to bother coming over here."

"Aw, for goodness' sake!" Marcus uttered, rising from the wicker chair. "He's your brother, Michelle. Why would you do that?"

"Because he's letting a murderer stay in his house!" Michelle retorted.

"We tried to talk to him," Angela added, rising to meet her husband. "He won't listen to reason."

"I'm gone a week and this is what happens?" Marcus asked, disapproval showing on his face.

"What was I supposed to do? Tell him that I approved of Whitney coming back into his life?"

"You were supposed to keep your nose in your own business," Marcus replied, pinning her with level stare.

Sarah started to fuss, and sighing, Michelle rocked her, trying to calm her down. She said, "Dad, you don't understand."

Angela placed a hand on her husband's arm. "Of course

we love Javar. But after we showed him the pictures and he chose to ignore our concerns, we felt—''

"Those stupid pictures," Marcus said scathingly. "When are you going to get over this?"

"Our son is going to ruin his life if he reconciles with Whitney!" Angela's tone rose an octave.

Sarah burst into tears. Groaning, Michelle stood and walked out of the room.

Curtis followed her, leaving Angela and Marcus arguing in the garden room. When he caught up with Michelle, he said, "Sooner or later, Michelle, you're going to have to grow up. Accept responsibility for your life, not Javar's. He's a grown man. As much as you may not like his choices, you cannot meddle in his life."

Shaking her head, Michelle rolled her eyes again. "He's my brother," was all she said before she stalked off.

Curtis grunted when she was out of sight. Her obsession with Whitney Jordan was taking its toll on their relationship. He guessed it was also taking a toll on Angela and Marcus's relationship, as well.

Javar was at the door of his office when the phone rang. He stopped mid-stride, contemplating whether or not he should answer it. It was already early evening, although he had only planned on spending half a day in the office. Taking care of business had taken more time than he had hoped.

Turning around, Javar decided to answer it. Another message on top of the ones he already had was not what he needed. He grabbed the receiver. "Javar Jordan."

"Ja-va-r!" his brother almost sang. "What's up, guy?"

Javar's face broke into a smile. "Hey, Khamil. I'm fine, man. Fine."

"You still coming to New York?"

"Oh yeah," Javar replied, his tone saying that the possibility of doubt didn't exist. "I'm leaving Sunday night."

"I was beginning to wonder. I hadn't heard from you. . . ."

"I know. I've been busy. Real busy."

"So I hear. What's this about Whitney being back in town? Mom told me she's staying at your place."

Javar groaned. "Don't start. I've heard enough from Mom and Michelle, man."

"Start what?" Khamil asked. "I'm not going to give you a hard time. You know me better than that."

Nodding, Javar said, "Yeah, I do." His brother had let him live his own life, and if he had any opinions of what Javar did or didn't do, he kept them to himself. "It's just that Mom's driving me crazy here. I can just imagine what she told you about Whitney. . . ."

"Hey," Khamil said, cutting him off. "I'm a lawyer, remember? I'm good at sifting through fact and fiction. Don't sweat it."

"Sorry," Javar said.

"So, how is Whitney? She had an accident?"

"Mmm hmm." Javar explained to his brother the events of the past week, and how Whitney was now recovering.

"That's great to hear." Khamil paused. "So, does this mean that you two are getting back together?"

"Is that what Mom told you?"

"Forget what Mom said. I'm asking you."

Javar exhaled deeply. Despite last night, it was too soon to say what would happen for him and Whitney. He said, "We're seeing if we can work things out."

"All right, J." The enthusiasm in Khamil's voice indicated his sincerity. "I always did like Whitney."

"You mean you've gotten over the fact that she chose me over you?"

"Hey . . ." Khamil protested, but there was laughter in his voice. "I *let* her choose you. I had too many other women, remember?"

Javar chuckled. "Sure. Speaking of women, anyone you're serious about yet?"

"I'm serious about my work."

"All right," Javar said, agreeing not to press his brother. One of these days he would find the right woman. "Sooner or later you're going to have to give up that playboy lifestyle."

"Just let me know if things don't work out with you and Whitney," Khamil said, mirth in his voice. "She still as fine as she used to be?"

"What do you think?" Javar asked, a vision of Whitney's long smooth legs invading his mind. His wife was fine all right.

"You better hold onto her, J. You may not luck out and find a woman as hot as her a second time."

"Really?" Javar said, lowering himself into his swivel chair. He had a feeling this conversation would not end soon.

"Hey, you can't help it if you weren't born with my good looks." Khamil was laughing.

"Remind me not to invite you to our second wedding," Javar said. But he was laughing too.

Whitney sensed Javar's presence before she actually heard him. Sitting up on the lawn chair, she turned around.

Javar's lips curled into a smile as he looked at her. "Hi."

Relief washed over Whitney. Seeing Javar now, smiling at her with such warmth, she knew that he cared deeply for her. He was not responsible for any attack on her life. "Hi," she said softly.

Javar walked toward her. He held his blazer over a shoulder, and the top buttons of his cotton shirt were undone. As usual, he looked incredibly sexy. As usual, she felt drawn to him.

When Javar reached the lawn chair, he reached out and stroked Whitney's face. "I take it you're feeling better."

"Yes," Whitney replied, holding Javar's hand against her

face. Bringing his hand to her lips, she kissed his warm flesh. A hint of his musky cologne flirted with her nose, and Whitney took a deep breath, trying to ignore the feeling stirring in the pit of her belly.

Javar squatted, then leaned forward and planted a soft kiss on her lips. "I missed you today."

"I missed you too." Whitney smiled. "How was work?"

"I did something that I think you'll be proud of."

"What?" Whitney asked, her eyes narrowing as she flashed Javar a quizzical look.

"Today, I offered my senior associates a partnership in the company."

"What?" Whitney's mouth fell open.

"I said, I offered my senior associates a partnership in the company."

"You're not kidding?" Whitney asked, stunned. Jordan & Associates meant everything to him, and before, Javar hadn't even wanted to consider giving up his majority share.

"No," Javar said, "I'm not kidding. I meant it when I said that I wanted us to save our marriage. Having a partner or two will mean less work for me, and more time to spend with you."

Touched was how Whitney felt. Genuinely touched. And dare she think it, loved. She framed Javar's face with both hands. "Javar . . . I know how much your firm means to you."

"But you mean more." Rising, Javar changed the subject. "There's still some time before the sun sets. How about going down to Grant Park? The Taste of Chicago is still going on."

Grabbing Javar's extended hand, Whitney stood. "Oooh, you sure know how to tempt me." The Taste of Chicago was an annual affair, where culinary delights were served by more than seventy of Chicago's finest restaurants. Whitney and Javar had gone together for the two years that they were married, feasting on the extraordinary food as well as enjoying the various entertainment. Looking down at her white sundress, Whitney asked, "I don't have to get changed, do I?"

"No," Javar replied, wrapping his arms around Whitney and pulling her close. "But I do."

"You look fine. Great, actually."

"But a little too formal for where we're going." He kissed her forehead. "Want to come with me upstairs while I change?"

Whitney chuckled. "Oh, I don't think so. We could get . . . delayed."

"Some delays are good," Javar said, cocking his head to the side.

Whitney pulled out of his embrace. She was tempted. . . . But no. They should go out. Sex was only one part of their relationship, and they had proven that they were still compatible that way. They needed to prove that they could spend an evening together, doing something as a couple and still enjoy each other's company. "Go get changed. I'll meet you in the foyer."

Biting on his lower lip, Javar flashed Whitney a mock-dejected look. Whitney smiled wryly, then shook her head. Javar turned, jogging into the house.

It took him only minutes to change and meet her downstairs. "Want to take the BMW?" Javar asked.

"Your car was found?" Whitney asked.

"Mmm hmm," Javar replied. "I've got it back and it's as good as new. I'm itching to take it for a spin."

"Sure," Whitney said.

Javar slipped his hand into hers, holding it tightly. "It's in the garage."

They shared a look then, a look that said they'd both like to forget the festival and go back upstairs. Whitney swallowed, trying to shake the feeling.

"Let's go," Whitney said to Javar. She giggled as he groaned.

Seconds later, they were at the garage door. Javar closed

the door, then entered the security code into the box on the wall. While he fiddled with that, Whitney walked ahead of him into the garage.

Her eyes roamed the four-car garage, but she didn't see the black BMW. The red Viper was there, the gold Jeep Cherokee, the black convertible Mercedes, and . . .

Whitney froze. Her eyes focused on the car that looked familiar, the one that looked like the BMW Javar loved. But the car she saw was not black.

It was the same 700 series BMW, she suddenly realized, but it was now a deep maroon as opposed to its original black.

Oh, God, Whitney thought, her stomach fluttering as the implication of the realization hit her.

God help her.

Chapter Nineteen

Whitney's eyes darted to Javar's. "You . . . you painted your car?"

Javar nodded. "Yeah. You don't like it?"

Whitney walked down the garage steps, moving to the BMW. With a fresh paint job, the car looked brand-new. She didn't know why, but an icy numbness spread through her body, enveloping her in fear.

Yes, she did know why. Because Derrick had said that the car that had run her off the road was black. Because Javar's car was conveniently reported stolen around the time of her accident. And now, it had a new paint job, erasing any possible evidence.

"Whitney? Is something wrong?"

When Whitney looked up, Javar was already at the driver's side door, while she stood at the base of the steps, immobile. "Why?"

"Why what? Why'd I paint the car?"

Whitney nodded.

"Because there was some damage to the car when the

police found it. I figured I may as well paint the whole thing a new color. I was getting tired of black, anyway."

"Oh."

"Well, are you coming, or are you waiting for me to come and get you?" Javar raised a suggestive eyebrow.

Okay, Whitney. Don't drive yourself crazy. This doesn't mean anything. And it didn't. This was just a coincidence. The new paint job had nothing to do with her accident. Deep down, she would know, feel it in her gut if Javar was lying to her. She wouldn't be falling for him . . . again.

Javar was walking toward her. "You *do* want me to come get you?"

Whitney shook off the unpleasant thoughts and forced a smile just before Javar wrapped an arm around her waist and drew her close. He planted a soft, lingering kiss on her lips, and despite Whitney's thoughts of only a few minutes ago, her body warmed.

Javar broke the kiss and locked eyes with hers. "We can always go back upstairs. . . ."

Shaking her head, Whitney said, "No. I'm looking forward to the festival." Slipping out of his embrace she moved to the car. "Let's go."

Their bellies full—his anyway—Javar and Whitney now lay side by side on a blanket in Grant Park. Each propped up on an elbow, they looked out at the water and the various boats sailing in the distance.

There was a light breeze that played with Whitney's raven hair, tossing it every which way. Whitney had long given up trying to keep it down. Whether a perfectly styled coif or a wind-messed one, his wife still looked gorgeous. With her facial bruises covered by makeup, she looked healthy. The only sign that she'd been in an accident was the bandage on her forehead.

Javar reached out, stroking her face. Whitney's eyes turned to him, and she smiled.

"I want to ask you something," Javar said.

"Go ahead."

"Next week, I have to go to New York on business. I was wondering if you'd come with me."

Whitney's eyes narrowed. "Really? You never used to—"

"I know, but that was before." He trailed a thumb over her lips, tempted to replace his finger with his mouth. "I have to leave Sunday night, and I was thinking that if you went with me, we could check out a Broadway play, or something. Oh, and Khamil says he'd like to see you."

"Khamil . . . How is he? I haven't seen him in ages."

"He's fine. Busy."

"Does he have a girlfriend yet?"

Javar rolled his eyes playfully. "You know Khamil. He's like Teflon when it comes to women. Nonstick."

Whitney chuckled. "Yeah, I remember. New York . . ."

"It would only be for a day. I'd really like you to come with me."

"And while you're doing your business?"

"You'll be getting pampered. How does a day at the spa sound?"

Whitney moaned. "Mmm. That sounds wonderful."

"So you'll come?"

"Do I look like I'm crazy? Of course I'll come!" She laughed.

Whitney's enthusiasm was addictive. Javar laughed along with her, leaning close and pressing his nose against hers. God, it felt so good just sitting around like this and laughing. How had he ever lost sight of the important things in life? What good was working hard, earning a ton of money, if you couldn't share it with someone you loved? If you couldn't laugh or love?

As Javar pulled back and stared into the eyes of his wife,

he knew without a doubt that their days ahead would be filled with plenty of laughter. And love.

"Grandma Beryl!" Whitney exclaimed, jumping up from the quilt on which she sat. "What are you doing here?"

Grandma Beryl cocked a slim hip as she flashed Whitney a mock-indignant look. "I have to eat, too, now don't I?"

Chuckling, Whitney drew Grandma Beryl into her arms for a big, warm hug. "It's so good to see you, Grandma."

Grandma Beryl squeezed Whitney tightly. "Whitney, dear. Oh, I'm so happy to see you up and around." Slipping out of Whitney's arms, Grandma Beryl moved to Javar and wrapped her arms around her grandson.

"Hey, Gram," Javar said, stooping to kiss her on the cheek.

"Javar, I can't believe you're here watching a sunset, instead of at the office."

Javar chuckled, then flashed Whitney a look that said his new outlook on life was because of her. Turning back to his grandmother, Javar said, "Well? Aren't you going to introduce us to your . . . friend?"

Grandma Beryl turned back to the elderly gentleman who was with her, placing a hand on his upper arm. The man was probably just shy of six feet, and slim. His skin was the shade of a shelled almond, and his eyes were a distinct green. "Henry," Grandma Beryl began, a hint of pride in her voice, "meet my grandson, Javar. The one I've told you so much about."

"Good things, I hope," Javar said.

Henry chortled. "Of course." He extended a hand and Javar shook it. "Pleased to meet you, Javar."

"Likewise," Javar said.

Grandma Beryl smiled as she waved a hand in Whitney's direction. "And this is Javar's beautiful wife, Whitney."

"Hi," Henry said, shaking Whitney's hand firmly.

"Hello, Henry," Whitney said, a bright smile on her lips. To Grandma Beryl, she raised a curious eyebrow. Grandma Beryl averted her gaze, seeming to blush. Whitney would have to ask her about Henry later. He seemed nice enough, still extremely attractive despite a few wrinkles, and judging from the way Grandma Beryl was holding onto his arm, he was someone special.

"It makes me so happy to see you two out, *together,*" Grandma Beryl said. "I take it things are going well?"

Whitney glanced up at Javar and found him looking at her too. His eyes seemed to ask her if she was going to answer the question or if he should.

Javar took the lead, nodding as he returned his gaze to his grandmother. "I'd say ... things are going very well. Wouldn't you, Whitney?"

Forced to answer his question on the spot, unwanted questions and doubts suddenly invaded Whitney's mind. She wanted things to work out, and they seemed to be. . . . Smiling shyly, she replied, "Yes. Things are definitely looking up."

Grandma Beryl squealed with delight. "Oh, I knew it. I'm so happy for you. A love like yours doesn't come along twice in a lifetime . . ." She paused, then cast a sidelong glance at Henry. "Unless you're extremely lucky."

So Henry was a *very* special man in Grandma Beryl's life. As Javar pulled Whitney closer, she smiled at the thought that her grandmother had found happiness again. Grandma Beryl definitely seemed to be in love. If anyone deserved to be happy, it was Grandma Beryl.

Would she find that kind of happiness again, Whitney wondered fleetingly. With Javar? They were getting closer, but . . .

"What were you two doing?" Javar asked, interrupting Whitney's thoughts.

"We were going to walk along the beach," Grandma Beryl replied. "Burn off some of the calories we just ate!"

"Feel like company?" Javar asked.

Grandma Beryl's thin lips lifted in a wide smile. "You bet."

"What a day, what a day," Derrick said, plopping himself on the plush sofa in his small living room. Evan Whitfield, Chicago's biggest cocaine dealer, was now behind bars.

His heart still beat rapidly from the excitement of the hunt, then the catch. Having found Whitfield's 'warehouse,' Derrick and five other detectives were able to catch Whitfield red-handed. Twelve kilos of cocaine had been seized, with a street value of more than three hundred thousand dollars.

Derrick threw his head back. His sense of victory was minimal. Yes, he was thrilled that Evan Whitfield was behind bars, but there was another pressing concern. Whitney. He needed to tell her about the latest development in her case.

Raising his head, Derrick glanced at the wall clock. It was eleven thirty-three. It was late, but he still had to chance calling her. In the long run, despite her doubts now, she would thank him. Javar was a dangerous man.

Derrick reached for the phone on the end table. Cradling the receiver between his ear and shoulder, he punched in the digits to Javar's home.

The phone began to ring.

When Whitney and Javar stepped into the house through the garage, the phone was ringing.

Javar's forehead wrinkled with speculation. "Who's calling here this time of night?"

Whitney shrugged. "Hmm. I wonder. Aren't you going to answer it?"

Javar looked down at her, his eyes getting a shade darker as his desire pooled in their depths. "Nah."

"But it could be important."

"If it's important, whoever it is will call back," Javar said simply. "Preferably tomorrow." As he pulled Whitney into his arms, he made it clear that he had other things on his mind. Things much more important than answering the telephone.

Whitney swallowed as the flame of passion stroked her body. After a wonderful evening, she now wanted to be with Javar. No intrusions.

"Okay," she whispered, slipping her hands around his neck. "Let it ring."

Chapter Twenty

Soft, whimpering sounds lured Javar out of sleep. Bolting upright, he realized that Whitney wasn't beside him.

The bathroom light was on. Jumping out of bed, Javar ran into the ensuite bathroom, the sense of déjà vu hitting him as he saw Whitney naked on the floor, crouched over the toilet . . . again. The stench of vomit filled the air. What was happening to her, Javar wondered as he ran to her side. The distressed moans coming from her lips pained him as though someone had stuck a knife in his gut.

"Whitney." He felt so helpless as he looked at her and the vomit that covered the floor. "Oh, God."

She wrapped an arm around his neck and sagged against his chest. "Javar. I feel . . ."

"Shh. I'm here now. It's going to be okay." A reaction to alcohol, his foot. Last night, Whitney hadn't had a drop of alcohol. If she was in this kind of pain, then there was something else wrong besides mixing alcohol with her medications. He was taking her to the hospital. God, what if she had internal injuries from the accident?

"Hang on, honey," Javar said, bringing her to the bed

so that he could put some clothes on her. "I'm going to get you some help."

An hour after Javar had brought Whitney to Rush North Shore Medical Hospital, he paced the floor in the waiting room, anxious to see the doctor. Dr. Adu-Bohene, whom he would have preferred to deal with, was not working this early in the morning, so Javar had no idea who was supervising Whitney's care.

Hearing footsteps, Javar turned around. A tall, lanky gray-haired man approached him. Dressed in a white lab coat with a picture ID on his lapel, the man was clearly a doctor.

"Mr. Jordan?" the physician asked.

"Yes." Javar nodded. "Yes, that's me. How is my wife?"

"Your wife," the doctor announced, a grim expression etched on his pale face, "is suffering from an opiate overdose."

"Wh-overdose? What are you talking about?" Javar asked.

"Morphine," the doctor said, explaining the type of overdose in layman's terms. "Urine tests determined that your wife is suffering from a morphine overdose. That's what's causing the nausea."

"My God."

"We've got her in a room, and we're administering the antidote, naloxone, through an intravenous tube to counter the effects of the morphine. She can't go home yet."

Javar was too stunned to speak. An overdose? How, why? What on earth was going on?

The doctor spoke. "Do you know anything about this?"

Javar flashed the older man an incredulous look. "Of course not. My wife . . . she was recently in a car accident, and she's been under the care of a nurse." He paused, ran a hand over his face. "None of this makes sense. The nurse was regulating her medications. As far as I know, she wasn't even taking morphine."

"Not even for pain?"

"No," Javar said, resolutely. "She was taking Tylenol for pain. Penicillin for an infection. And a stress tablet, lora—"

"Lorazepam," the doctor completed. "You say she had a nurse supervising her care."

Nodding, Javar said, "Yes." His breaths were shallow as he faced the fact that this wasn't a nightmare. Somehow, Whitney had suffered a morphine overdose. "Is she going to be okay? I have to know."

"Yes. She'll be fine. A morphine overdose usually causes nausea, grogginess, a sense of euphoria sometimes, but it can also lead to death. Your wife is very lucky."

Javar grunted, squeezing his forehead with a palm. "Damn it! Why is this happening?"

"I'd like to speak to the nurse, verify the medications she gave Whitney."

Javar swallowed. Tried to relax. "Okay. Sure. You can call her. She should be home." He gave the doctor the number. "If she doesn't answer the phone, let me know. I can . . . go wake her."

"Thanks."

The doctor turned to leave, but Javar darted toward him, placing a hand on his arm. "I . . . can I see her?"

"Not yet, Mr. Jordan. But the moment we've stopped the antidote, someone will come out and get you."

After being assured that Whitney would be asleep for hours, Javar decided to return home and question Elizabeth himself. It didn't matter that it wasn't quite six A.M. He stormed down the hallway to her room, pounding on the door when he got there.

Elizabeth opened the bedroom door moments later,

holding the two open ends of her pink robe closed. "What's going on?"

"Why don't you tell me?" Javar asked, stalking into the bedroom.

The nurse flashed him a perplexed look. "What are you talking about?"

"Whitney is in the hospital," Javar announced, glowering at her. "She's apparently overdosed on morphine. Care to explain that?"

"Morphine? I have no idea—"

"Don't you? You're her nurse."

"Yes," the nurse said, taking a step backward. "But I didn't give her any morphine. She was taking Tylenol for her pain."

"That's what I thought," Javar hissed. "Until I found out otherwise."

The nurse seemed flustered, speechless.

Someone was trying to poison Whitney. Trying to kill her. The realization knocked the air from Javar's lungs. God, how had this happened? Had the nurse been paid off by somebody to switch Whitney's medication? She had to have been, because she didn't know Whitney personally. But who? Stephanie?

"Who paid you?" Javar asked, anger causing his voice to rise.

"I . . . I work for you, Mr. Jordan."

Javar took a threatening step toward the nurse whom he had trusted. The nurse who had betrayed him. "Stop lying to me! Who paid you to poison my wife?"

Tears glistened in Elizabeth's eyes. "I . . . I don't know what . . ."

Unable to look into the woman's face, Javar turned around and walked to the bedroom door. "I want you out of here Ms. Monroe. I'll give you an hour."

Then he was out of her room and making his way to his bedroom. There, he collected the bottles of medication that Whitney had taken on a daily basis since the nurse's arrival. Javar pocketed the three bottles, then headed back downstairs. He was going to get to the bottom of this, if it was the last thing he did.

Whitney awoke slowly. Her eyelids were heavy and hardly wanted to open, but sensing unfamiliar surroundings, she opened them wide and looked around.

She was in a hospital. Again. Why?

Glancing to the right, she saw Javar's form by the window, where the early morning sunlight was beginning to light the sky. She called to him. "Javar."

Javar whipped his head around, moving to Whitney's bed in three quick strides. "Hey," he said, smiling. "You're finally awake."

Whitney looked at Javar through narrowed eyes, knowing that with his cheeriness he was trying to avoid the reason that she was here. Well, she would get the answers she needed. "Javar, why am I here?"

Pain crossed over his features, and Javar released a hurried breath.

"What is it?" Whitney asked, her heart racing. "What?"

Javar lifted her hand into his, staring into her eyes. "Whitney, the reason you've been feeling so sick, vomiting . . . is because you've suffered a . . . a morphine overdose."

"*Morphine?* I haven't been taking morphine."

"You thought you weren't, but apparently, you were. I brought in your medications, and the doctor has confirmed it. The stress tablet and the painkiller had both been tampered with, consisting of morphine instead of what you thought you were taking. The penicillin was the only pill not tampered with."

She heard his words, but her brain didn't want to accept what he was actually saying. "Wh-what do you mean, tampered with?"

"I fired the nurse," Javar said in response. "I figure

someone, maybe Stephanie, paid her to switch your medications." Javar sighed. "Gosh, I don't know."

No. Whitney shook her head, unable to believe Javar. Oh, God. Someone really wanted her dead. Someone really was going to stop at no lengths to make sure she was out of the way.

Derrick believed that person was Javar. Pinning him with a suspicious gaze, Whitney stared into his eyes, hoping to find the truth there. Could it be true? Could Javar want her dead?

Motive, means, opportunity. Javar had them all.

Javar's eyes narrowed as he analyzed her gaze, then widened in disbelief. "Tell me you don't think I had anything to do with this. . . ."

Whitney tore her eyes from Javar's, her heart aching. "I . . ." Her voice faltered, but somehow she found the strength to continue. "I don't know what to believe."

Javar rose, indignation flashing in his eyes. "C'mon, Whitney. You know I had nothing to do with this."

Did she? Her heart didn't want to believe the horrible possibility, but her brain . . . God help her, she didn't know what to believe. She didn't trust Javar. "I don't . . ." Whitney's voice broke. "Too much has happened, Javar. Too many crazy things since I moved into your house."

"Our house," Javar retorted, stressing the words. "And I'm as baffled by all this as you are, believe me."

"I need time." Whitney couldn't look at him. It was too painful.

"Time? For what?"

"To think, Javar!" Whitney replied, frustration evident in her voice. "Please, just go."

"No. I'm not going to leave you. Not now."

Whitney whimpered. Her heart was breaking and she couldn't do anything to stop it. "Javar . . . please."

"Why are you doing this?" he asked, sounding sincerely perplexed. "I love you, Whitney."

Those were words she had longed to hear, yet Whitney

cringed, her stomach aching. They had been trying to work things out, and Javar's proclamation of love should have warmed her heart. Instead, she was so confused that all she could feel was pain. If Javar had been behind the attacks on her life, then everything he had said about wanting to reconcile was a lie, and that hurt more than she thought she could bear. This was what she had feared most; trusting Javar again, giving him the power to crush her heart.

"If you really care about me, you'll leave."

Javar shook his head. "No. I'm not going to leave you. Not until you tell me that you don't think I would ever hurt you."

Whitney met his eyes then. She thought she saw genuine distress there, as well as confusion. God, this was so hard. She wrenched her gaze away, settling back on the bed.

"Whitney?"

She said nothing, unable to give Javar what he wanted. How could she, when she didn't know the truth?

Javar groaned, and Whitney sensed resignation in his tone. Finally, she heard his soft footfalls as he walked away.

When he left the room, the tears came. Didn't stop. Couldn't stop.

Letting Javar back into her heart had been a mistake. They didn't have a future.

Let that be Whitney, Derrick thought as he rushed out of his apartment bathroom and hurried to the living room phone. *Please.*

Grabbing the receiver, he brought it to his ear. "Hello?"

"Derrick."

She sounded breathless, like she had been crying. Derrick propped himself against the arm of his sofa. "Whitney, is that you?"

"Yes."

She *had* been crying, Derrick realized. Instinctively, he

knew that Javar had caused her tears. "What happened Whitney? What did Javar do?"

"I'm in the hospital," Whitney explained. "I've overdosed . . . on morphine."

"What?" Whitney overdosed on a painkiller? He found that extremely hard to believe.

"I didn't take it. Well, I didn't know I was taking it. I thought I was taking my prescribed medications, but instead . . ."

"Someone tampered with your medication?"

"Yeah," Whitney replied softly.

"And you think it was Javar?"

"I don't know," Whitney admitted. "I don't know what to think. I keep thinking about what you said."

Derrick paused, preparing for the next blow he would deliver. "There's something else you should know. About the accident."

"What?" Whitney asked, the pitch of her voice rising.

"Well," Derrick began, somberness lacing his voice. "I've got a definite lead in your case."

"You do?" She almost sounded like she didn't want to know.

"Yeah. I spoke with a witness to your accident yesterday. She says she definitely saw a car tailing you that night. Her impression of the event was that someone tried to run you off the road."

"Oh, don't say that, Derrick. Don't tell me that."

"Whitney, I know this isn't easy, but from what you've told me, it's pretty obvious now that someone has been out to get you since you came back to Chicago. And the witness's version of events makes that fact even harder to dismiss. I don't know. Maybe the accident wasn't deliberate. Maybe it was some teenager out for a joyride who got a bit stupid."

"The accident happened more than a week ago. Why didn't this witness come forward sooner?"

"She was frightened. She thought maybe the driver of

the other car got a look at her, and would come after her if she went to the police."

"And now?"

"Now, her conscious was getting the better of her."

There was a pause, then Whitney asked, "Well, did she get a look at the driver?"

Derrick shook his head. "No. But she did get a look at the car."

Whitney blew out a hurried breath into the receiver. She asked, "What kind of car was it?"

"A late model, top-of-the-line BMW. Definitely black."

Whitney felt a sharp pain in her chest, and she brought a hand to her heart. "Oh, no. No."

"What is it?" Derrick asked. "What's the matter?"

"Javar . . . he . . ." This was too hard. So many coincidences! Or were they? Was Javar as guilty as he now looked?

"What? Javar what?"

"His BMW . . . it was black. Now, it's maroon. He just had it painted."

"What hospital are you at?" Derrick asked, the words coming out in a rush.

Whitney told him the hospital, and the room number.

"Have you called the police yet?"

"No," Whitney replied, hardly able to breathe.

"Okay. Hang tight. I'm on my way."

Whitney replaced the receiver, then lay back on the hospital bed. Her lungs hurt as they strained to take in air, as the oxygen strained to flow through her blood. Her mind pounded as it searched for answers, searched to make sense of this whole sordid situation.

Javar . . . What hurt the most was that she had allowed herself to hope, to dream. And now, that dream had come crashing down. Maybe Derrick could take her to Javar's to collect her things. She couldn't stay at his house any longer; that was certain. Not when she knew the truth.

No, she conceded with a frown. She didn't know the truth. She knew what Derrick suspected. She knew what Javar said. And man, was she ever confused.

She heaved a wistful sigh. Just a couple of nights ago, she and Javar had gotten over a hurdle and come close to recapturing what they had lost. How could she believe that the Javar who had courted her so lovingly in recent days could possibly want to kill her? Remembering those days, her mind couldn't even contemplate that reality.

But then there was the Javar who had lost his son, the Javar who blamed her for J.J.'s death. Could his sweet words and whispered promises really be some sick plan to get her to trust him again, only so that he could get close enough to kill her?

Her heart fluttered in her chest, as if telling her that it couldn't believe that. But her brain . . . There were facts she couldn't deny. Regardless, this test of her faith had proven to her one crucial thing: she didn't have a future with Javar. How could she, when she couldn't truly trust him? There were too many complications in their relationship, and with Javar in her life—along with his interfering family—she would never truly be able to get over her demons.

But if the answer was so simple, then why did Whitney's heart ache at the very thought of walking away from Javar and never looking back?

Why did she feel as if her whole world was coming to an end?

When the phone rang, Javar nicked his chin with the razor, muttered a curse, then ran into his bedroom to answer the phone. He said anxiously into the receiver, "Hello."

"Javar. Hi."

The sound of his father's voice, not Whitney's, caused Javar to groan. Not that he wasn't happy to hear from his father, but he was concerned about Whitney, and was hoping desperately that she would call.

Javar said tightly, "Hi, Dad."

"I sense that I've caught you at a bad time," Marcus Jordan said.

Javar blew out the air in his cheeks. "Kind of. I was expecting a call."

"I won't keep you. I wanted to call and say hi since I'm back in town, and I also wanted to say bye, since I'm heading out again tonight."

"Wow. You've been pretty busy. Another conference?"

"Yeah. This one's in Hawaii, so I'm looking forward to it."

"I bet."

An awkward silence fell between them, and Javar didn't know what to say. His father had never been a big supporter of Whitney, and he had no doubt heard his mother's version of what Whitney had and had not done. He loved his family dearly and wanted them to accept the woman he loved.

Marcus cleared his throat. "I heard about the fight you had with Michelle and your mother."

Javar was immediately defensive. "Dad, if you're going to tell me to apologize—"

"No," Marcus said quickly. "I'm not going to tell you to apologize." He sighed. "In fact, I'm calling to apologize . . . on your mother's behalf."

Surprised, Javar's eyebrows rose.

Marcus continued. "Look, I admit that I was worried when you started dating Whitney. She came from the projects . . ."

"Neither you nor Mom was born with silver spoons in your mouths," Javar said, thinking that that was the worst part of all. While his parents hadn't come from poor backgrounds, they had certainly worked to acquire their status among the upper-middle class.

"I know. And I wasn't finished. What I was going to say

was that even though I originally had my reservations, I respected your decision to marry her. And I respect your decision now. If you want Whitney in your life, then I will accept her in mine . . . with open arms.''

The revelation was so unexpected that Javar was speechless. Sure, his mother had been the more vocal opponent of his relationship with Whitney, but he hadn't expected his father to embrace her with open arms. Closing his eyes for a second, Javar opened them, truly feeling touched. "Thanks, Dad. That . . . that means a lot."

"I'm tired of the quarrels, all the resentment. Whitney has suffered enough. So have you. We all have."

Javar shook his head at the irony. Now, of all the times for his father to make this call, it was when Whitney might finally want him out of her life. Javar silently groaned.

"Something's bothering you, isn't it?" Marcus asked. "More than this problem with your mother and Michelle."

"Yeah," Javar admitted, clenching a fist. "A lot has happened. Too much to get into over the phone. But Whitney and I may be going our separate ways after all."

"I'm sorry," Marcus said. "I mean that."

"Thanks." Javar moved to his bed and sat on it. "That's who I was hoping would call. . . ."

"I won't keep you then. I'll see you when I get back."

"Okay. Enjoy your trip. How long is it?"

Marcus replied, "Five days." He paused. "By the way, I've spoken with your mother about this whole . . . mess. She should be calling you, to apologize personally."

Javar rolled his eyes and wanted to say, "When pigs fly," but instead said, "Thanks again, Dad. I really appreciate having you in my corner."

Javar ended the call, feeling a modicum of satisfaction. The conversation with his father meant a lot.

Rising from the bed, Javar returned to the bathroom and picked up the razor he had thrown in the sink. His eyes met their reflection in the mirror, and for a long moment he stood there, staring.

Yesterday, his brown eyes had had a spark, life. Today, that spark had been replaced by sadness. After everything, getting close again, making love, the dream was still out of his reach. It loomed before him, teasing him, taunting him.

He had lived without his wife for almost two years. Two long, painful years. He had been too stubborn, too hurt to seek her out and try to save their marriage. Now that he had put his heart on the line once again, and now that they had almost seized the dream, fate had dealt their relationship an almost deadly blow.

Not fate. Someone. The person who was trying to harm Whitney—*kill* her, for God's sake. Javar was paying for that person's actions.

His stomach churned when the next thought hit him. Someone didn't want him and Whitney to be together, and would stop at nothing to fulfill that goal.

"Damn!" Javar slapped a palm against the sink's marble counter. Whoever was doing this was very clever. Whoever was doing this was setting him up to take the fall!

Chapter Twenty-One

"I don't want to call the police," Whitney announced, running a hand through her hair.

Derrick, who sat on the edge of her hospital bed, looked at her as if she had completely lost her mind. "Whitney, you can't let him get away with this."

"He said he would never hurt me." She sounded like a woman in denial, she knew, but she just couldn't convince herself of Javar's guilt.

"What did you expect him to say?"

Whitney drew in a deep breath and shrugged. "Look, I've made my decision."

Derrick stood, paced the floor for a few seconds, then sat again. "You know that someone tampered with your medication. You know that someone attacked you while you were sleeping. You know that someone ran you off the road." He paused, reached for Whitney's chin and tilted it, forcing her to look at him. "Javar had access to your medication. He had access to you in your bedroom. That we know for sure. We also know that he drove a black BMW, which he reported missing around the time of your accident. He could have hired a thug to attack you, then let him get away. Whitney, he has the motive, the means—"

Whitney dug her fingers into his arm. "Derrick, please. I can't. I just can't." She paused, grimaced. "The doctor probably thinks I'm a druggie. Let's leave it at that, okay? I just want to . . . get on with my life. That means leaving Javar . . . leaving this whole affair behind me." She sighed, frustrated. "I don't want to have to see him every day for months in a courtroom. Don't you understand that?"

Derrick flashed her a look that said he didn't understand. "I'm a cop. I like to see the bad guys put behind bars. But," he shrugged, "I guess I can understand your position."

Whitney placed a hand over his. "Thanks, Derrick. You're a dear friend."

"I know." He smiled.

Whitney returned his smile with a weak one. "Hey, I'm waiting on the doctor to come back and give me the okay to leave. The morphine is out of my system, but he . . . Well, I should be out of here soon. And I'm going to need a ride to Javar's." She hesitated. Swallowed. Tried not to cry. "To get my things."

"Hey," Derrick said, stroking her arm. "Don't worry about it. I'll take you to Javar's and help you pack. Whitney, don't cry. . . ."

But she couldn't help it. A hot tear escaped her eye and spilled onto her cheek. With the palm of her hand she brushed it away. But then there was another one in its place. Angrily, she brushed that one away too.

"Come here," Derrick said, offering Whitney his arms.

She went to him, pressing her face into his jacket. "It's just so hard, you know."

"It's going to be okay. You'll get over this," Derrick told her. "Everything's going to be fine."

Whitney accepted the comfort he offered, but she

doubted there was any truth in his words. With Javar out of her life, how could anything ever be right again?

Javar's heart leapt to his throat when he heard the phone ring. Moving from the window in his office, he ran to the black cordless phone at the corner of his mahogany desk.

"Whitney?" he said into the receiver.

"Uh, no. This is your sister."

"Oh." Javar's already foul mood plummeted even further. "Michelle. Hi."

"Let me guess, you're not happy to hear from me."

"Weren't you the one who told me you didn't want me in your life if Whitney was still in mine?"

Javar heard his sister's sharp intake of breath. "That . . . that's why I'm calling," she said. "I want to apologize. For being so . . . unreasonable."

Javar heard a voice in the background, Curtis's voice. He chuckled inwardly. So, this was why Michelle was calling. She certainly didn't seem to be doing it of her own free will.

"You do?" Javar asked.

"Yes," Michelle said. "I shouldn't have given you that ultimatum. It was childish."

"That it was."

"Anyway, I just want to say that you're welcome to come over anytime you want. Michael misses you."

The mention of his nephew's name made Javar smile. "I miss him too."

"And . . . Whitney . . . she's welcome too."

Twice in one day. The gods of cruelty were certainly laughing at him. "Thanks, Michelle. I hope you mean that."

"Why would I call if I didn't?"

"Okay," Javar conceded, giving her the benefit of the doubt. "Well, since you'll probably hear this from someone else, I may as well tell you that things between Whitney and me . . . well, I don't think they're going to work out."

"Oh." Michelle sounded surprised. "Why not?"

Because someone has screwed up my life royally, he wanted to say. But he said, "It's a long story. Another time."

"Well," Michelle sounded infinitely more cheery than when she had first called. "Like I said, you're welcome to come over. I'm sorry for being so pigheaded."

"Apology accepted. Listen, tell Curtis I said hi. I've got to run."

"Sure."

Javar ended the call, holding the receiver against his chin. Could his sister have been responsible for the attempts on his wife's life? She certainly hated Whitney enough to do it. Or was it Stephanie, as he had originally thought?

What did it matter? Whoever was responsible for the attempts on Whitney's life had succeeded in ending his relationship. That was all that mattered now.

"Are you sure?" Cherise asked, hugging Whitney tightly.

Pulling from her cousin's embrace, Whitney nodded. "It's definitely over."

Whitney took a seat on the rose-colored sofa, and Cherise sat down beside her. Then she told her cousin everything. About the accident that wasn't really an accident, about the attack in her bedroom, about the morphine overdose and her hospital stay, about Derrick's suspicions that Javar was behind everything.

"You don't believe that, do you?" Cherise asked, her forehead creased with disbelief.

Whitney shrugged, then brought a leg up onto the sofa with her. "What Derrick says sounds plausible, but . . ."

"But you don't believe it."

Admitting what her heart knew to be true, Whitney shook her head. "I think Stephanie Lewis is behind all of this. She hates me for 'killing' her son. And when I first went to Javar's after the accident, she threatened me. Javar was there."

Cherise reached out and patted Whitney's leg. "Then why? Why are you giving up on your relationship?"

"Because," Whitney said quickly, inhaling a steadying breath. "Because ever since the accident, there's been nothing but pain. And we can't seem to get past it, Cherise. We tried, but it didn't work. And I can't do it anymore. I just can't."

"I hear you," Cherise said. "It's kinda like me and Paul, you know. There was love there, but we lacked something else. And the relationship died."

Now that Whitney had retrieved her belongings from Javar's, she wanted to forget about him. She wanted to forget about the attempts on her life. She asked, "Where are the kids?"

Cherise chuckled mirthlessly. "With Paul. They'll be home later tonight."

"Good," Whitney said. "I can't wait to see them."

Maybe surrounding herself with her family would help her forget the man she was leaving behind.

Hours later, Whitney woke up to a quiet apartment. Never in her entire life had she slept as much as she had in these last several days.

Yawning, Whitney rolled over in the bed. She should call her mother and let her know what had happened, that she was no longer at Javar's.

She knew what her mother would say. That as much as it was hard to fathom, Whitney couldn't ignore the evidence. The pills. The new paint job on the BMW. The accident . . . It would be too easy to call it all coincidence, her mother would say. Which was true. And, God help her, Derrick made a pretty convincing argument for Javar's guilt.

"But why?" Whitney asked aloud, knowing that the four walls would not whisper the answer to her question. Why pretend he wanted a reconciliation? Why take her into his home to heal? Why hire a nurse?

To get close enough to kill me. That thought caused a shiver to snake down her spine. As much as she wanted to deny it, it *could* be true. The Javar she had known years earlier would never have been capable of anything so heinous, but maybe the loss of his son had been too great. Maybe that loss had changed him, made his heart so cold that only the thought of vengeance would ever warm it.

If only she could make up her mind as to what she believed, instead of teeter-tottering between arguing for Javar's innocence, then arguing for his guilt.

The only thing she knew for sure was that she had made the right decision leaving Javar's home.

Sitting up on the twin bed, Whitney fought the overwhelming sadness and reached for the phone. She placed the receiver to her ear and was about to punch in the digits to her mother's number when she heard a voice.

". . . treating me like this? Why're you acting so holy now, like you never wanted me? Because of her? She doesn't even want you, for God's sake."

Whitney knew she should have hung up the phone, but for some strange reason, she was compelled to listen. If Cherise was talking to Paul, her ex-husband, then it was obvious that despite the tough attitude and tough face she showed the world, she wasn't really over him.

"Answer me," Cherise demanded. "Why are you dissing me for someone who doesn't even appreciate you? If it's because she was hurt . . ."

The strangest, eeriest feeling passed over Whitney. Her hand tightened around the receiver as she waited to hear the man's response, needed to hear it.

Finally, he spoke. "Cherise, I already told you how I feel. I'm trying not to hurt you, but you're giving me no choice. I want to be with Whitney. Only her."

Whitney opened her mouth to gasp, but no sound would come out. The voice was unmistakable from the first moment he'd spoken. And when Whitney heard it, she froze, and a numb feeling enveloped her body. The strength came now, propelling her to act. Hastily, she replaced the receiver and sprang from the bed. Grabbing her purse, she ran to the bedroom door.

She halted. Clutched her stomach. God, was there nobody she could trust? First Javar, now Cherise . . . Who next? Derrick? Her mother?

Shaking her head, Whitney swallowed against the lump in her throat. Never her mother. That much she knew. And that was the only safe place she could go before she could make arrangements to go back to Louisiana.

She threw the door open, then stopped mid-stride. Dark brown eyes pinned her to the spot.

"Whitney, wait," Cherise said, her voice softer than the look in her eyes. "Let me explain."

Chapter Twenty-Two

"Get out of my way," Whitney said, moving forward.

Cherise blocked her path. "No, Whitney. Not until you let me explain."

"Explain? I may have hit my head in that car accident, but my hearing is perfectly fine!"

"I . . . you weren't supposed to hear that."

"No doubt!" Whitney took a step forward, but Cherise was in her face, stopping her.

"Listen to me. Whitney, I'm sorry . . ."

"Like hell you are!"

Cherise glanced down the narrow hallway. "My kids are sleeping."

"I don't—"

Forcefully, Cherise took Whitney's arm and dragged her into the bedroom. Then she closed the door behind them.

Whitney crossed her arms over her chest. "Save it, Cherise. I already feel like a fool!"

Approaching her slowly, Cherise's lips pulled into a taut line. When she was about a foot away from Whitney, Cherise spoke. "Whitney, it's not what you think. Javar . . ."

Stepping backward, Whitney said, "Don't. Oh God, I've been a fool!" She squeezed her head with both hands. Cherise and Javar . . . Suddenly, she needed to know. She deserved to know. "How long, Cherise? How long has . . . *this* . . .been going on?"

As Cherise stood, her arms wrapped around her torso, her bottom lip quivered. Finally, she spoke. "You have to believe that I'm sorry, Whitney. I don't know what I was thinking."

"Neither do I," Whitney retorted. "How could you? How? You're my cousin. You're my family. How could you do this to me, lie to my face . . ."

"Because!" Cherise's eyes were now misty. "Whitney, you don't even want him . . ."

"And you acted like you couldn't stand him! Like you were angry with him for how he'd turned his back on me! Now you want him?"

"Well if it's any consolation, he doesn't want me," Cherise spat out.

Turning, Whitney marched to the bed. Dropped down on it. "Why? Why Javar?"

Cherise brushed her tears away. She no longer seemed apologetic, only angry. "Why not?" she challenged. "You don't want him. Or do you?"

Her heartbeat accelerating at the thought, Whitney avoided the question. "Javar is not a commodity. Even if I don't want him, I can't just give him to you." Glancing up, Whitney saw the defiance in Cherise's eyes. Her cousin had always been pigheaded, feisty. "Besides, given our history, why couldn't you have gone for someone else? There are other fish in the sea."

"Not like Javar."

Whitney cringed. This all had to be some horrible nightmare. "I guess if you gon' do wrong, do wrong right, huh?"

Cherise continued, "That's not what I mean." She sighed. "What I mean is that I have two children to think about. Look at where I'm living. A man like Javar could give me the kind of life I deserve. Why are you the only one who should have that kind of man?"

"I don't have him. And I'd never want a man who didn't want me."

Cherise's face contorted with sarcasm. "Oh, that's right. I forgot you live in a friggin' fantasy world. Well I live in the real world, and in the real world I have two kids to look out for."

Whitney whispered, "Sounds like you're the one living in a fantasy world."

"Look, I apologized—"

"Did you?"

Cherise groaned. "There's no pleasing you."

Whitney was about to respond, but bit back her retort. This was getting nowhere. She was the fool. She should have seen the signs. Ever since she and Cherise were young, Cherise had always coveted the nice things she had, even the simple things. Now, she wanted her husband, and in her own crazy way, she was justifying her lies.

Rising, Whitney stared at Cherise long and hard. "Just how badly did you want Javar?" At Cherise's perplexed look, she asked, "Badly enough to try to kill me?"

"You're crazy!"

"Am I? You were there, in my room at his house. You could have tampered with the pills. You knew the moment I arrived in Chicago. How do I know you didn't try to run me off the road?"

"Whitney, I would never do that!"

Oh, God. It could be true. Cherise could have wanted Javar badly enough to want her out of the way—permanently. Whitney headed for the door in long, quick strides, knowing she couldn't spend another moment here with Cherise.

When she opened the bedroom door, Cherise was at her heels. "Whitney—"

Whitney kept going. Hustling as quickly as her legs could take her, she ran to the apartment door, grabbing her suitcase that still sat in the vestibule. She didn't look back as she jetted through the door and down the apartment hallway. It was only when she reached the main street that she stopped to catch her breath.

Where was her mother? Whitney stood on the porch of her mother's town house, straining to hear a sound inside the house. The interior hall light was on, as always, to keep unwelcome visitors away, but the house was quiet.

Whitney knocked again. Waited. Still, no response.

She fished into her purse for her key. Opening the door, Whitney went inside.

At a moment like this when her heart was racing and her nerves were frazzled, Whitney didn't welcome the eerie quiet of the house. She wanted noise, happy voices, loud voices, to distract her from her thoughts. Even a crying baby would be welcome at this moment.

Placing her suitcase on the floor beside the stairs, Whitney sighed. Her mind worked a mile a minute, trying to make sense of tonight's events. Trying to dismiss the new, devastating possibility. Could Cherise be behind the attempts on her life?

Biting her bottom lip, Whitney sauntered into the living room and sank into the worn, comfy sofa. She reached for the television remote and hit the "power" button.

A late news broadcast was in progress. ". . . dead tonight in more gang violence. The young boy was apparently hit by a bullet meant for someone else. . . ."

Whitney shivered. She changed the channel. Normally, she watched the news, depressing as it was. But tonight, the last thing she needed was to be reminded that there were bad people in the world, some of whom might actually want to kill her. Pulling a leg up onto the couch, Whitney flipped through the channels. News. More news. A late-night trashy talk show. Groaning, she switched off the television.

As she walked through the small dining room and into the adjoining kitchen, Whitney thought she heard a sound. She paused. It was faint, but someone was knocking on the front door. Slowly, she walked through the kitchen to the main hallway and went to the door.

She glanced through the peephole. Javar!

"Whitney," he called softly.

Should she say something? On one hand, she wanted to tell Javar to get out of her life, but on the other, she didn't know whether she could trust him. If she let him know she was in here, would he bust down the door and try to harm her?

"I know you're in there. I saw you through the window."

Her body grew rigid. This wasn't right, being afraid of her own husband. But although her mind told her she should be cautious, her heart told her she had nothing to fear. There was no way Javar could hurt her, at least she didn't want to believe he could. Even if he did, would he be foolish enough to try and kill her, right here at her mother's home? She doubted it.

"Please, Whitney. I just want to know that you're okay."

With that, Whitney threw caution to the wind and opened the door. There stood Javar, one arm above his head resting against the door's frame. His eyes showed concern as he looked down at her.

She met his eyes with a hard gaze. "What did you think, Javar? That I would be in here crying my eyes out?"

"Cherise called me. She said you were . . . distraught. That you left and didn't have a ride. She was worried."

"Yeah right."

Javar stepped into the foyer then, closing the distance between them. "She told me that you heard . . . our conversation."

"Oh, yeah. I certainly did."

"It's not what you think." Javar's eyes implored her to believe him.

"So Cherise said." Whitney turned, walked a few steps,

then faced Javar again. "How long has . . . has she *wanted* you?"

"I don't know," Javar said. "I don't care. All I know is that I never encouraged her advances. Ever."

"Then why didn't you tell me? God, you could have at least saved me from making a fool of myself with her."

Javar shrugged. "I figured since there was nothing going on, there was no reason to tell you. Besides, we were trying to work out *our* problems. Cherise has nothing to do with us."

Her face hurt from frowning. Her head hurt from pounding. She heaved a long-suffering sigh. "Fine. You've made your point. Now leave."

"I meant what I said before. I love you, Whitney. God knows, I'm telling you the truth."

"It's over." But she couldn't meet his eyes as she lied and said. "I've . . . called a lawyer. I'm filing for divorce."

Javar closed his eyes pensively, and Whitney watched his Adam's apple rise and fall as he swallowed. Slowly, he opened them. "If this is about Cherise—"

"It's about us," Whitney replied quickly, her throat constricting. "It's not gonna work. It's not."

"How can you say that? We were getting so close. . . ."

This hurt; there was no denying it. Pushing her husband away when her heart ached to embrace him . . . Her nerves were frazzled from the anguish of this moment, and she didn't know how much longer she could handle being in the same room with him, staring at the man whom she could no longer deny she still loved.

"Please, Javar. Don't make this any harder than it already is. Just go."

Javar's eyes held hers for a long moment, and when she saw the sheen of tears her breath snagged in her throat. God, she wanted to go to him, tell him that nothing else mattered but how they felt for each other. But she couldn't. Because the cards were stacked against them and they were just too high to leap over.

"Just tell me . . . tell me you don't believe that I tried to hurt you. . . ."

Whitney's body shook as emotions overwhelmed her. Her throat was so tight she didn't even know if she would be able to speak. Her voice a mere whisper, she finally replied, "No. I-I don't believe that."

Javar nodded tightly, then quickly turned on his heel, heading for the door. The gasp that wanted to escape got lodged in Whitney's throat as she pressed her lips together. She covered her mouth with one hand and held onto her torso with the other, the physical pain wrenching her insides into a tight knot.

Javar never turned around, not even when he grabbed the doorknob and closed the front door.

And finally, Whitney couldn't hold back the gasp. It escaped her lips as a flood of tears escaped her eyes.

Javar was gone from her life. Forever.

Summoning all her courage, Stephanie walked up the stairs to Javar's monstrous home. The home that could have been hers if she'd had the chance to regain Javar's love. But he had fallen in love with Whitney. And because of Whitney, her son was dead.

She pushed that thought from her mind. She had a job to do. Soon enough, she would have her revenge. Javar would know that he couldn't get away with dissing her for their son's murderer.

Stephanie looked back at the car where both her brothers sat. Kevin nodded, silently encouraging her. Part one of her plan was about to be executed. Her brothers would execute part two. This was Javar's own fault. He had driven her to this.

Stephanie raised her hand, rang the doorbell. Moments later, Carlos swung the front door open.

Stephanie pushed past him, stepping inside. "Where's Javar?"

"You are not welcome here," Carlos told her.

"Yeah, yeah, whatever. Get Javar for me."

"If you do not leave—"

"Get Javar," Stephanie repeated, louder this time. "I won't leave until you do."

Carlos glanced around worriedly, as if unsure what to do. *Let him glance all he wants,* Stephanie thought. *I'm not leaving until I accomplish what I came to do.* She had to get Javar into the foyer.

Javar must have heard her, because he was in the hallway now, walking hurriedly toward her from somewhere on the first floor. "I told you not to come back here."

"Yeah, well, too bad. I want to talk to you."

"I have nothing to say to you. Get out."

"No." Firmly, she stood her ground.

Javar turned to Carlos. "Carlos, will you please excuse us?" There was no mistaking his anger.

"What do you want?"

"My son's things. Everything. You're disrespecting his memory by having his killer right here in this house."

As Stephanie had hoped he would, Javar grabbed her forearm and led her out the front door. At that moment, Keith lunged at Javar, snaring him in a headlock. Although she was expecting the action, even Stephanie was surprised when it happened. With his hand securely around Javar's neck, Keith, who was almost as tall as Javar, ushered him down the front steps. Before Javar could react, Kevin was there, planting a sucker punch in his solar plexus.

Javar groaned, but fought back then, squirming in an effort to free himself of Keith's powerful grip. Kevin leapt at him, tackling him to the concrete. When Javar landed on the hard surface, Keith kicked him in the rib cage causing Javar to writhe in pain.

Stephanie stood to the side and watched.

Keith said, "Next time you think about attacking my sister, you better think twice."

His breath coming in ragged gasps, Javar looked from Stephanie to Keith to a now-standing Kevin, his eyes narrow slits. The anger in his gaze was so strong it seared Stephanie's skin.

"That's right," Kevin added. "You want to get to Stephanie, you have to go through us. Remember that."

Grunting loudly, Javar lunged for Kevin's legs. He surprised Kevin, knocking him to the ground. Stephanie screamed. Moving quickly, Keith nailed Javar with a boot in the back. Javar yelled out in pain, releasing his hold on Kevin as he did, falling to his side.

"Okay," Stephanie said, grabbing Keith's arm. "That's enough."

Blinding pain was all Javar could feel spreading through his entire body with the force of an electrical charge. He clutched his side, willing the agony to subside. "Cowards," he spat out, eyeing Stephanie, whose face was contorted in a grimace.

"Stay away from Stephanie," Kevin said, meeting Javar's eyes with hatred in his own. "This is the only warning you'll get."

Javar wanted to lurch forward and rip that devilish smirk off Kevin's face. But he was no fool; he was outnumbered. Besides, his side hurt. He wondered if a rib was broken.

He watched as Stephanie and her brothers ran to the Ford Tempo parked in his driveway. Inhaling deeply to keep his mind off his body's physical suffering, Javar got to his knees, watching helplessly as the trio sped away, tires squealing.

Javar was in the midst of standing when Carlos ran through the front door and down the concrete steps, a harried expression etched on his features. "Sir! Sir, are you all right?"

"Call the police," Javar said, wincing as he stood to his full height.

"I called them from my room when I heard the commotion,'' Carlos replied, moving to stand beside Javar and offering him an arm for support.

"Good," Javar said, before groaning.

Stephanie and her brothers would see who had the last laugh.

Chapter Twenty-Three

Long after the word came that Stephanie and her brothers had been arrested, and long after Javar had given the police a formal statement, the pain lingered. And not the pain from the actual assault—nothing was broken, only bruised—but the pain in his heart. Pensively, he sat in the leather recliner by the floor-to-ceiling fireplace in his den, trying to come to terms with the foul events of recent days. Trying to come to terms with his loss.

Javar had tried to reach Whitney after the attack, but each time he had called her mother's, the answering machine had come on. At this hour, he was sure she was there, but she was most likely deliberately avoiding his calls. Like almost everybody in America, her mother probably had a call-display feature on her phone that allowed her to see who was calling.

He needed to reach her, needed to let her know that Stephanie and her brothers had been arrested. He needed to let her know that the people who had tried to harm her were behind bars.

He needed to tell her that he loved her, always would.

That without her, his life wasn't complete and never would be. But she wouldn't even talk to him.

With a moan, Javar wondered if there was even any point in trying. Whitney had made herself very clear. She didn't want him in her life.

So, since he hadn't been able to reach her, he did the only thing he could: he left a detailed message on her mother's answering machine, letting her know about the turn of events and ultimate arrest. At least that should stop her worrying, if she was indeed worried about someone trying to "finish her off". Stephanie's arrest should give her some much-needed peace of mind.

Javar reached for the glass of straight Scotch on the table at his side, but his hand stopped in the air. He recoiled it, brought it back to his side.

Forget the Scotch, he decided. It might help ease his physical discomfort, but it would never numb the ache in his heart.

Whitney heard the soft protest of the door's hinges as it swung open, but she didn't turn around. Quietly, she sat on a wicker rocking chair, her legs curled under her as she stared out the window at the activity of the morning. Staring, but not seeing.

"Whitney," her mother said softly. "You need to eat something."

"I'm not hungry, Mom."

Carmen's clothes rustled as she walked toward her daughter. She placed a hand on her shoulder. "Honey, you can't sit here like this all day. You've got to get out, get on with your life."

Whitney didn't reply.

Carmen sighed. "Cherise called for you."

"I don't care."

There was silence for a moment, then Carmen said, "Well, I think you need to hear this. Javar called—"

"Mom—" Whitney protested, casting a sidelong glance at her mother.

"Hear me out," her mother stated firmly. "Javar called with some news. He said that Stephanie Lewis and her two brothers were arrested last night. Apparently, they went to his home, beat him up pretty bad."

Whitney turned and faced her mother then, her heart leaping into her throat. "Oh, my God. Is he okay?"

"In his message, he said he was." Carmen paused, raised a speculative eyebrow. "He also said that the police believe they were the ones who tried to kill you."

"I knew it," Whitney muttered, rising. Her heart was beating wildly in her chest, concern for Javar taking precedence in her mind. "I . . . should c-call him." She moved to the phone on the night table, reached for it, but didn't lift it.

She couldn't call Javar. How could she, after last night? Her body ached to lift the receiver and see for herself how he was doing, but after last night, she realized that it was best to let things be. Not only did she not want to give Javar false hope with her concern, but it would be too difficult to talk to him. To hear the deep, sexy voice of the man who was no longer hers.

As she recoiled her fingers, Whitney silently wondered if time would ever numb the pain in her heart.

Three days later, Javar still hadn't been able to reach Whitney. On a couple of occasions, he had spoken with her mother, who surprisingly, did not seem as bitter when she spoke with him as she had been right after the accident. In fact, Carmen seemed apologetic when she told him that Whitney didn't want to talk to him.

Today, Javar was missing Whitney even more intensely than the last few days. Today, she was supposed to accompany him to New York for his business trip. Instead, he was going alone.

It was poignant, tangible, the desolation he felt now that she was gone from his home, his life. After Stephanie's arrest, he had hoped that Whitney would take his calls, that she would be willing give him another chance.

Instead, she was going ahead with her plans to become his ex-wife.

Javar almost didn't want to go to New York; it wouldn't be the same without Whitney. But he had to. Just because Whitney didn't want him anymore didn't mean that he had to let his business suffer. Without Whitney, his business would become his first love again. Because without Whitney, there would never be another woman in his life. As final as it might sound to others, Javar knew he would never love again.

The phone rang, and for a split second, Javar allowed himself to hope. But as he reached for the receiver in his home office, Javar braced himself for the reality that Whitney probably was not the person on the other end of the line.

She wasn't. "Hello, Javar," said his mother.

"Mom."

"I heard about Stephanie. I'm sorry."

"Yeah, so am I." More than his mother would ever know.

"To say the least, I was very surprised. I never thought she would resort to physical violence. How is Whitney?"

Javar rolled his eyes to the ceiling. "Mom, I'm sure Dad told you that Whitney and I are . . . that things aren't working out."

"Well," Angela began sheepishly, "he did mention something about that. But I thought that after the arrest, you would have spoken to her."

"No," Javar said quickly. "I haven't. She won't take my calls."

"She's at her mother's, I guess."

"Yup." Out of his house, out of his life.

"Hmm," was all Angela said. Then, "Stephanie . . . What

a story. Has she admitted to running Whitney off the road
and causing that horrible accident?"

"To be honest, Mom, I don't know. She didn't even
want to admit that she had her brothers attack me. But
the police believe the case against her is pretty strong."

Angela sighed. "Well, at least that's over now."

"Yeah."

"Look, there's another reason for my call. I . . . I'm
calling to apologize," she said cautiously. "I'm sorry we
fought last week. I'm sorry I was intruding in your life. I
just love you so much that I get carried away sometimes."

Javar hesitated before answering, debating whether or
not to let his mother off the hook so easily. Sighing, he
decided there was no point in continuing the feud. He
had enough stress to deal with. "Apology accepted."

"Oh, good. Look, maybe we can get together later
tonight, have some dinner. Your father has gone off again,
so I'm here alone."

"Actually, I can't," Javar replied. "I have an evening
flight. I'm heading to New York on business. But maybe
later this week."

"Sure," Angela said. "That would be fine."

"Great. I'll be in touch when I get back. Take care,
Mom."

"Take care, dear."

Javar ended the call and headed upstairs. He may as
well double-check that he had everything he needed for
his trip.

Anything to keep his mind off Whitney.

Whitney didn't know how she got through these last few
days since leaving Javar's home. Looking for a lawyer had
drained her, left her feeling empty, and she still hadn't
found one that she was happy with. Most wanted to go
after Javar for half of this and half of that, but all Whitney
wanted to do was go on with her life. She didn't care about

maintaining the kind of lifestyle she had been accustomed to while she was with Javar.

Some lawyers had smiled at her and told her not to think of her life as coming to an end, but as a new beginning. Somehow, Whitney found that extremely hard to do.

So, after a couple of days, she had given up on the search for a lawyer—for now—and instead had done the one thing she thought would take her mind off Javar. She had gone to the All For One community youth center in Chicago's Near West where she had volunteered years earlier.

Meeting with her old friends and making some new ones, Whitney had smiled for the first time in a long time. Being with the children energized her, but still, when she came home in the evening, Javar invaded her mind. Javar kissing her. Javar making sweet love to her. Javar telling her that he loved her.

It would never be easy if she stayed in Chicago, Whitney realized. There were too many memories here, too many ghosts. What she needed to do was head back to Shreveport and resume the life she had been living there. Getting back to work at the youth center there would help her concentrate on other things. Help her forget Javar.

Restless, Whitney lay on the couch, her thoughts of Javar more poignant today for some reason.

Maybe it was because her mother had just left with Robert for an evening of dinner and dancing, leaving her feeling alone because she didn't have a man in her life.

Maybe it was because it was Sunday, the day she should have been going to New York with Javar.

Her stomach fluttering, Whitney realized that that was what was really bothering her. All thoughts led back to Javar. Would she ever forget the way his eyes crinkled when he smiled, the way his gentle touch ignited her skin, the way she felt when wrapped in his powerful arms? God, would she ever get over him?

"I have to," she said, standing. "I have to."

When the phone rang, she was so thankful for the welcome distraction from her thoughts that she just grabbed the receiver. "Hello?"

"Whitney. Hello."

Whitney's back stiffened when she heard that voice. Angela Jordan. Why was she calling her?

"Whitney? Are you there?"

"Yes," Whitney replied, her tone guarded.

"This is Angela Jordan."

"I know who this is."

"Good." Pause. "I guess you're wondering why I'm calling you."

"Mrs. Jordan, I don't have time for games."

"I understand." Her tone was syrupy, and Whitney wondered all the more why her soon-to-be-ex mother-in-law was calling her. "I'm calling because . . . I want to apologize."

"Apologize?" Whitney asked, a bit incredulous.

"Yes. Please, hear me out. Over the years, I haven't exactly been nice to you."

"That's an understatement," Whitney threw in.

Angela cleared her throat. "Well, you know the situation. I don't have to regurgitate the facts. I only wanted to say that I heard about the whole mess with Stephanie, and that I'm sorry about it."

"Why are *you* sorry?"

"Because I don't think I made things any easier. Perhaps even added fuel to Stephanie's fire."

Whitney drew in a deep breath and let it out slowly. "Mrs. Jordan, I just want to forget everything. Okay?"

"I understand, dear. This isn't working. I should do this face to face."

"Do *what?*" Whitney asked. Javar's mother had never liked her and probably never would, and she didn't see the point in having a conversation with her.

"Whitney, I would really appreciate it if you gave me the opportunity to apologize in person. That way, you'll know I'm sincere."

"It really doesn't matter," Whitney said.

"But it does, Whitney. I'd really like to get over the bitterness of the past and let bygones be bygones. Please, say you'll come over tonight. If not for dinner, then for tea."

Whitney found the whole idea of having tea with Angela Jordan a little daunting. "I . . ." Her mind scrambled for a logical excuse. "I don't have a car."

"Oh, I can have a driver come and get you." Pause. "Whitney, I think this is very important, for both of us. Please don't say no."

The words "No, thanks" were on the tip of Whitney's tongue, but she held them back. Angela Jordan was one of her "demons". One of the demons she had to face sooner or later. Maybe spending time with her would help Whitney face one demon and move on.

She was crazy for even considering this, Whitney knew. Still, she said, "All right, Mrs. Jordan. I'll come."

Chapter Twenty-Four

Something wasn't right. Javar felt it in his gut, in his soul. Something . . . But he couldn't put his finger on what.

It was just after six-thirty in the evening, and his flight was in a couple of hours. Driving along I-90, Javar looked out at the steady flow of traffic, trying to shake the wary feeling in his gut.

The feeling wouldn't go away. "What is it?" he asked aloud, speaking only to the windshield of his BMW.

It hit him then, the cause of his anxiety. His mother. Or rather, their phone conversation. His mind worked frantically like a computer virus program to isolate the one piece of information that nagged him.

They had spoken about Stephanie and Whitney. She'd apologized for interfering in his personal life.

Stephanie. That was part of it, Javar realized. But what about her?

Has she admitted to running Whitney off the road and causing that horrible accident?

The words came into his brain clearly, almost as if his mother spoke them from within the car. Icy fear slithered down Javar's spine, as he considered the implication of that question.

How did his mother know that Whitney had been run off the road? Even Javar hadn't been sure about that, and he certainly hadn't mentioned that possibility to anyone.

Definitely not to his mother. Or his father. Or his sister or brother. So how did his mother know?

Maybe someone else had told her. Derrick maybe. Stephanie? But those options didn't seem likely.

Javar signaled and veered his car to the right, exiting the I-90 before he reached Chicago O'Hare International Airport. He had to turn around and head east to his mother's.

He had to find out the truth, once and for all.

When the driver pulled into the driveway of the Tudor-styled home in Highland Park, one of the wealthiest suburbs of Chicago, Whitney looked out at the grand house she hadn't seen in more than two years. Surrounded by lush forests, the home was ultimately private. She remembered that this house had every luxury known to man, from gold fixtures in the bathrooms to a private bar in the master bedroom. Her in-laws also had a fifty-foot yacht in the boathouse, a boat she recalled they hardly used.

The driver pulled the Mercedes to a stop in the winding driveway, then exited and opened the back door closest to where Whitney sat. The driver was a young black man, probably no more than thirty, and definitely not the man she remembered as being the Jordans' driver.

Whitney stepped onto the pastel-colored interlocking stone cautiously, her hands shaking from a bout of nervousness. *I can do this,* she told herself, annoyed with her fear. Angela Jordan was a woman just like she was, albeit a very controlling one. *Just get this over with, let her say what she has to, and then get out.*

The driver escorted Whitney to the front door, which swung open as she arrived. Angela Jordan flashed a smile as wide as the part in the Red Sea, and to a stranger, it might look as if the woman was genuinely happy to see her. But Whitney doubted that.

"Whitney, come in," Angela said, waving her arms in invitation.

As usual, Angela looked dazzling in a flowing red pant-suit, her preferred style of clothing. Her ebony hair was styled in an elegant chignon, and simple pearl earrings dangled from each ear.

Whitney looked around the massive foyer. A gigantic brass-and-crystal chandelier hung from the top level of the house to just below the railing of the double staircase. The beige-colored marble floor, highlighted by a rose-colored marble trim, glistened beneath the artificial light from the chandelier. Everything was spotless, from the floor to the exquisite paintings on the walls.

Angela placed a hand on the back of Whitney's arm, gently leading her down the great hall. "Why don't we go to the sunroom? The sun is setting, but the view of the lake is breathtaking this time of evening."

It was. The sky was a dazzling array of oranges and reds, just above the peaceful-looking water. The backyard was pretty impressive, too, Whitney thought, looking out at the large oval-shaped pool illuminated by night-lights. There was also a pond in the distance, and an array of colorful flower gardens.

"What can I get you to drink?" Angela asked. "Tea? Gretta made some fresh lemonade before she left for the night."

"Uh, lemonade sounds great."

Smiling, Angela scurried off, leaving Whitney to explore

the sunroom. The room was made totally out of windows, except for the ceiling, but that even boasted a skylight. French doors trimmed in polished oak led to the backyard and the pool. The room boasted high ceilings, over which looked part of the upstairs hallway by way of a balcony. It was absolutely gorgeous.

"Here you go," Angela almost sang.

Whitney turned to face her, immediately reaching for the extended tall glass of lemonade. Until now, she didn't realize how dry her throat was and how in need it was of quenching. "Thanks."

"Please, take a seat." Angela motioned to the cream-colored sectional.

Flashing a timid smile, Whitney moved to the comfortable-looking sofa and sat. Angela took a seat next to her.

"I'm glad to see you're looking wonderful," Angela said.

Whitney took a sip of the lemonade, wetting her throat before speaking. "Thank you, Mrs. Jordan. You look great. Red really suits you."

Angela nodded her thanks for the compliment. "Well, I won't bore you with mindless chatter. I'll get right to the point." She adjusted herself on the sofa so that she could face Whitney head on. "Whitney, I am truly sorry for the way I've treated you in the past, even very recently. I know I hurt you, and I can only hope that you can find it in your heart to forgive me."

At Angela's words, Whitney exhaled a gush of air. Never had she expected to hear her mother-in-law say anything like what she just had, especially not face-to-face.

The effort must have taken a lot of courage, Whitney realized, and to her surprise, Angela seemed sincere. Whitney had always wanted a mother-daughter type relationship with her mother-in-law, but while married to Javar they had never achieved that type of closeness. There had been much bitterness, anger, regret. Now more than ever, Whitney wanted to put the negative feelings behind them.

"Thank you for that," Whitney said softly. "I appreciate your effort."

"After what happened with Stephanie, I realized that life is just too short to waste being angry for foolish reasons."

Whitney put the glass to her mouth and took a large gulp of the lemonade. "I have to admit, I was a bit wary of coming over here. . . ."

Angela chuckled. "You were? Well, you needn't have been." She rose, saying, "I've got some spring rolls warming in the oven. Nothing much. Just something Gretta made to nibble on. Care for any?"

"Sure," Whitney replied.

Twirling around, Angela glided out of the room.

Whitney drank some more lemonade. Then widened her eyes as her lids suddenly felt very heavy. *Whoa.* She felt strange all of a sudden.

Rising, Whitney stretched, then stumbled backward onto the sofa. Her head was spinning.

What was wrong with her?

Oh, God! Whitney's mind screamed, fighting off the impending darkness. She'd been set up!

And as the darkness crawled into her brain, numbing her mind as well as her body, Whitney's last conscious thought was of Javar. Of what a fool she'd been to push him away.

Javar.

Javar heard Whitney's voice in his mind, almost like she was calling out to him, asking him for help.

His heart pounding, Javar floored the accelerator. Quickly gaining speed, he drove toward Highland Park like a madman. A madman on a mission.

This time, if he got stopped for speeding, he would gladly accept a ticket.

Because he knew in his gut that Whitney needed him. And he sensed that time was running out.

"Is she out?" Angela asked Steve, the young man she had hired to help her do this deed. It was amazing how far people were willing to go for a few thousand dollars.

Steve lifted Whitney's eyelids, then let them close. "Yep. She's out cold."

Angela blew out a relieved breath. "Good. She'll be out for awhile. Let's get her out to the car."

She watched as Steve lifted Whitney's limp body and threw it over his shoulder. He seemed to thrive on this kind of activity, but then for what she was paying him, he should.

"Let's go," he said.

Angela hurried ahead of him, leading him to the door that led to the garage. A sense of satisfaction flowed through her blood, but she wouldn't allow herself to celebrate yet. The deed wasn't quite done. But this time it would be. She would make sure Whitney died if it was the last thing she did.

And Whitney deserved to die. She was a gold digger who wasn't fit to be her son's wife. And as far as most people were concerned, she was also a murderer.

That was the only part Angela regretted. Even now, it made her incredibly sad when she thought about it. Javar Junior should not have been in the car that day; when Whitney had left her house that day almost two years ago, J.J. hadn't been with her. How was Angela to know that Whitney would stop and pick him up on the way home?

Angela popped the trunk on her black Mercedes, watching as Steve dropped Whitney's body inside. J.J.'s death was still Whitney's fault, regardless of the fact that the brakes had been cut. If Whitney had had him buckled in, J.J. would still be alive today, as was Whitney.

Steve closed the trunk with a thud, then hurried around to the driver's side door. Pushing the painful memories of her loss aside, Angela followed him.

Tonight, it would all be over. Tonight, vengeance would be hers.

Chapter Twenty-Five

Almost all traces of the sun were gone from the sky when Javar turned onto the street where his parents lived and headed toward their grand home. Because he was in a residential area, he was forced to slow down, but he was still anxious to get to his mother's home and question her about their earlier phone conversation.

As his hands clenched the steering wheel, the wary feeling in his gut intensified. Whitney was in trouble. He knew it, sensed it. But he prayed his worst fear wasn't true. He prayed his mother wasn't involved.

He was almost there. The large oak tree he had climbed as a child loomed in the distance, and he increased his speed a little. As he was almost at the winding driveway, he saw his mother's black Mercedes Benz pull onto the street and turn right, heading north. Heading away from him.

Javar's stomach tensed. Watching the car gradually pick up speed, he aborted his original plan. He was sure his mother was in that car. Stepping on the gas, he followed her.

*   *   *

After about a ten-minute drive, the car ahead of him slowed, turning into a dark, secluded area along the coast of Lake Michigan.

Javar slowed his car, not wanting his mother or whoever was in the Mercedes to realize that their car had been followed. Pulling to a stop, Javar killed the engine and parked. Then he hopped out of the car, following the trail the Mercedes had taken by foot.

The foliage at this part of the beach was thick and dense. Fear prickled Javar's nape, as he knew instinctively that whatever was going on here was not good. Crouching as he jogged, Javar advanced to some bushes so that he could watch without being seen.

Parked amidst high bushes, the Mercedes's lights were off now, but Javar could hear the steady hum of the car's engine. Then, the driver's side door opened slowly and a well-dressed man exited and looked around cautiously.

Javar ducked, straining to see through the bushes. The man walked toward the back of the car. Moments later, he popped the trunk.

That was when Javar saw his mother exit the car from the passenger's side door. Also eyeing the area with caution, Angela crept to the trunk of the car.

His mind knew then what his heart wanted to deny, and when he saw the man extract a body from the trunk, his whole being shook.

It was Whitney. Limp and seemingly lifeless.

Javar held back the well of emotions that wanted to overflow. Instead, he acted, charging through the bushes and shouting an angry cry.

Angela whirled around, clearly stunned, and as he neared the two, absolute horror passed over her face as she realized who the intruder was.

The man, who'd been holding Whitney's body against his, let her drop to the ground when he saw Javar charging toward him. As Whitney landed on the hard earth with a thud, the man was already sprinting through the bushes.

Javar didn't care about the man, whoever he was. Running to Whitney, he dropped to the ground beside her, scooping her up as quickly as he could.

"God, oh God," he muttered as he took in her features. Her lips slightly parted, her eyes closed, she looked . . . "No. Oh, God."

Anxiously, he pressed his ear to her face, desperate to find a sign of life. He was trembling, fear spiraling through him from the inside out. If Whitney was dead . . .

"Sweet Jesus," he murmured, "please don't let her be dead. Oh, please!"

Drawing in a deep breath, Javar held it, realizing that he needed to be still. And then he felt it. It was soft and faint, like a whisper, but it was there all the same. She was breathing.

Looking heavenward he said, "Thank you. Thank you." But he knew the battle wasn't over. He had to get Whitney out of here, get her to a doctor.

He was lifting her from the ground when his mother said, "Javar."

He looked at her then, saw the anguish in her eyes. But beneath the anguish, he saw the hatred. The hatred that had led her to try to commit murder.

"What did you do to her?" Javar asked.

"It's just a . . . a strong sedative . . ."

"What were you going to do? Throw her in the lake while she was helpless?"

"I'm sorry," was all his mother said.

Anger consumed him then, like flames blazing out of control. "*Sorry?* My God, you tried to *kill* her, and you're sorry? Sorry for what? That you got caught?"

Angela whimpered, then threw a hand to her mouth.

Javar started off, Whitney in his arms. If Whitney had only been given a sedative, then he could bring her home—were she belonged. As long as the paramedics said she was okay.

Angela ran in front of him, blocking his path.

"You don't understand," she said, sounding hysterical. "I was doing this for you, don't you see? Sh-she was using you. Sh-she killed your son!"

"Get out of my way," Javar said slowly, unable to look at his mother. This was a nightmare, so incredibly hard to fathom that he wanted to put as much distance between him and his mother as possible until he'd had a chance to think.

Javar moved forward, and Angela matched his movements, stepping backward ahead of him. "God, Javar! Don't look at me like that! I did this because I love you. I wanted to protect you!"

Her line of reasoning was so pathetic, Javar didn't even bother to respond. Brushing past her, he ran with Whitney to his car.

She may be his mother, but she had tried to kill his wife. After securing Whitney in the backseat, he reached for the car phone on the front seat.

While he dialed 911, his mother sat on the ground, bawling like a spoiled child.

Wet. Something wet was dripping on her face. Whitney stirred, moaned softly. She wanted to open her eyes, but her lids felt so heavy. . . .

Man, was she ever groggy! When was she ever going to be herself, feel one hundred percent again?

She bolted upright as a memory hit her. A memory of Angela Jordan, of being at her place. But it was Javar who was with her, pressing a wet cloth to her face.

Where was she? Narrowing her eyes, Whitney glanced around. Her breathing calmed as a sense of relief washed over her. She was at Javar's place. Javar was with her, comforting her.

He took her in his arms, hugged her, holding her so tight that she didn't think he wanted to let go. He held her even tighter, relief evident in his grasp.

Whitney held onto him, drew from his strength for a long moment. It felt so good to be in her husband's arms.

When Javar pulled back and looked at her, Whitney's body immediately yearned for his. God, she was a fool. And a liar. There was no way she could live without Javar. How had she tried to believe that she could?

"How do you feel?" he asked.

"I'm okay," Whitney replied, resting a head on his strong shoulder.

"I was so scared. . . ."

Lifting her head, Whitney looked at him. Something horrible had happened, she knew that much, but she couldn't remember a thing. "What happened? I remember being at your mother's, but . . ."

A frown tugged at Javar's lips, and melancholy flashed in his brown eyes. "You—you're not going to like it."

He explained to Whitney the events of the evening, ending with the horror he felt when his mother admitted being behind all the attacks on Whitney's life; his mother and some hired thug. He was only glad that he wasn't too late. As he spoke, his voice broke, and Whitney's heart ached. Though her own life had been jeopardized, she felt the need to comfort him. Reaching out, she gently stroked Javar's face, bringing a finger to his mouth.

"You saved my life," she said softly.

Javar nodded, the grim expression still etched on his face. "The story gets worse."

Whitney cocked an eyebrow. She wondered what could be worse than learning that his mother had wanted his wife dead. "Worse? Worse how?"

Javar drew in a deep breath, then covered her hand with his, holding it against his lips. Suddenly, his face contorted as an internal struggle played out on his features.

Whitney's brow furrowed in concern. "What? Javar, you're scaring me . . ."

He closed his eyes then, sniffling as he opened them. A tear escaped, slowly trickling down his cheek. Whitney watched him, baffled, feeling as though someone was squeezing her heart, cutting her life source.

"J.J.," he finally said. "She . . . she killed . . ." His voice trailed off.

But he had said enough. Enough to cause the eeriest sensation to sweep over Whitney, making her body tremble. "What do you mean?" Whitney asked, the words barely leaving her throat.

Javar sighed and said, "She admitted everything. All this time, I was angry with you . . . but she did it. She cut the brakes . . ."

This was too unreal, too unbelievably horrible. As Whitney looked into her husband's eyes, saw the torment in their depths, she almost couldn't breathe.

Somehow she found her voice. "You mean . . . ?" Her head was shaking, and her body felt so incredibly cold.

"Yes!" Javar exclaimed. "Damn it, she did it. She killed him. She killed my son!"

It all seemed too bizarre to be true. For so long, Whitney had blamed herself for J.J.'s death. If she had only buckled him in, if she had only been able to stop the car from spinning out of control. . . . She remembered hitting the brakes, but that they had not wanted to cooperate with her efforts to control the car. But she had blamed herself even for that.

And now . . . It wasn't her fault. That first accident had been sabotage.

Oh, God.

"She wanted to kill you," Javar was saying. "But she— she killed my son."

It was like reliving the whole horrible nightmare over again, watching Javar grieve as he had two years ago. Fighting her own tears that threatened to fall, Whitney framed Javar's face with both hands, forcing him to look at her.

"Everything was a lie. It was all a lie," he said.

"Oh, Javar. I'm sorry."

"No," he said sharply, taking her hands in his. "I'm sorry. I'm sorry for being so blind. Why didn't I see this? Why?"

"It's not your fault." Whitney's reserve of strength began to crumble. "Oh, God." Slipping her arms around his neck, she pulled him close. "Oh, God."

And there they stayed, in each others arms, grieving anew for what they had lost. Grieving for little J.J., the innocent victim who had died because they had loved. Grieving for the years of misplaced guilt. Grieving so they could start to heal.

That night, two hearts reunited. Two lost souls found their way home.

Epilogue

Whitney glanced up at the jib and watched the wind play on the small orange ribbons that she and Javar had used to trim the sail. There was a light breeze, but it was enough to move the sleek white boat through the water. Beside her, Javar controlled the sail, much like he controlled her heart.

Her husband . . . this time forever.

Javar cast a sidelong glance in her direction, smiling as he caught her staring at him. They had come a long way; her round belly was a testament to that fact.

It was almost a year to the day when Javar's mother had made a final attempt on her life. The Jordan family was stunned and hurt by the news, and shortly after Angela's arrest, Marcus filed for divorce. Even Michelle, who had never liked Whitney, disowned her mother when she learned what her mother had done. Michelle had explained to Whitney and Javar that although she and her mother had hired a detective to investigate Whitney, she hadn't been part of her mother's warped murder plan. Both Whitney and Javar believed her.

Initially Angela had pled temporary insanity in court, but later changed her plea to guilty. She was convicted of murder and attempted murder, and was now in prison for at least the next fifteen years.

Despite everything that happened, Whitney and Javar had triumphed, beating all the odds against them. Because instead of concentrating on the obstacles, they had remembered their love for each other, the very love that had brought them together in the beginning.

"My ears are burning," Javar said.

"At least your ankles aren't swollen," Whitney retorted playfully.

"You're beautiful," Javar said, and the spark in his eye told her his words were one hundred percent true.

"Come here," Whitney said, patting the tramp beside her.

Javar fiddled with the sail, then joined his wife, placing a hand on her belly as he sat beside her.

"I know we said we'd never keep anything from each other," Whitney began, "but there's something I have to tell you."

Javar arched a thick eyebrow, his lips pulling into a tight line. His tone guarded, he asked, "What do you mean?"

"I mean," Whitney replied, her lips curling into a smile, "that I haven't been completely honest with you."

Javar sensed she was being playful, but was still confused by her riddle. "Okay. What haven't you told me?"

"Oh . . . that we're having two babies." She wrinkled her nose, then said coyly, "Please don't be mad."

Javar's mouth fell open and his eyes grew wide. "Twins? We're having *twins*?"

Whitney nodded, then squealed. "Yeah. I just found out."

"Sweetheart!" Javar wrapped her in an embrace—as much of an embrace as he could, considering her belly. "Oh, that's fabulous news!"

"Yeah, I thought so."

Javar planted a kiss on her lips, then pulled away to look at her. The smile was gone, replaced by a more serious expression. Whitney knew he was remembering J.J. They would never forget him; he had a permanent place in their hearts. But they were moving on, together.

"I have news of my own," Javar said.

"You do?"

"Yes." He took Whitney's hand. "Remember when my firm didn't get the Li bid, I told you I wasn't upset because I was working on something else? Something much more important?"

"Yes."

"Well, that 'something else' is finally coming together. I've found the perfect place."

Whitney eyed Javar quizzically. "What are you talking about?"

"It isn't finalized yet, but there's an old house close to Burnham Park that I want to buy. It's big. I want to fix it up, and . . ." He paused, then continued, ". . . turn it into a youth center."

"Javar?" Whitney asked, surprised.

"I'm going to name it the J. Jordan Jr. Community Center . . . as a tribute to J.J. What do you think?"

Whitney reached out, ran her fingers over the planes and grooves of Javar's face. "I think that's an absolutely wonderful idea. J.J. would be so proud."

Javar smiled weakly. "I know."

"I love you, Javar Jordan," Whitney said, trailing a finger along the outline of his full mouth. "So much."

"I love you too."

And then their lips met in a soft, lingering, breathtaking kiss. A kiss that spoke of their promise, of their profound commitment to each other.

A kiss that spoke of everlasting love.

Kayla Perrin lives in Toronto, Canada with her husband of four years. She attended the University of Toronto and York University, where she obtained a Bachelor of Arts in English and Sociology and a Bachelor of Education, respectively. As well as being a certified teacher, Kayla works in the Toronto film industry as an actress, appearing in many television shows, commercials, and movies.

Kayla is most happy when writing. As well as novels, she has had romantic short stories published by the Sterling/MacFadden Group.

She would love to hear from her readers. Mail letters to:

Kayla Perrin
c/o Toronto Romance Writers
Box 69035
12 St. Clair Avenue East
Toronto, ON Canada
M4T 3A1

Please enclose a SASE if you would like a reply.

COMING IN AUGUST . . .

LOOK FOR THESE ARABESQUE ROMANCES

WHISPERED PROMISES   (0-7860-0307-3, $4.99)
by Brenda Jackson

AGAINST ALL ODDS   (0-7860-0308-1, $4.99)
by Gwynn Forster

ALL FOR LOVE   (0-7860-0309-X, $4.99)
by Raynetta Manees

ONLY HERS   (0-7860-0255-7, $4.99)
by Francis Ray

HOME SWEET HOME   (0-7860-0276-X, $4.99)
by Rochelle Alers